DOUBLE BACK

SHANNON BAKER

SEVERN RIVER

PUBLISHING

Severn River Publishing
www.SevernRiverBooks.com

This is a work of fiction. Names, characters, businesses, places, events and incidents are either the products of the author's imagination or used in a fictitious manner. Any resemblance to actual persons, living or dead, or actual events is purely coincidental.

ISBN: 978-1-64875-418-0 (Paperback)

ALSO BY SHANNON BAKER

The Kate Fox Mysteries

Stripped Bare

Dark Signal

Bitter Rain

Easy Mark

Broken Ties

Exit Wounds

Double Back

Bull's Eye

Close Range

Michaela Sanchez Southwest Crime Thrillers

Echoes in the Sand

The Desert's Share

The Nora Abbott Mystery Series

Height of Deception

Skies of Fire

Canyon of Lies

Standalone Thrillers

The Desert Behind Me

To find out more about Shannon Baker and her books, visit

severnriverbooks.com

1

With lights flashing, I whipped my cruiser to a stop outside of the Long Branch and jumped out, heading for the front door. Most Thursday evenings, or any day, really, you could find me at home spending quiet—excessively quiet—time with my dog. That didn't mean I'd rather be dealing with a barroom brawl to break up the monotony. But I'd learned that sheriffing in Grand County was nothing if not unpredictable.

A half dozen or so people had gathered in the dusk up the street from the only restaurant and bar in Hodgekiss, Nebraska, population around one thousand dear souls, and a few less than dear. The warmth of the sunny early June day had nearly vanished, leaving a chill that would deepen as the night wore on.

Some people wouldn't consider Hodgekiss much of a town, consisting of only a handful of businesses that mostly carried the bare necessities. The railroad stretched east and west, running parallel to the highway bisecting the town. Most buildings nestled on a steep hill to the south of the highway. The Legion Hall reigned at the top of Main Street, and the Long Branch anchored the highway at the bottom. A half dozen streets spoked from the highway up the hill on either side of Main Street. One long street outlined the north side of the railroad bed. Old cottonwoods and elms bunched here and there to differentiate civilization from the grassy rolling hills that stretched for miles in every direction.

If the Long Branch wasn't the oldest building in Hodgekiss, it had stood on this corner at least as long as the first photos taken in the late 1800s. Two stories of weathered beige stucco, and in the old days it had a balcony where the working ladies kept an eye on the street. For most of the last century and into this one, a few hotel rooms occupied the second floor, with the bar and restaurant on the ground floor.

A tall figure hurried from the opposite direction, and I didn't stifle my eye roll and a muttered, "Of course."

We hit the door at the same time, reaching for the handle and brushing hands. Neither of us let go, but we didn't pull open the door either. I wasn't about to let him take the lead, even if touching him sent an uncomfortable pulse of familiarity and repulsion through me.

I peered through the glass into the vestibule, not giving my ex-husband, Ted, another glance. "What are you doing here?"

He tugged at the door, but I pushed to keep it closed. "We're here for supper, and I heard a gunshot," he said.

An obvious lie, since if he'd been here when the trouble broke out, why was he only now reaching for the door?

When Aunt Twyla had called, she hadn't mentioned gunshots. But it had taken me nearly ten minutes to drive in from my house on Stryker Lake, so the situation might have escalated since then. Fat chance Ted happened to arrive at the Long Branch now. But that could be sorted out once I got this situation under control. "I'll go around back and come in through the kitchen. You wait here until I give you a signal."

Close to a foot taller than me, Ted frowned down. Thankfully, his Ben Affleck good looks no longer made my knees weak. "What kind of signal?"

I was already on the run toward the alley that would lead me to the back door. "I'll holler loud enough or call your cell. Just wait."

I'd been tilling my garden all day and hadn't taken the time to change out of my shorts and T-shirt; I'd stepped into old cowboy boots and buckled on my utility belt with gun and cuffs.

Before I'd been elected sheriff in Grand County, Ted had held the job for eight years. Now, much to my annoyance, he was sheriff in the next county over.

I hurried to the back alley. The smell that billowed out seemed like that of a million burgers and fryer grease in need of changing. I paused to listen for danger, then eased open the screen. The door was an old-fashioned wooden frame without a latch, and except for those days below freezing— of which there were too many for my tastes—it was the only barrier between the noisy kitchen and the alley.

My uncle Bud sat on the floor, his greasy apron—years from actually being white—puddling between his legs while he smoked a cigarette and looked bored.

Aunt Twyla, who only weighed a hundred pounds if she carried a commercial-sized bag of flour, paced toward me. Her Wranglers hung on bony hips, and her thick ponytail, with an impressive ratio of brown to gray, hung down her back. "Those damned fools are still at it. One of 'em fired into the ceiling and, by God, they're going to pay for that."

Damn it. The last thing we needed was two armed Vietnam vets going at each other. An old sheriff once told me the job was ninety-five percent boring and five percent "Oh, shit." The banging of my heart told me this was in the second category.

I motioned for Twyla to get down, with as much effect as I usually got telling Poupon, my standard poodle, to get off the couch. "Anyone staying upstairs?"

"I should be so lucky."

I must have given her a shocked look because she fired back, "If I had someone renting a room, you wouldn't have to clear those yahoos out of the bar so fast. I need to get my paying customers back in here drinking beer and whiskey." She whipped a ropy arm out to indicate Bud. "And he's got to flip some burgers. We ain't made of money."

I doubted Twyla's income was in jeopardy. As soon as news of a shootout hit the gossip trail, which no doubt was already happening, folks would be flooding to the Long Branch to get in on the hoopla. It might make a dull Thursday rival a hopping Saturday. "What's the situation in there?" I nodded toward the bar.

From family photo albums I'd seen, Twyla had been a looker in her youth and still kept that youthful mane. But a diet heavy on Jack Daniel's and light on vegetables, and years as a smoker, had left her shrunken and sallow, but not lacking in vigor. She scowled in the bar's direction, as if the men inside could see her. "Who knows what got 'em going? We're havin' a decent night. I was training a new gal, and she knows how to take an order, for pity's sake."

Alarmed, I scanned the kitchen. "A waitress? Where is she?"

Twyla waved her arms, maybe trying to swat away her irritation. "Said she could wait tables but doesn't have the sense to get herself out of the way. I think maybe she's hiding under something out there."

Great. Someone who could get caught in the crossfire. What next?

Twyla growled at me. "So's we're all busy and not paying attention, and all the sudden one of 'em shoves the other, and then both of 'em are up with fists flying."

"That's not unusual."

"It's when they threw the table—" Bud started before Twyla interrupted.

"And broke the beer bottles to use as swords."

I hadn't ever seen them use more than fists on each other. With a clearer picture, I continued past the grill and deep fryer, heading for the opening to the bar and the distinct odor of a hundred years of beer and whiskey.

"I ain't never." The words, though not shouted, sounded weighted with warning.

"I seen you. And I'm sayin' it ain't right." The answer came back punctuated with heavy breathing.

From the kitchen, I entered behind the wooden bar and squinted into the scant light. Two men, looking like flip sides of the same tarnished penny, faced off in the center of the room. Flimsy pedestal tables were upended, and glasses and bottles littered the floor. Broken shards caught light from the dim overhead fixtures.

The Johnson brothers. Newt and Earl. Around the same age as Dad, they were less than a year apart in age. Never married, it was uncommon to see one without the other. And though they often disagreed, tended toward bickering, and often fell into shoves and fists, they seemed devoted to each other.

Except now, each held a revolver pointed at the other. Probably the same make and model, both guns had long barrels. I'd guess they bought them to resemble movie cowboys. The guns looked bigger than either could hold up for long, but they were making a heroic effort.

I'd dealt with Newt and Earl many times, and I used the same tone as I did when my nine-year-old twin nephews got out of hand. I figured my voice booming in the empty bar would break their focus on each other. "Okay, boys, put the guns down."

Neither of them flinched, keeping their focus with an intensity that implied only one would come out alive.

This would require some finessing. If I surprised them too much, it might cause one or the other to squeeze the trigger. I took a moment to consider.

A moment too long.

2

The glass front door thrust inward, and amid a flurry of shouts and warnings, Ted crashed into the bar. "Sheriff. Hands in the air."

He was halfway into the room when the first shot rang out. The slug whizzed past me and struck a bottle on the back wall. A shower of glass and whiskey rained down, washing me in alcohol. A contact drunk might not be a thing like a contact high, but the smell stung my nose.

The second shot hit the plate glass door, probably missing Ted's stupid head by inches. It surprised me that the glass didn't shatter, just a few shards fell, leaving a hole about head height. I only hoped the bullet lodged itself in the restaurant wall on the opposite side of the barroom and didn't pass into the street.

Ted threw an arm around the brother closest to him. Since I couldn't see their ears in the dim barroom, I couldn't tell which brother was which. When the boys were toddlers, Earl bit a chunk out of Newt's right ear, giving the rest of us an easy way to tell them apart.

Before things got worse, I scooted into the barroom and grabbed the other brother around the shoulders, pulling his gun arm behind his back and loosening his grip enough for the gun to drop to the floor.

Even though he wasn't a big man, his wiry frame felt hard as iron, and I had little doubt that if he really wanted to, he could throw me off. Newt or

Earl, whichever one I held onto, spent the bulk of his day bending, sorting, lifting, and hauling. He did his share of driving, since dumps and estate sales were miles apart in this rural country, but there was nothing soft about him.

Both brothers tugged and tussled a bit before eventually calming down. Being up close gave me a chance to see I held Newt, the younger of the two.

Ted had succeeded in relieving Earl of his revolver.

"Okay," I said, loosening my grip but not releasing him. "Are you two good?"

Newt and Earl, together weighing no more than a bucket of rocks and measuring little more than ten feet if stacked on top of each other, grumbled some syllables that sounded as if the danger had passed.

I glared over Newt's head at Ted. His barging into the Long Branch had created the kind of mayhem I'd hoped to avoid. It was a minor miracle no one had been killed—assuming that last bullet hadn't hit a bystander on the street. It'd be nice to brain Ted as soon as I got Newt and Earl corralled.

Tentatively, I eased my hold on Newt and then stepped back. I gave a curt nod to Ted for him to do the same.

With the swift moves of an attacking hawk, Earl flew at Newt. "You can't take what's not yours."

Newt ducked and parried and came back barreling into Earl's gut, throwing them both to the floor, now covered with glass and beer. "Not yours neither!"

Ted and I both dove for them, wrangling them apart.

"I shoulda let you die in that firestorm."

"You'da never made it back without me, and now I'm plumb sorry."

This sounded deadly, way more serious than I'd ever heard them before. While we succeeded in separating them, it took as much muscle as wrestling a steer.

Ted and I shoved each of our charges to opposite sides of the bar.

While Ted talked to Earl, I tried to calm Newt. In a commiserating tone, I said, "He's got you pretty riled up."

Newt looked over my shoulder at Earl. "What lies is he spreadin' to Ted?"

I leaned into his line of vision. "Don't worry about that. Why don't you tell me what's got you both so steamed?"

With some reluctance, Newt turned his attention to me. He lifted his hand to poke gently at the soft spot under his eye where it had already started to swell. "The pinhead gave me a shiner."

I took hold of his chin and tilted his head to get better light. "Yep. Gonna be a good one. What did you do to get him so testy?"

Newt scowled over my shoulder again and sucked his lips into his mouth as if stopping up the words.

"Newt? Tell me what's going on."

He shook his head, and I didn't think he was answering me. I glanced to the other side of the bar at Ted's back and Earl's face, focused on Newt. They were communicating in their weird way. Whatever dire disagreement they'd had, they seemed to be determined to keep it to themselves.

Newt shifted to me and with a firm voice said, "That's between me and Earl."

"Not if you're shooting up the Long Branch."

"Be that as it may..." Apparently, he thought that explained enough, and his face shut down.

Ted turned to us, and maybe we had a weird communication, too, since we both stepped back and let Newt and Earl slowly meet in the middle of the room.

The brothers shrugged and resettled their shoulders, letting their plaid cowboy shirts fall into place.

Something didn't seem right with them, and it took a second to register. They still wore their more-salt-than-pepper hair in buzz cuts. But they weren't wearing their oversized camo shirts and pants, their usual outfits since coming back from Vietnam all those years ago. Their faces weren't smeared with grunge, their Levi's were freshly laundered, and their shirts looked ironed.

The biggest difference from their normal state was that they weren't surrounded by a cloud of odor. Sweat and dirt, as you'd expect from two men who made their living sifting through dumps, but they often carried other, less identifiable smells, maybe from skinning muskrats, or their general avoidance of teeth brushing or showering. Their regular state made them seem as if they'd grown from the dumps and sheds they rummaged through. But now, they seemed downright domesticated.

"What's the problem, boys?" I asked.

Newt looked down at his boots and mumbled, "Sorry 'bout that, Sheriff."

We all managed to keep a straight face when he used my title, despite me wearing gym shorts, cowboy boots, and a heavy utility belt.

Earl flashed a stink eye in Newt's direction. "He got carried away. Won't happen again."

Newt's head snapped up. "It wasn't my fault, you darned peckerwood."

Earl puffed his chest. "Hope you're not sayin' it was mine."

Ted held a hand up. "Whoa, now."

I stepped between them. "That's enough." I didn't have kids of my own, but I could call on a mom voice when needed. "I'll take those guns."

Both their mouths opened, and they started some form of protest, but they hadn't let loose more than a squawk before my half-pint of an aunt whooshed from the kitchen in a rush of indignation. "What the hell do you think you're doing? You chased my customers out, and look what you've done to her." Twyla thrust her arm toward a dark corner of the barroom where one table had survived the battle.

We all turned to look. Squeezed between the pedestal and the corner, a lump huddled in the dark. As if terrified by our attention, it let out a peep.

Newt slapped a hand over his mouth, his eyes round with horror. Earl leaned over with his hands on his knees and spoke slowly to the dark mass. "We're sorry if we scared you. We didn't mean no harm."

Twyla marched past us to the table and stood beside it. "Come on out, Donnell. They're done with their shenanigans. Folks'll be coming back in, and they'll be thirsty."

Donnell didn't move.

Twyla planted her hands on hip bones sharp enough to cut glass. "You traumatized her, and if she ain't fit to wait tables now, I'm gonna take that out of your hides. And you're already into me for a couple bottles of Four Roses and a new door. And that don't count the damage I haven't discovered yet."

Newt's eyes shimmered. He fitted himself next to Earl as if trying to coax Donnell from hiding. "We'd never hurt you. Just a stupid fight between us."

I crossed the barroom and squatted down by her side. This close, I could see she'd wound herself tight, on her side with her arms hugging her legs, her cheeks squished with her knees. Only her eyes shone out at me, looking a little like a 'coon hiding in a tree at night.

I held my hand to her. "It's safe. Don't be afraid."

Donnell slowly uncurled and took my hand. I helped her stand, surprised that after she'd stretched to her full height, she towered over me, with the girth and build of a heavyweight wrestler. With one swipe of a well-aimed arm, she'd have been able to flatten both Newt and Earl. She focused on Twyla and with a shaky voice in the tenor range said, "I quit."

Twyla held her hands up and stepped between Donnell and the door. She had to tip her chin back to see into Donnell's face. "I know you're spooked. And I'm already banning those lunkheads from the Long Branch, but you don't have to go. I'll match all the tips you get tonight. Kind of combat pay, like."

Donnell hesitated. Twice the size of Twyla, her light brown hair in a messy bun, she swiped at tears and cast a nervous glance at the brothers. She seemed like a Great Dane of a person: big enough to overpower, but too timid to try.

Newt and Earl spoke almost simultaneously. "We're sorry."

Donnell sniffed and pushed straggling hair from her face. "Can I have a dollar more an hour?"

The look Twyla aimed at the Johnson brothers could have stopped a charging rhino. She gave Donnell a tight smile. "Sure, honey. Just be ready to take orders when they all stampede in here." Twyla hated to wait tables more than a cat hated a bath.

That taken care of, I turned to Newt and Earl. "Hand over your guns."

Ted opened his mouth. "You ought—"

The look I shot him shut him up, possibly saving his life.

Earl said, "Aw, Katie, we learnt our lesson. Gotta pay for all the damage from Newt losing his head and shootin' up the place."

"Shooting up the place?" My temper shifted from Ted to the brothers. "You could have killed someone. And not only each other."

Newt scowled at Earl but didn't argue or throw a punch. "Look it, Sheriff." He put an emphasis on my title, probably to correct Earl calling me by my name. "You needn't take our sidearms. We'll take 'em home and put 'em away. We promise."

I held out my hands. "I'll hang onto them for a while until I'm sure you're over this nonsense. What are you fighting about?"

Ted started in. "Doesn't matter what it's about, you can't go around shooting off guns in public. I have half a mind to arrest you both. Spending a night or two in jail might help you cool off."

I took in a long, loud breath and nailed Ted with a stare I wished had fists...with iron knuckles. "Since this is my county, I'll decide how to deal with these two reprobates."

Earl drew his head in. "Repro-whats? We're proud soldiers of the United States Army. So you can call us veterans, but I'm guessing what you called us doesn't mean that."

Newt set his lips into a pout. "You've known us your whole life. We don't need to be *dealt* with."

Ted's smirk ignited my temper, but I held it down. I addressed the Johnsons. "I'm gonna need your guns. And then I want you to go home and stay out of trouble."

Twyla huffed. "That's it? You aren't gonna throw 'em in jail or give 'em a ticket?"

Maybe Aunt Twyla expected me to be the niece who recognized her authority. When I turned my warning gaze on her, she raised her brows in silent rebuff and folded her arms.

Newt's eyes fluttered with panic. His voice quavered. "We can't go to jail." He spun toward me. "Don't put us in jail."

Ted inserted his opinion. "You ought to teach them a lesson so it won't happen again."

Throwing Ted in jail would give me a lot more satisfaction, but that situation was for another time.

I gave each brother a reprimanding glower. "You're not going to act out again, right?"

They shook their heads. "No, Sheriff."

"You're going to pay Twyla for any damage or loss, and you're going to make all the repairs needed, subject to my inspection."

They nodded. "Yes, Sheriff."

"Give me your guns."

Newt thrust out his lower lip and cast puppy eyes at me before slowly bending down to pick up his gun and offer it to me. He watched as I unloaded the cylinder, the bullets clacking in my hand until I shoved them in a pocket of my utility belt. I fitted the gun into a snug loop on the side of my belt.

Earl stood in front of Ted until Ted handed over the revolver with a show of irritation. When he gave it to me, I unloaded and stowed it on the opposite side of my belt, making me feel like a gunslinger.

I nodded at them. "Apologize to Twyla."

Newt lowered his head. "I'm sorry. We shouldn'ta let our tempers get the best of us in your place."

Twyla harrumphed.

Newt nudged Earl, and I was relieved it led to Earl clearing his throat instead of another round of violence. "Well, dang, Twyla. You know we're good for the damages. But do you have to kick us out for good?"

Twyla glanced at Donnell. "You can get to-go but not after three in the afternoon."

Newt brightened as if she'd given him a million dollars. "We'll be good. I promise."

The two of them shuffled toward the door. Earl elbowed Newt, and they both turned, looking like they suddenly remembered something. "Don't suppose we can wait for our to-go burgers," Earl said.

Twyla shouted, "Git!"

They tipped their heads together, clearly partners again, and mumbled between themselves as they crunched through the glass on their way out.

Twyla bent down and set a table upright. "Bud, get a broom, and let's get this place set to rights."

Donnell shoved chairs around and helped arrange tables. Bud sauntered in from the kitchen, cigarette tucked into the corner of his mouth.

Twyla looked over her shoulder at me. "We could use some help here."

She tossed off to Ted. "You. Get out there and tell them folks the show's over and come on in."

Ted started for the door, but I stopped him. "Hang on. Tell me the real reason you showed up here so fast."

His eyes flicked toward Twyla and Donnell before resting on me, a clear signal he was about to lie. "I told you. Came to town to have dinner with Dahlia and Dad."

It had always seemed strange Ted called his mother by her first name. I assumed it was Dahlia's idea but was never sure if she thought *Mom* made her sound too old, if she thought using her first name made her seem cool, or if there was some other reason. "You weren't here when the fight broke out. My guess is that Dahlia called you even before Twyla called me."

"Why would she do that?"

Bud had swept up the glass by the front door. A small area, like a vestibule, about the size of three old-time phone booths smashed together with doors that opened one way into the bar and the other into the restaurant side. One front door led to the street from the vestibule. Bud leaned against the outside door and waved an arm in the direction of the small crowd up the street. He came back and continued sweeping up glass while Twyla and Donnell set the rest of the chairs and tables upright.

Ted avoided denying my accusation, which was his usual technique to save an outright lie. I answered my question for him. "She called right away so you'd handle the conflict and she could tell everyone I wasn't doing my job. Then she'd let everyone know you'd be a better sheriff than me, and when you run against me in another year, she can brag about this."

He tossed his head back and scoffed. "You've got a good imagination."

Before I could press the issue, people poured into the barroom like cows into a fresh meadow after the gate was opened. There was at least double the amount as had been on the sidewalk when I'd arrived.

Shorty Calley, one of Dad's oldest friends, walked in with Bill Hardy. They both ranched miles away from town but maybe had been to the fairgrounds for a roping now that the days were getting longer. Every summer cowboys banded together to buy a bunch of calves. A few times a week, they'd bring in their good horses and throw their ropes. Some practiced for rodeos and paying events; others just loved the sport. "By God, smells like the inside of a bourbon bottle in here."

Bill laughed and pointed behind the bar, where Twyla stood amid the bottle massacre, waiting to get the party started again. "They didn't get the tap or I'da had to shoot them both," he said.

"That's right," Twyla said. "Sit on down, and Donnell'll bring you boys a pitcher."

Shorty raised his eyebrows. "On the house?"

Twyla cackled. "Hell, no. How'm I gonna afford repairs if I give away booze?"

Newt and Earl are going to take care of that part. I kept my mouth shut and let Twyla run business her own way.

I realized my T-shirt was damp and I probably smelled like I'd been on a three-day bender. Add to that my bare legs and old boots, and I felt less than lovely. My wild hair escaped a messy ponytail, and I felt the burn on my cheeks from a day in the sun.

Whatever else I might say to Ted wouldn't get said because Dahlia shot from the front door on a beeline to her little prince—even if he was over forty years old and tall enough to see the top of a refrigerator without a stool.

She wore a bell-sleeved, crushed-velvet shirt the color of merlot and had a silver concho belt that might have challenged a conquistador with its weight draped on her hips. Her tight jeans tucked into tall cowboy boots with paisley tooling completed the cowgirl-chic look that might have been appropriate for a woman half her age. With her bobbed hair curled into ringlets and enough makeup to drywall a living room, she was decked out for a night on the town. Too bad the Long Branch was the best she could do.

What didn't fit with the ensemble was the squalling toddler fighting to free himself from her grip. With his red face pinched and his mouth open and slobbery with sobs, Ted's son, Beau, was clearly not happy.

Breathless, Dahlia seemed close to losing the battle to hang onto the little guy. In a voice loud enough for everyone in the room to hear her above Beau's wailing, she said, "Thank goodness you were here, Ted. You saved us."

Typical drama for Ted's mother, and at least he had the awareness to look embarrassed.

Before either of us could respond, Beau took account of his surroundings, blinked in the dark, and focused on me. He immediately reached in my direction and kicked Dahlia like a bronc rider spurring a horse. "Kay-Kay-Kay!"

Beau launched himself at me, and I grabbed him under his arms just as Dahlia lost her grip. I swung him into the air and planted him on my hip. "Hi, little man." Beau and I had bonded a few weeks after his birth in a situation that still torqued me off. I didn't hold it against Beau, and we'd grown to be great friends in his almost two years on the planet.

All agitation vanished, and Beau's sticky hands patted my cheeks. "Kay-Kay."

A venomous glitter flashed across Dahlia's face before she resumed her performance. "This county is becoming a lawless frontier. Gunplay, criminals at large, no consequences for violating the law. We're so lucky you were here to restore order, Ted."

Most of the folks streaming back into the Long Branch didn't pay any attention to Dahlia's carrying-on. They were more interested in getting the skinny from Aunt Twyla and being next in line for drinks.

While Beau tugged at my hair, pulling curls from my ponytail and babbling happily, only adding to my stickiness and disarray, I faced Dahlia with my most patronizing manner. "No one was hurt. Some property was damaged that will be restored. Why don't you have Donnell bring you a glass of wine to calm your nerves."

Ted couldn't hide the amused twinkle in his eyes. He might be a mama's boy, but he enjoyed seeing someone needle Dahlia.

She didn't take my condescension with grace. Dahlia looked down her nose at me. Literally. She had a sloping, regal nose. Some might call it beak-like if they weren't being kind. I didn't feel like being kind. And she stood several inches taller than my five foot three. "My nerves are fine, thank you. But it's a wonder the whole county isn't in a panic. You've been sheriff for nearly three years, and in that time, we've been riddled with murders and crime, and you haven't seen fit to do anything about it."

It seemed like a good time to give Beau a few playful bounces and make a silly face that set him to giggling. Still engaging Beau by wiggling my eyebrows, I addressed Dahlia. "I solved a murder when Ted was still sheriff here and kept him from going to jail. I think you'd be happy about that."

She tossed her head, sending her ringlets bouncing. "Ted was in the hospital, but we all know he was calling the shots on that."

Arguing with Dahlia was as productive as wearing sunscreen at night. I bent over and set Beau free to toddle over to Ted and hug his leg. When I straightened up, ready to head to the courthouse to lock up the Johnsons' guns in my office, I faced Ted's wife, Roxy, who had appeared like a cloud of noxious gas.

Like Dahlia, Roxy had fixed up for coming to town. Every bit as tall and statuesque as Dahlia, Roxy's hair was longer, making her curls bigger but no less bouncy. She wore a black sheath that she saved from being classy by heaping so many multicolored beads around her neck, it made me wonder how she kept her head up. She finished the look with black tights and boots with such colorful tooling they might require a seizure warning.

Roxy threw her arms around me and pulled me into her impressive cleavage. That she'd managed to lose all the baby weight but keep her boobs didn't seem right. "It's so good to see you!"

I succeeded in pulling free before she smothered me. With fake enthusiasm I said, "What are you doing in Hodgekiss?" Maybe I was checking up on Ted's story about meeting Dahlia for dinner, because I normally wouldn't bother asking.

"Oh. It was the luckiest thing. Dahlia and Sid are watching Beau so Ted and I can have a date night in Broken Butte." She paused and slapped her palm on her chest as if she'd realized something. "I know you would probably have wanted to babysit, but Ted thought you were on call, and since it's Thursday night..." She tilted her head as if asking for forgiveness for not saddling me with her kid.

Assuming my pardon, she rushed on in her Roxy way. "We had already gone through town when Dahlia called. So, we turned around and came back. I imagine date night is off." She cast a fake pout on Dahlia. "But I hope you'll still keep Beau so we can at least get a steak here and have a little 'us' time at home." She winked at me. "If you know what I mean."

Since Ted was my ex, I knew more about what she meant than I wanted to.

Dahlia wasn't done with me yet and nudged Roxy aside. "As soon as you stole the job from Ted, all of a sudden your brother is involved with Mexican cartels, and *voila!*" She swatted the air. "No charges filed. And then the next thing we know, your mother turns out to be a terrorist, and she miraculously disappears."

Brave Ted tipped his chin up in a wave to Tuff Hendricks, who had walked in the door. Ted acted like Tuff wanted to talk to him, even though Tuff didn't seem to notice him. Ted rushed away, abandoning Dahlia to her stage.

Roxy shifted her attention to little Beau, who was patting my legs to get me to pick him up again.

Twyla saved me. "For pity's sake, Kate, get back here and help me."

Slinging a few drinks might not be another great way to spend a summer evening, but at least it might keep me from murdering my former mother-in-law.

3

My alarm pulled me from sleep way too early. I didn't mind beating the sunrise by an hour or so, but this felt like the middle of the night. Probably because it wasn't far off from midnight. My phone showed 3:30 a.m. when I reached over to silence the darned thing.

By the time I'd made it home from the Long Branch, it had been nearing 11:00. Maybe that didn't sound late to most adults, but for someone like me, whose habits resembled those of a chicken more so than a thirty-four-year-old single woman's, it was well past time to hit the rack.

I stumbled out of bed and planted my feet on the cold oak floor on my way out of the bedroom to the kitchen. My bungalow, built in 1912, was tucked under a hill with a shallow lake fifty yards from my front porch. Even back then, it was probably considered cozy, with its two bedrooms and one bathroom small enough that you could sit on the toilet, brush your teeth, and dip a toe in the bathtub at the same time. The front door opened to a living room that ran alongside the bedrooms with no hallway to separate them, and it opened into the kitchen. An archway divided the long room in half, to make the front a living room and give the back bit just enough space for a dining table and chairs. As the biggest room in the house, the kitchen held my pride and joy: a refrigerator with a bottom-drawer freezer and ice and water in the door. It was a luxury I'd never had while living with Ted and managing his family ranch.

A front porch that looked out on the lake made up for any shortcomings my bungalow held. It was my favorite part of my house.

The light above the stove glowed from the kitchen.

"I started the coffee."

The voice startled me, and when I looked up, I spotted Dad's silhouette in his pajama bottoms, making his way from the kitchen toward the other bedroom, or what used to be my office.

I was so tired I hadn't realized I smelled coffee. And something else. Suspiciously as if someone had baked something.

After a week of him staying here, his presence still surprised me. "Uh. Thanks."

He walked past me in the darkened living room and slapped on a light in his room. "We'd better get a move on if we're going to get there in time to round up."

I bit back my response that I knew how long it took to get to my brother and sister-in-law's ranch and we'd be there in plenty of time to bring the cows and calves in for their branding. Dad was dealing with a bigger adjustment than I was, and he deserved my patience. He was my guest, even if there were other of his kids with bigger houses and more space that he would certainly be more comfortable staying with.

I walked back to the couch and tugged on Poupon's collar. "No dogs on the furniture." It was my usual way to greet my standard poodle in the morning.

After ushering him outside for his constitutional, I spoke to Dad as I passed his door. "I'll be ready in ten minutes."

I stumbled through the kitchen—noting the coffee grounds spilled on the floor and water splashed across the counter—and into the bathroom. Dad's razor rested on the narrow lip of the pedestal sink, and I shifted it to the shelf above the toilet that I'd cleared for his things.

It wasn't that I was a neatnik, but in my private, petite house—the only place that had ever been mine alone—I felt invaded. And that made me feel guilty for being so selfish.

After Mom had left a year ago last fall, it had taken Dad several months to shed the shell-shocked look. Then, he'd assessed his choices and decided he could no longer tolerate staying in the home he'd shared with her for forty years. He'd passed the house to my oldest sister, Louise, and her family, who had been crowded into an old cookhouse on a ranch just outside of town.

After that he'd moved into a room above the Long Branch. That had only lasted a few weeks before his sister, Twyla, had booted him out in favor of paying customers.

He'd stayed with my brother Douglas on a ranch thirty miles from town, but making his calls to work at the railroad was iffy. He'd only lasted a few weeks with my brother Michael, Douglas's twin, but he said Michael's two girls created too much noise and confusion for him. That last bit didn't make sense to me because Mom and Dad had raised nine kids in a house bursting with chaos. My guess is that my sister-in-law, Lauren, made him nervous with her constant motion.

For the last several months, he'd rented a single-wide mobile home in town and seemed content. But Shorty Calley's hired man came home from a bender a week ago and ran his Ford F-250 into Dad's kitchen, creating more fresh air than necessary. After that, Dad had ended up at my place.

By the time I'd dressed in old jeans, worn boots, a few layers of shirts, and topping off with a frayed hoodie, Dad was back in the kitchen pouring coffee into thermal cups. "Heard Newt and Earl got fired up last night."

I brushed my hair from my forehead. "Don't know what got 'em going."

He considered it. "Love or money. Everything comes down to that."

I dumped kibble into Poupon's dish, and he commenced to gobble. "Can't imagine the Johnsons have much of either."

He set the empty carafe on the counter. "Those boys don't spend much, so maybe they've saved a bundle." He paused and looked me in the eye. "As for love, all of us could use more of that."

He turned away and left me to wonder if he'd meant that last bit for me, to encourage me to start looking again. Or if he meant it to warn me that he didn't intend to be alone forever. Either way, it made me squirmy, and I didn't answer.

Dad spoke over his shoulder. "I'll get the dessert."

I spied a double-crust pie on the counter, no doubt the reason for the lingering aroma. "You made pie?"

"From those cherries I found in your freezer. Good thing you had them, or we wouldn't have anything to bring to the branding."

Telling Dad I didn't always take a dish to brandings would launch him into a lecture on how real Sandhillers treat people. It was far too early in the morning for that business.

"I didn't know I had cherries. Maybe Louise stuck them in there sometime."

"You're out of lard, by the way." He scrounged in the fridge for the half-and-half.

"I don't know as I've ever bought lard in my life, so I'm not surprised I'm out."

He doctored both our cups before putting the half-and-half back. "I borrowed the cup I needed for the crust from Wanda Jenkins."

Wanda Jenkins? She lived in town and used to run a hair salon. At one time, she'd been married to the owner of the lumber yard. After that she'd run off with a rancher from Broken Butte. "I didn't know she was back."

He screwed the lids down. "Yep. Opened up the salon again. Grab that Jell-O salad from the fridge." He handed me my cup and picked up the pie. "Let's go."

I opened the fridge and located a foreign Tupperware bowl a shade of pink that told me it was practically an antique. "Is that mandarin orange salad?" I snagged it.

He was halfway through the living room toward the front door. "With the Cool Whip, yeah."

I hurried after him. "I've never known you to make that."

"I didn't make it, but I mentioned to Trudy Drake that I always liked it, and she whipped some up for me. No way you and I could eat it all, so we're taking it to the branding."

Trudy Drake? She was the postmistress, Barby Drake's sister-in-law. When her husband passed away last year, she'd moved back to Hodgekiss after thirty years living in South Dakota.

I trailed him down the front porch to his pickup. Poupon, who would rather ride in the luxury of the back seat of my sheriff cruiser, hesitated a moment to confirm that I really meant for him to jump into the beater that was older than most of Dad's grandkids.

I gave him a firm choice. "Get in, or stay home alone."

He seemed to weigh his options. Poupon placed one paw, then the next on the floor of the cab, and with as little effort as possible, bumped himself in and onto his spot in the middle of the bench seat.

We settled in for the half-hour drive to the ranch. The best thing about Dad and me was that we didn't need to carry on conversation if we weren't in the mood. Even though I wanted to quiz him about Wanda and Trudy, I would rather ride along in silence.

There is a special silence in the early morning. Before the sun rises, when everyone except the kangaroo mice and owls are sleeping. When it's closer to daylight than sunset, a kind of hope that no matter what challenges I must face in the coming day, I have the opportunity to do some good. Conversation had the potential to extinguish that spark. There would be plenty of time to figure out why my newly single, looking-at-the-tail-end-of-his-sixties father was finding more romance than I was.

It was still dark thirty minutes later when we made our way between two tall hills and kept straight down a rough dirt road that opened into a wide valley with a well-lit single-story house huddled into a stand of cottonwoods on the other side. The hay meadow along the valley floor attracted herds of deer that Sarah loved to gaze on, even while hating the damage they did to the hay crop.

The Nebraska Sandhills take up about a third of the state, and it's a big state land-wise, if not by population. It sits on top of the deepest part of the world's largest aquifer, and on wet years, the groundwater touches the surface, creating numerous shallow lakes, which are home to a surprising number of birds. But with a population density of 0.9 people per square mile, it gave me the kind of space I could breathe in. More cows, deer, birds, 'yotes, and other critters than people, it could be the most peaceful place on Earth.

Except when brothers got to shooting at each other in the bar or when families crowded too close.

We pulled into the ranch and wound past the house to the barn. Bright lights spilled from the open doorway, and figures moved around, hauling saddles to horses tied to the fence in front. Dad parked next to several other pickups, close neighbors who would also help with the first chore of the morning, rounding up the pasture and bringing in the cow-calf pairs.

By sunup, the herd would be in smaller holding pens temporarily set up in a corner of a pasture. The rest of the crew would arrive there. About two dozen usually showed up. Family, friends, neighbors, folks visiting from far away, they'd take on the jobs of roping, branding, vaccinating, castrating, and removing horns. Today, it was Robert and Sarah's turn. Over the next few weeks, they'd help out at other ranches, and the scene would be repeated all over the Sandhills.

Dad balanced the pie on the salad bowl and took off to drop them at the house. He'd probably have a cup of coffee with Sarah and Louise, who would be peeling bushels of potatoes and starting preparations for the feast they'd provide the workers. He'd given up riding for the roundup and would meet us at the pen.

A whistle caught my attention, and I followed the signal to a horse trailer, where my favorite niece—and yes, I did have a favorite—Carly held the reins of a tall bay.

When I got close, she said, "I brought Spitz for you." In the soft glow from the barn light, her teasing wickedness shone at me.

I glanced into the trailer at the rear end of a roan. "Isn't that Cactus?"

She thrust Spitz's reins at me. "Rope's been riding him all winter. He's much more settled than last year." Rope was the foreman at the Bar J, the ranch Carly had inherited from her grandfather.

I cocked my head. "That would be last year when he dumped my butt on the ground and took off, leaving me to walk a mile back to the house?"

When she lit up with a mischievous spark, it was all I could do to keep from grabbing her and hugging her close. I'd come so close to losing her. But for the last two years, she'd been enrolled at the university in Lincoln (Go Big Red), and it hadn't been until this last year that I'd seen some of the heaviness lift from her spirit and her impish nature return. I kept my hands to myself, because we were Foxes, for Pete's sake, and we didn't do things like spontaneously hug.

I stepped into the trailer and eased around Cactus to untie him. "You can show me how well behaved Spitz is now. I'll take Cactus."

"Old lady," she teased.

She might be right. By the calendar, I wasn't that old, but something in me felt ancient. I'd failed at one marriage and definitely made a mess of dating. I'd managed to alienate the man who felt so much a part of me, that after almost two years I still dreamed about him. I probably would never have children of my own. If someone was concerned about overpopulation of the planet, the Foxes had filled their quota in my generation, so being content to be auntie to so many nieces and nephews ought to satisfy me.

While we finished saddling up, Carly said, "You did talk to Diane about getting the stroller for Zoe's shower, right?"

I hefted the saddle onto Cactus's back and straightened the blanket under it. "I texted her. She's got nearly two weeks."

Carly fiddled with the stirrups on her saddle. "I'll remind her."

I didn't really feel jealous of Diane and Carly's closeness. But they shared secrets that made me nervous for Carly's safety. Trying to keep my mother-bear tendencies in check with my fully capable and fully grown niece was a struggle.

Robert, my older brother by less than a year, strode to us. He carried his daughter, only three weeks younger than Ted's son. Brie rested her head on Robert's shoulder and gazed around with sleepy eyes, her thumb planted in her mouth. "I need to take Little Bit back inside. You can head out and get started." He didn't need to give us any more instruction. We'd followed this routine for the nine years Robert and Sarah had been at this ranch.

The ranch technically belonged to Sarah's father. Just one of three he'd inherited and built up. With only one brother, Garrett, who was an attorney in Scottsdale, Sarah assumed she and Robert would eventually run all the ranches, if not inherit them outright.

Carly watched Robert hurry toward another pair of riders, singing a made-up song about bunnies to his daughter. "He's nuts over that kid." The sadness in her voice told me she was remembering her own father and their closeness.

Again, I had the urge to hug her. "At that age, your mother and father had you in the saddle in front of them. I imagine Robert would like to do the same."

Carly yanked on the girth strap to suck up the slack when Spitz let out a breath. "Sarah must be like a caged tiger in the house with Louise, cooking dinner and taking care of a baby."

Branding day was where my sister Louise shined. Most days she was about as irritating as a canker sore, but she could organize and manage a branding dinner like she was born to it.

Much like me, Sarah would rather be in the branding pen, covered in dirt and cow manure, wielding a branding iron or squeezing a vaccine gun, than stranded in the kitchen basting a roast and stirring up macaroni and cheese. Before she'd had a baby, Sarah left the dinner to Louise. A good friend would spend the morning with her, not sneaking off to work cattle.

"There are disadvantages to having kids." I placed a boot in the stirrup and pulled myself into Cactus's saddle.

The back screen door slammed, and a figure marched from the light cast through the kitchen windows into the shadow of the yard at a fast pace toward us.

I'd faced down lots of trouble as sheriff, but this put the fear of God in me.

4

Sarah's thick ponytail swung from side to side, and her long legs carried her to where Carly and I sat on our horses.

"Where do you think you're going," she said to me. Sarah and I had been best friends since we'd started kindergarten and sat at the same desk. We'd shared a whole lot since then, including being suspended in high school for protesting global warming during the homecoming parade. The Kyoto Protocol had just convened, and we were wise beyond our years—or so we believed. We were college roommates and now sisters-in-law.

"I'm rounding up cattle." So much for my chicken-hearted hopes of escape.

Robert joined us, passing off Brie so she could snuggle into Sarah's chest, nudging her head into the curve where Sarah's neck met her shoulder. With her thumb still in her mouth, Brie's eyes closed.

Sarah and Robert shared a brief kiss, so natural and effortless it sent a sharp arrow of longing into me. I couldn't imagine I'd ever have that kind of love. Robert said, "She was pretty busy here. She'll probably take a long nap."

"Unless she's overstimulated." Sarah rubbed Brie's back. "But if she doesn't sleep, Auntie Kate will take care of her."

I sat up taller, as if ready to ride away. "Got to get moving to round up those pairs."

My brother Jeremy and another cowboy passed by, urging their horses into a trot.

Sarah's laugh had an edge to it. "Nice try. If I have to be at the house, you do, too."

My voice sounded whiny in the still morning air. "Come on. I didn't have a baby."

Robert considered me, then Sarah with an uneasy air.

Carly nodded at him. "If you know what's good for you, you'll back away and let them deal with it."

I was sunk and knew it. I couldn't say no to Sarah any more than she could when I asked her to do a three-day trail ride with me. She'd wanted to go to a street dance in Bryant, but I'd broken up with a boyfriend and didn't want to see him there with his new girlfriend. So I'd begged Sarah to have an adventure with me. A thunderstorm the first night soaked our sleeping bags and spooked the horses, so they ran off. And still, when I'd pleaded with her to continue, Sarah hadn't let me down.

I slid from the saddle.

Carly kicked Spitz, and he jumped, rearing to go. "You two girls be sure to cook up some tasty vittles."

"Screw you," Sarah said, making Carly's laughter ring out as she trotted after the others.

Robert hadn't backed away fast enough. Sarah glared at him. "Glass ceilings shatter for everyone, women CEOs and politicians. And in the Land That Time Forgot, you get to direct our branding and I'm stuck serving up homemade dinner rolls and taking care of the children."

"You baked dinner rolls?" Now I was excited.

Robert rubbed her shoulder. "It's not fair, but we're not going to take down the patriarchy this morning. Your father would keel over dead."

Sarah patted Brie's butt. "Dad, sure." Resigned, she started for the house. "Come on, Kate. Maybe Louise will let you grate the cheese."

We spent the morning setting up tables in the shop, stirring, chopping, slicing according to direction from Louise.

Sometime well after the sun had risen, we'd succeeded in getting Brie to sleep, and Sarah and I retreated to the front porch with a cup of coffee.

Haze rose from the alfalfa field, smearing the green leaves and smattering of purple flowers into an Impressionist artist's fondest dream. Blackbirds kibitzed with the sparrows and yellow finches, while the savory smell of roast beef mingled with the fresh scent of the still dewy prairie.

Sarah leaned back on the porch swing and closed her eyes. "Did I tell you Garrett flew in for the branding?"

I sat back in a padded chair and put my boots on the railing. "Lord Gary came home to wear the crown for a day?" No one, ever, called him Gary.

"Alden and Ellie drove to Broken Butte to get him last night." A strain of bitterness crept into her voice. "They wanted me to go with them, but someone had to get things ready for the branding."

Alden was Sarah's father, who ruled his kingdom with a sometimes capricious hand. Ellie, Sarah's mother, had doted on Garrett since the day he'd nearly been strangled by the umbilical cord and arrived from the womb blue and weak.

"At least he didn't bring Sheila." That was Garrett's wife, a pale, skinny woman terrified to let the sun strike her skin. She didn't cook, do dishes, chat with the branding help, or venture far from her laptop, where she managed her real estate business. "I'm surprised he had the nerve to come back after last time," she said.

That made me laugh. "When was that? Four years ago?" Sarah had been wielding the branding iron, and Garrett had tried to take over. She'd responded by branding his boot. He'd been mad enough he'd driven to Denver and flown back to Arizona that day, which I thought was an overreaction, since the iron hadn't penetrated to his foot.

I didn't blame Sarah for not being a big Garrett fan. Her parents never passed an opportunity to brag on their successful son, who bought a McMansion on the third green of a Scottsdale golf course, served on the board of a few charities, and was a named partner in an international law firm. Garrett blew into town every few years, wowed the peasants of the Sandhills, and blew out again, leaving Sarah to deal with her aging and, to my way of thinking, cranky parents.

The screen door opened, and Louise rolled out, dragging her chins with her. "Here you are."

Sarah gave her an uncharacteristically guilty look. "Taking a break. Should we be doing something?"

Louise plopped down next to Sarah, making the swing dip. She skewered me with her gaze, surely hoping for inside information. "I heard Newt and Earl got into it last night at the Long Branch."

"Yep."

My terse response didn't daunt her. "I heard Ted was there being all official."

Sarah let out a breath that sounded like, "Asshole."

Louise gave her a side-eye. "I don't know how Dahlia could have arranged it for him to be there, and maybe it's coincidence, but I have to warn you, Kate. Dahlia is bad-mouthing about you all over town."

I sipped my coffee and watched the sun warm the hay pasture in front of the house. A doe and fawn grazed, not at all concerned about us. "She's never liked me."

Louise liked to dispense wisdom almost as much as she loved to dole out her baked goods. "If you'd made even the smallest effort to get along, you wouldn't have made such an enemy."

Sarah laughed. "Being hated by Dahlia is a badge of honor."

Louise didn't argue, and I could tell she was working her way to another topic, one that might even be more annoying.

"So, Kate." Not a promising start. "How's Dad getting along?" Her attempt at casual chitchat was unconvincing.

I stayed still, hoping that like a T-rex, she wouldn't attack if she didn't see movement. "Fine."

She shifted, causing the swing to jar and Sarah to grab the armrest. "You need to talk to him."

"I talk to him all the time."

Sarah's eyes twinkled, and I wondered if she knew where Louise was heading.

Louise leaned forward, tilting the seat of the swing and almost tossing Sarah to the deck. "About his behavior."

"No." I stood, clutching my coffee mug.

Louise jumped up, too, bouncing Sarah back. "He's drinking too much, staying out late. He's been going around with…" She lowered her voice and managed to look scandalized. "Women."

I opened the door and stepped inside. "Not my business." I shut the door on whatever else Louise said, and from the sound of her raised voice, it was plenty.

Not long after, I was dispatched to the branding pen to get a head count.

We'd had our typical Sandhills spring, some teaser days in March when the temps climbed to the high sixties for a few hours. Just enough to drive us all into despair when the remainder of winter settled in for the last few weeks. Then April, with its increasingly warmer and sunnier days, topped off by that last heavy snowfall designed to break the hardiest spirit. We'd recently kissed May goodbye, who'd taken her chilly, gray days that struck with unpredictable cruelty but sprinkled in seventy-plus-degree days with skies so blue it could break your heart. And now we welcomed June, like a newborn with all the hope and promise ahead of her.

Today, a few hours after sunrise, the sun had already coaxed the first layers from the branding crew, leaving them in sweatshirts that they would probably shed in another hour. If it hadn't been for the roar of the propane branding fire, we'd have been serenaded by meadowlarks, blackbirds, sparrows, and all their cousins.

I climbed from Dad's pickup and made the count, texting Sarah the results. Twenty-seven out there, Louise, Sarah, and me, and we could count on a few of the closest neighbor women showing up with pies and salads to help serve and gossip.

The herd was bunched in one corner with three ropers moving stealthily through them, picking out calves. All the others worked their jobs like a pit crew on a NASCAR track. Vaccinators, branders, and all the others descended, and in a matter of seconds the work was completed and the dazed critter released to find its mama.

The whole place smelled of burning hair and had a team atmosphere. Roaring propane stove, cattle bawling, people yelling, it would seem like chaos if you didn't understand the process. The work was hard, but with neighbors and friends gathered, there were plenty of jokes and teasing. All ages participated. The youngest and least skilled were put to work wrestling calves.

Robert stood by the temporary panel fence. He watched me drive up and park next to the pickups and SUVs of the neighbors and friends who had arrived after the cattle had been rounded up. I sidled up to him amid the organized chaos that marked any branding corral. "You shirker. Are you now the big boss and don't have to work?"

Robert, tall and lean, a dusty, well-worn black hat securely on his head, surveyed the operation. "I had a job." He spoke with uncharacteristic bitterness. "But I was relieved of it."

Sarah and Robert ran the ranch as a true partnership, but because Robert was the man, the branding fell under his charge. Not all ranches operated with this patriarchy, but Sarah's family clung to it. He'd called the neighbors, handed out the assignments for vaccinating, roping, wrestling, and tagging. And, since Sarah's father's minor stroke had left him tottery and not safe around a herd of agitated cows, Robert's job as surrogate ranch owner would be wielding the branding iron.

I located the person who now held the iron. Ah. The grating tone of Robert's comment made sense.

Garrett Haney hefted a branding iron from the fifty-five-gallon barrel where the propane fire heated it. He had the same brown hair as Sarah, tailor-made for a shampoo commercial. His was shaped with some kind of precision cut that kept it perfect, barely ruffled by the breeze. Smooth skin that hadn't seen years of weathering as had most of the faces in the pen. He was tall and toned, broad shouldered, with a physique, according to Sarah, curated in an expensive Scottsdale gym.

"Sarah told me he'd made it for the big day," I said.

Robert glared at him. "Showed up about an hour ago. Alden chauffeured him in, no doubt after mimosas and eggs Benedict."

"It's his family's brand, guess he's got the right," I baited Robert.

It worked, and his jaw clenched before he grumbled, "When he's out here in a blizzard pulling a calf and warming it in the bathtub at two in the morning, then I'll say he's entitled to play rancher at the branding."

He finally turned his scowling face to me to catch my grin. His face relaxed. "Got me. But, damn, it torques me when he acts like he's the boss."

"He's not around much, so you can either get over it or die." I gave him the usual dose of Fox sympathy.

Robert nodded across the pen, and I peered through the crowd of cows and branding help. A skinny boy, around the same age as our nine-year-old nephews, pressed close to the temporary fence. His jeans and tennis shoes showed not a speck of dust or manure. He looked terrified. "Garrett's son, Tony. The poor kid doesn't know what to do."

He grew up in Scottsdale, Arizona. Maybe he'd seen a horse at a petting zoo. I didn't remember him visiting the ranch many times. "Why don't you help him?"

"I'd rather stay here and sulk," Robert said. He winked at me and pushed from the fence to make his way to Tony.

My youngest brother, Jeremy, rode his steady paint into the bunch, Carly next to him. Tuff Henderson threw his rope and snagged a small calf. He dragged it out toward Louise's nine-year-old twin hellions, Mose and Zeke.

Once they'd struggled to get him down, Garrett approached with the branding iron. Branding was a prestigious job. Not only were brands precious and handed down for generations, but the branding laws also stipulated the location of the brand, whether left or right, hip, middle, shoulder.

Garrett planted a shiny cowboy boot on the calf to steady it and pressed the branding iron into the hide.

Jeremy hollered, a few others joined in, a horse neighed, and Mose and Zeke, being kids, turned their focus from the calf to the ruckus in the bunched cattle. The calf gave a kick and unsettled Garrett, who only had one foot on the ground. He fell backward and landed on his butt.

Meanwhile, Spitz was in the process of making a liar out of Carly, who'd called him settled. He'd reared up and now was giving his best impression of a bucking bronc. Carly had both hands on the horn and her knees clenched, but she was losing the battle. The cows and calves were stampeding the temporary panels of the corral. Everyone was running and yelling, some trying to herd the cows on foot toward the center of the pen so they wouldn't break out. It seemed everyone had a mission, but not necessarily the same one, creating a riotous pen of disorganization.

About the time Carly sailed over Spitz's head, a cluster of cows knocked over a panel, and the whole bunch streamed out on a dead run away from the melee.

This was a disaster, as the panicked herd would take hours to round up and the branded calves were mixed in with the unbranded, requiring another level of sorting.

While chaos streamed around me, I hurried to Carly, getting there in time for her to push herself upright and rub her shoulder. No blood, all her limbs working, she'd survive with a few bruises and sore muscles. I gave her a gloating snort. "I can see how Rope's got Spitz calmed down."

Robert appeared, holding the reins of a calm and spent Spitz. "I'd be embarrassed if I were you. Look at this sweet boy."

Carly chucked him on the arm. "You wouldn't have lasted half as long as I did."

I nodded. "She'd have made the eight plus. Last time you rode a bronc, you got thrown right out of the gate."

Before Robert could respond, Garrett stormed up, his arm around Tony's shoulders and the boy being dragged along. "What the hell? Is this all a joke to you?"

Robert's chin rose and his face hardened, leaving no trace of humor. "You have to admit Carly looked pretty comical trying to hang on."

Garrett yanked Tony closer, his hand white on the boy's shoulder. He thrust his face toward Carly with hot rage shooting from him. "Someone could have been hurt."

Without thinking, I shoved between Garrett and Carly. "Hey. No need for that."

Garrett took a moment to study Carly over my head. "It's irresponsible to bring a skittish horse to a branding."

"Whoa," Robert pushed back. "We're working with animals in the great outdoors, not documents in a climate-controlled office. Unexpected things happen."

Garrett's face, so familiar to me because he looked like Sarah, had the hard eyes and stern set of a headmaster. "She should have ridden a more reliable horse. Or let someone else rope."

"No one got hurt," I said, though I probably should have stayed out of it. "Lighten up."

Garrett narrowed his eyes at me, then shifted to Carly and landed on Robert. "Foxes. You're always about the laughs."

Excuse me? I opened my mouth to ask what he meant by that when I felt the vibration in my shirt pocket. With a flick of my fingers, I whipped the phone out and answered, "Sheriff."

In the second it took me to turn my back and start walking away, I saw surprise in Garrett's brown eyes.

5

I recognized the number and expected Marybeth, the usual dispatcher. She came back with, "We've got a 10-18. Creekside Golf Club. GM says there's been a robbery."

I'd finally gotten the hang of most of the ten codes, but like a second language, I still had to translate. For instance, 10-18 meant urgent. Not a law enforcement code, but I had to think to translate GM to general manager. "Is the thief there?"

She sighed and let down her professional tone. "No. The GM thinks because the golf course is big money and big names, they're more important than us local yokels. Not sure when the theft took place, but the urgency is questionable."

A real crime took precedence over what Garrett Haney considered criminal here, so there wasn't a reason I couldn't head to the golf course now. "I'm on my way."

Already on a trot for the fence, I stashed my phone and hollered at Dad, who was helping set up the panel fence. "You need to catch a ride to town. I've gotta go."

Garrett's mouth dropped open, and eight kinds of irritation lined his red face. I supposed he felt I was abandoning a hairy situation. Maybe he thought I ought to arrest Carly for negligent mischief. Sarah was right; he was an entitled rich guy. Probably like the GM at the Creekside club.

Dad raised his hand in acknowledgment, and I leapt to the steel rung of the fence and vaulted over, my boots plopping in the pasture as I took off for his old pickup.

The rolling hills sported a soft blanket of green from the adequate spring rains and abundant sunshine. As long as the summer didn't get stingy with storms, Grand County might grow a fine crop of beef this year. Now that the day had warmed, I rolled down the window. The wind rushing in couldn't create more noise than Dad's rumbling and grumbling old Dodge. Hopefully Dad wouldn't forget to collect Poupon when he caught a ride back to town. I squinted into the bright day, sorry I hadn't grabbed sunglasses when we'd left in the darkness.

I loved this time of year in the Sandhills. Much as I felt about dawn, early summer lent itself to irrational hope. A little sunshine and optimism would do me good. I'd been far too long feeling the stab of loss and longing.

It took nearly forty-five minutes to reach the Creekside golf course going south on the one-lane blacktop road after I left the branding pen and traversing along a gravel back road that could have used a blade to smooth out the washboards. Herds of Black Baldy cows and their frolicking calves dotted the pastures as I topped one hill and descended into a valley, over and over.

People were often surprised to learn about the world-class golf course built in what many considered a desolate patch of prairie. The scheme to construct it there arose with developers scanning the globe to find terrain that most closely resembled the first courses in Scotland. Apparently, with the choppy, grass-covered hills, this landscape fit the bill. Although I'd never been to Scotland, my impression of the country was a green, overcast, chilly landscape, the air full of moisture, the ground spongy. Here, we had blazing sunshine most of the time, wind a good portion of days, only fourteen inches of annual rainfall, and winters cold enough it could make a polar bear shiver.

Several years ago, investors hit on what they considered golfer heaven right here and hired Gary Player, a retired golf pro, to design one of the courses. They'd brought in developers and turf experts. They'd installed rustic-looking cabins along the bank of the Creekside, built a glass-and-river-rock clubhouse with fat pine beams and pillars, laid down a landing strip, and opened for business.

What a business. At least, we all assumed it was an amazing venture, since mostly us peons were kept at a distance. The goings on at the Creekside course didn't affect the normal Sandhiller's daily life. The rich and famous, celebrities, sports legends, those with wealth we couldn't fathom flew in on private jets, played golf, stayed at their faux-rustic cabins, associated with each other, and flew out. We didn't see them; they didn't know we existed. It worked out well.

The restaurant and cleaning staff were local women. Yes, all women because Sandhills men didn't do that sort of thing. The caddies and course maintenance workers were mostly college kids home for the summer and an occasional high schooler. The chef and groundskeeper, as well as any of the management, were hired from the outside. They appeared in the spring, lived at the course, and hightailed it in late fall. On occasion, Gus MacMartin, the groundskeeper, made his way to the Long Branch. He was a colorful character with a boisterous laugh and quick jokes.

If the Sandhills were Italy, the Creekside club was Vatican City. They were completely autonomous from the rest of us. A few of the more affluent and social of the locals, including Sid and Dahlia and Dahlia's sisters, had memberships. Needless to say, it was pricey. Unless you ponied up the annual fees, you couldn't eat at the restaurant or golf the beautiful course— if you can call a course with natural prairie roughs, no trees, and nature-made sand bunkers beautiful. (I did.) If I were to take up golf, though, I'd like to be surrounded by lush green living things under the shade of leafy trees.

If isolation was one of the draws, the Creekside club came up a winner. It truly would be easier to hire a plane to fly me in than it was to drive, especially in Dad's Dodge. The rough road wound down a crest through soft sand, with two detours veering me off course because of washouts. Dust puffed through my open windows, and about halfway there a bumblebee the size of a 747 Jumbo Jet flew through a hole in the floor. My ducking and wild swatting didn't do much to drive the bee away, but it did send me into a dune next to the road.

After digging out, my patience already growing thin, I continued on and made the last curve around a lone hill. With the vast prairie of wild grass in the rearview, in front of me lay the clubhouse like a glittering castle. The lawn so green and sweeping it would make Kentucky jealous, and pristine black paths lined with vibrant snapdragons, asters, and more marigolds than seemed possible made the place cheery and welcoming.

I eased Dad's pickup to a halt under the portico and almost felt the road dust settle onto the pavement like muddy footprints over a freshly mopped floor.

The crazy-tall and slender front doors of the clubhouse opened, and four middle-aged white men sauntered out. Golf shirts in pastels, khaki shorts, cleated shoes, and hair parted on the side with smatterings of gray. I'd have to look hard to distinguish them from each other, but the wealth wafting around them like spring pollen was obvious.

Before I climbed out, a younger foursome bounded from the clubhouse. More energy, brighter-colored clothes, darker tones of skin and hair, but the same confident and conquering manner. I figured the groups were heading for their starting tees.

As my dusty boots hit the drive, the slap of tennis shoes made me look up to see Opie Lundgren galloping my way.

Like his namesake, Opie had carrot-red hair, copper freckles splattered across his nose, and an easy smile that made him one of the most likeable of my younger brother, Jeremy's, friends. They'd palled around from grade school on and still raised their share of hell together. In a way, Jeremy and Opie might be considered related since Opie's sister was the mother of Jeremy's son, Mason. Mason was the result of a high school dalliance with a college girl home on Christmas vacation. The little guy was a treasure to us all and never once considered an "oops," as some biddies said. Mason's mother had married someone else and moved to Tulsa, and we didn't get to see Mason much.

With spindly arms extending from the short sleeves of a Creekside Golf T-shirt smeared with grease and grass, he waved at me. He rushed his words. "Hey, Kate. Let me park your rig." Opie had worked in the shop since before he'd graduated from high school.

I gave Dad's ride a once-over. "Don't want this vintage beauty stinking up the place?"

Opie glanced over his shoulder to the clubhouse; its doors opened to spit out a gaggle of women who no doubt paired up to the first foursome I'd seen. In their fashionable and crisp activewear, they skirted us with as much care as a mouse would pass a sleeping cat.

Opie nodded and smiled at the women and turned back to me. "Um. Valet service."

"You're a mechanic, not a valet."

He scrunched up his mouth. "Just, um, yeah. This doesn't fit the image."

"I can see that." I laughed. "Where would I find the GM?"

Opie tilted his head on his long neck, somehow reminding me of a giraffe. "Sherwood Temple?"

"Sheriff business."

Opie lifted his eyebrows at my faded jeans and manure-crusted boots.

"I was at a branding when I got the call."

Opie hopped into the Dodge and cranked the key. "Try his office. I've never been in there before." With self-deprecating humor, he added, "They like to keep it clean."

Another group of two couples passed me as I entered the front doors. Their not-so-discreet disapproving looks didn't faze me. They probably weren't any more comfortable with ranchers in dusty jeans and boots than I was with golfers with togs that cost more than my monthly salary.

The tall ceilings, flagstone floors, dark green walls, and deep wood tones gave the place such a rich feel. An unbidden thought of Glenn Baxter hit me. This would be his natural habitat, so different from my Sandhills life. He'd stride through places like this without a thought. I felt like a piece of macaroni on a string of pearls.

Soft footsteps brought another familiar face around a corner. Amy Klinger, a girl about Carly's age who had graduated from Dunbar High, carried a tray with two glasses of orange juice, two coffee mugs, a thermal carafe, and a cream pitcher. She drew up short with shock across her round face. "Kate?"

I didn't want to consider how out of place I looked in my branding get-up, so said simply, "Sheriff business. I'm here to see Sherwood Temple."

"They sent you? Wow. There's no conflict of interest or anything?" The orange juice sloshed a little but didn't spill.

Her reaction was curious, but since I'm related to half the population of the Sandhills, conflict of interest didn't seem unusual. "Yep. I'm here. Where's the office?"

She directed me down a hall and watched as my boots clacked, no doubt leaving bits of branding-pen debris in my wake.

I found Sherwood Temple in his office down the hall from the club-house kitchen. A silver-haired man I'd place in his mid-sixties, he towered over me when he opened the door. He reminded me of an aristocratic Dick Van Dyke, straight angles and athletic. His nose twitched, and I imagined he caught a whiff of the authentic Sandhills from my boots. "You are?"

I extended my hand. "Kate Fox, Grand County Sheriff."

Unlike Opie's humor at my appearance, Sherwood Temple didn't seem at all amused. "Sheriff, you say?"

We had a way of doing business in the Sandhills, and he might as well get used to it. "I was at a branding when I was called. Dispatch said you had a theft?"

With a grudging welcome, he stepped back and indicated a chair in front of his desk.

My boots sank into the high pile of the hunter green carpet, and the air conditioning immediately drew goose bumps as I sat on the smooth leather. Enticing smells of bacon from breakfast and whatever gourmet fare they prepared for lunch drifted from the kitchen, making me sorry to miss the branding dinner at Robert's. Though by the time they rounded up the pairs and finished up at the pens, I might be able to join them.

Sherwood's face wasn't so much a smile as a grimace. He folded his long-fingered hands on the empty green blotter in front of him. "I had expected the state patrol. And even then, I would have thought they'd be here much sooner."

Ooookay. Marybeth calling him arrogant was as understated as jeans at a gala. "The golf course is a long way from civilization. By design, if I understand it." The canned air didn't feel right, and his office didn't have a window, adding to my claustrophobia.

He waved his hand in dismissal. "If you can call the rest of Nebraska civilized."

If part of being civilized meant knowing how to be polite, then yes, we were a far sight more civilized than the likes of Sherwood Temple. "So. The theft?"

He rose. He wore camel-colored trousers in a fabric that looked so soft a bunny would be jealous, and a crisp white shirt and navy blazer. Sherwood wasn't hitting the links today; he was managing his empire and helping important people feel pampered. "It is a very expensive piece of art. Not large, so we had it on a shelf at the entrance, opposite the front door. Stolen some time in the last day or two. I'm sorry I can't be more precise."

He yanked open a drawer on a dark wood filing cabinet and rifled through it. "We're in the midst of our busiest time. Our players tend to like June as opposed to August, when it can be unbearably hot. We've been particularly fortunate this year with not much rain."

"Good luck for the golfers, maybe, but not so much for the cows." I couldn't help poking back.

He didn't respond to that, maybe because he didn't understand, but probably because he didn't care. "As I said, we've been busy, and it wasn't until this morning I noticed it missing."

He whipped out a folder and strutted back to his desk. When he opened the file and slid a page out and flipped it my way, I nearly choked.

I stared at the invoice he'd given me. The number of zeros on the total at the bottom was shocking enough, but the photo of the piece was what had stopped my breath with a lump like rising bread dough in my throat.

The bronze in the picture wasn't one I'd seen before, but the origin was unmistakable. Flowing lines of the abstract piece rose up like elegant flames. With sunlight or even electric illumination, it would feel alive and vibrant with energy. It punched a hole in my heart.

Chin raised, Sherwood gazed down at the page too. "I admit to a personal fondness for the piece, which is surprising, since we'd sought the artist purely because she is local."

"Was." My voice sounded strained. "Was local. She doesn't live here anymore."

He didn't appear interested in the details, which was a relief. "Since we can't obtain a replacement, it makes it that much more imperative you have the art returned to us. Our guests love the idea that someone with her reputation and obvious talent comes from this place."

How Sherwood Temple could have avoided the splashy headlines almost two years ago about the artist Marguerite Myers and her shocking past, I don't know. But it was my good fortune he hadn't put it together with the artist who created his pilfered sculpture.

I stared at the photo of the bronze, though I couldn't bring myself to touch it. I remembered Mom in her basement studio. The heat of her art causing her to shed her clothes and work without thought of eating or sleeping...or the fact she had nine children who needed her attention. How could I ache so much for a woman who had such little regard for us?

Sherwood frowned, and I wondered what emotions had crossed my face. "What do you need from me?"

Despite how rattled I felt, I managed to sound professional. "I'll need a list of anyone staying here since the statue was last seen. Any employees working those days, visitors, or anyone who was on the premises."

His aristocratic white eyebrows dipped low over cold eyes. "I'm afraid that will be difficult."

"Why is that?"

After an inhale that sucked oxygen from the shut-off room and an exhale full of hot air, he said, "We held our annual employees' day on Tuesday, and a local charity scramble yesterday brought in local members and guests. We're only recovering from the influx of..." He paused as if searching for a suitable term. "Well, not our normal caliber of guests."

Of course it didn't seem like a big chore to him. He probably didn't understand I had no deputy or undersheriff. I was the only law enforcement officer in Grand County, an area just slightly smaller than Rhode Island.

Sarcasm crept into my response. "You're thinking some of the Sandhills riffraff ran off with this pricey piece of art."

A lilting *huh* sounded like his version of Homer Simpson's *d'oh*. "While it's not unheard of for celebrities to have a bout of kleptomania, it doesn't seem the most likely scenario. Let's start with the Sandhills population. It shouldn't take you long to investigate, since there are so few. If you haven't discovered the culprit by then, we can work through the guests."

He rose to usher me out. "I'll have my assistant provide you the list of employees and local membership rolls." He stood by my chair until I got to my feet.

With an arm out to direct me to the door, he said, "I'm sure you understand we'd prefer to keep this investigation discreet. It's rare, but occasionally one of the guests will get chummy with an employee and they share information. Our business relies on word of mouth, and we can't afford for potential guests to think our staff is dishonest."

Mom had bred in us a distrust and maybe even revulsion for the monied class. It was a prejudice I'd rejected long ago, especially after knowing Baxter. And even though I hated agreeing with Mom on anything these days, it was hard not to dislike this stiff-backed snob. "I'll start by interviewing the staff now."

He held the door open and let his gaze slide up and down my rustic appearance. "It's probably best you aren't in uniform to keep from alarming our guests. But please, use the employee entrances and stay out of the public areas."

The door closed behind me, and I stood in the quiet hall, the sickly swoosh of air conditioning crawling across my skin.

6

I spent the next couple of hours talking to servers, housekeeping, and kitchen staff. The closest I came to any real information was Amy Klinger remembering she'd dusted the sculpture on the morning of the employee barbeque. That was two days ago.

I stood with Opie in the open door of the mostly empty cart garage. "You didn't see anyone unusual hanging around on Tuesday?"

He wiped his hand on a rag and laughed. "It was mostly Sandhillers. Everyone is unusual."

"Fair enough. Was it only employees?"

He scrunched up his face, melting some freckles together. "Some of the local members pitched in for setup and cleanup so the staff didn't have to do it."

Sherwood Temple strode toward us across the black tarmac. He walked as I'd expected, with military crispness.

I watched him approach and spoke to Opie. "Can you text me a list of everyone you remember helping out?"

Opie caught me eyeing Sherwood, and he spun on his tennis shoes, hurrying into the shadows of the cart shed with a "Sure thing," chasing him.

"Sheriff Fox," Sherwood drilled at me before he was close enough for conversation. "Have you made any progress?"

I tipped my head toward the sky as if gauging the time. "It's been two hours. I've talked to most of the staff here."

He folded his arms, hardly ruffling his blazer. "Well. I sent you the lists you requested nearly an hour ago. What do you intend to do? Simply *ask* people if they took it?"

How many investigations had he conducted? "It's where I'm starting. If you have suggestions, I'd be glad to hear them."

He rolled his head up and around. "I'm not the sheriff here. It seems you'd have a system. Taking fingerprints, for instance?"

"A big fan of *CSI*?" I shouldn't have, but I couldn't help it.

His tight-lipped response was all he offered.

I circled back to professional mode. "Since so many people have been in the lobby recently, fingerprints wouldn't gain much. Asking around, matching stories, seeing reactions, jogging memories, these things often sift out some clues."

He obviously didn't see me as a law enforcement authority. He twitched his shoulder and looked down on me. "And?"

I had an idea or two and wondered how to let him know I hadn't come up empty, but my phone vibrated in my jeans pocket. With one finger held up to him, I slipped my phone out and answered.

A woman's voice sounded put out, and it took me a moment to place it as Henny Markheim, co-proprietor with her husband, Dutch, of Dutch's grocery store on Main Street. "Sorry to bother you. I figure you're out to the branding." Of course she knew who was branding on what days because they sold all the groceries for the giant branding dinners.

"That's okay. What's up?"

Sherwood Temple's face pinched with an unmistakable offense. I supposed he wasn't used to being put off by public servants.

Henny continued. "I didn't know what else to do since those two old coots are having a standoff next to the Raisin Bran and they won't listen to me."

Old coots. I had a strong suspicion about who she referred to. "The Johnson brothers?"

A crash sounded from her end. "Lordy, that was a jar of applesauce, and they already hit the Miracle Whip. You'd best hurry."

"On my way. It'll be thirty minutes, so try to get them contained." I stashed my phone and trotted toward Dad's pickup, which Opie had strategically parked behind the cart shed.

Sherwood Temple raised his voice, but as well modulated as it was, I couldn't call it shouting. "What about the investigation?"

I wrenched open the pickup door. "I'll take a look at the lists and go from there."

He wrinkled his nose as I backed up around him. Maybe it was the look of Dad's old Dodge, maybe it was the smell of manure on the wheels. I thought it more likely his general distaste and distrust of Sandhillers, and specifically the Grand County Sheriff.

Since I didn't get another call on the twenty-minute drive—I cut ten minutes from the normal time by maxing out the speed on the open road— I assumed the brothers hadn't found more guns and were indiscriminately taking out jars of pickles and loaves of bread. Part of my brain kept a tally of calves in each pasture, the play of clouds across the expanse of blue, the level of water in the shallow lakes. I might not be ranching, but I was still acutely aware of the weather and land and situation of the ranchers.

Thankfully none of our senior citizens were out for a leisurely drive along the highway through town, as was often the case, so I didn't slow much as I hit the town limit and turned onto Main Street to the grocery store.

The scene in the alley next to Dutch's was unexpected. I eased Dad's pickup to the curb and shut it off.

Aileen Carson walked out of Dutch's front door with two bags of groceries hugged to her chest. She wore crisp jeans and a button-up shirt, her face made-up and hair curled. In her fifties, Aileen always made an effort to clean up when she came to town from the ranch, even if it was only for more flour and sugar.

She hesitated and took in the goings-on in the alley, then made her way to her pickup parked next to mine. She tilted her head to indicate the store and maybe the alley. "It's a mess in there. Between the spaghetti sauce and mayonnaise, it looks like a murder scene."

What could I say to that? I offered a polite nod and turned to the alley.

May Keller, who was old enough to have celebrated King Tut's coronation with a cold beer and cigarette, stood in the middle of the empty lot and faced the grocery store wall. Before her, flattened against the building and looking as if they'd like to evaporate into the wall, Newt and Earl stood motionless. They wore clean shirts. Their scuffed and nearly worn-out work boots had been replaced with cowboy boots that looked newly polished.

Newt's eye had blossomed to a rosy purplish hue where Earl had planted his fist last night, but he seemed otherwise unharmed.

May didn't so much as flick her gaze to me as I approached. She had the focus of a border collie guarding sheep. "'Bout time you got here." May Keller made an apple doll look young and supple. Even her voice, worn from so many cigarettes, sounded as if there wasn't an ounce of moisture in her whole body.

"How long have you held them like this?" I asked, surveying the Johnson brothers and their pleading eyes.

Newt drew in a breath and started to speak.

He didn't get out more than a peep when May thrust her chin. She didn't move any other bit of her withered frame that was even shorter than mine.

May spoke out of the corner of her mouth. "Twenty minutes, give or take. I been holdin' for you so you could begin the interrogation."

That was considerate of her. "If you could hang on to them for a sec, I'll talk to Henny and be right out."

May scowled at the brothers. "Get on with it, then. I ain't got time to waste."

I found Henny, a plump and normally pleasant woman, on her hands and knees next to a scrub bucket in the second aisle. Shattered glass and dill pickles mixed with exploded plastic Miracle Whip jars, making the place smell like a lunchbox massacre. Bits of cereal and raisins added to the montage. "'Clean up on aisle two' probably doesn't sound funny to you."

She sighed and turned a flushed face to me. "No. It does not. I don't know what got into those two. All the sudden they were yelling and throwing groceries."

I squatted down and picked up a whisk broom and dust pan and swept pickles and cereal into it. "Did you hear what they were arguing about?"

She tore a string of paper towels from the roll and scooped up the gooey mess. "Mostly about who stole something in the old days and who is stealing now. Who knows? But they acted like they wanted to tear each other apart. I'm not going to allow them both in here at the same time again."

Newt and Earl mostly kept their disagreements in the open air. And I hadn't known them to be this violent. "Get an accounting of what they damaged. I'll guarantee they make good on it."

She kept her head down, working efficiently. "I'd make them clean this up if I wasn't worried they'd start in again."

I didn't want to risk that either. I finished with the whisk broom and went back to deal with the miscreants.

I found May and the Johnsons exactly how I left them. "Let's start the interrogation."

May relaxed and stretched her neck. The brothers both inhaled but stayed pressed against the wall.

I paced in front of them to create some tension. "I thought after last night at the Long Branch, when I didn't throw you in jail, you were going to straighten up. But here you are, causing more trouble What's going on with you two?"

They stayed stock-still, their arms straight at their sides, pressed against the wall.

Newt puckered his lips together before he let loose. "It's his fault. I wanted to get the fancy salad dressing—the kind that's original, you know, Hidden Valley—and he was dead set on Dorothy Lynch."

Earl's eyes flew open in astonishment. "Anyone can get that old stuff. But Dorothy Lynch is made in Nebraska, and after you been away awhile, that's what you want."

"You want what the rest of the folks eat out in the world." Newt side-eyed Earl, his head tilting a tad to get a better view.

Earl's arm snapped to the side to bump Newt's. "You don't know nothing."

I raised my hands in the air. If they could come to blows over salad dressing, it seemed like they needed a real time-out. "Now you're into Dutch's to cover the cost of what you destroyed. Which you can pay for as soon as I release you from jail."

7

I could easily have walked Newt and Earl to the courthouse on my own. Their whining and pleading didn't sway me more than the soft summer breeze. But May Keller apparently had the time to accompany us. Maybe she wanted to make sure the brothers wouldn't overpower me. Being trained and experienced as a sheriff, including being shot at, nearly run over, and investigating murder scenes, didn't seem to make a lasting impression on someone who'd known me all my life and had seen me flub the free throw that would have won district championship, and get bucked off a horse because I was goofing around—more than once.

To May, I might always be a clueless kid. I let her trail alongside us. Since Newt and Earl dragged their feet the one and a half blocks up the hill, it gave May plenty of time to light up and suck down her unfiltered Camel. She ground it into the pavement before we entered the back door of the courthouse, which opened into the basement. Sounding like stampeding buffalo, we clattered up the stairs.

The county clerk-assessor's office and the treasurer's office faced off on the west side of the main story across a linoleum floor the color of caramel and just as shiny as if it'd been licked. A wider corridor swept toward the double glass doors and out to the front of the brick building. The commissioners met once a month in a good-sized room that contained not only a sturdy table large enough to seat them and guests but also what served as a break room for me and the two county officials.

The brothers slowed their steps even more when we reached the main floor. Newt swung his head toward me, sounding on the verge of tears. "Aw, Sheriff. You don't have to do this."

Earl stopped and took a backward step into me. "We learned our lesson. We promise not to fight no more."

"At least not in public," Newt added, probably understanding no one would believe they'd get along forever.

I nudged Earl to get him moving again. "You already promised. Now I'm going to drive the lesson home." I didn't intend to keep them long. An afternoon spent locked up on one of the year's finest days ought to be enough to straighten them out.

May added her take. "You two fools are old enough to know better. Why the hell are you worried about salad dressing? Eat some damned French fries and leave that rabbit food to city folks."

My office, a converted storage room, was at the east end of the hall. Only big enough for a desk and two ancient metal filing cabinets. One tiny holding cell had been built behind a heavy door. The only natural light seeped in from narrow windows close to the ceiling.

There wasn't much cause to lock up criminals in Grand County, so I mainly used the cell for storage. May kept an eye on the culprits while I emptied the boxes of old phones and cords, office supplies, and detritus collected over the years. It wouldn't hurt to toss all of it in the Dumpster later on. Maybe I ought to thank Newt and Earl for prompting me to sort and clean.

The brothers started in again when I ushered them to the cell. With a metal sink in the corner and a rickety cot that could probably be used as a weapon if I ever had a dangerous person locked up, it wasn't exactly posh accommodations.

Earl hit on a bribe. "We'll clean out this stuff for you. Haul it away."

Newt nodded with enthusiasm. He paused at the doorway to the cell. "That's right. And we can come out and clean your basement and that old shed of yours."

I encouraged him into the cell with a wave. "I've only been there for two years. Haven't had a chance to accumulate junk."

Since I'd bought my bungalow on Stryker Lake from May Keller, I supposed she felt obligated to chime in. "That's right. And there wasn't any junk laying around when she moved in. I wouldn't tolerate a mess."

She said that pointedly, surely to emphasize the mess Newt and Earl lived in. They were junk men. Made their living from pawing through other people's discards. It made sense their home wouldn't be pristine. Unlike May's ranch yard, where not a single blade of grass dared to grow out of place.

They kept up their pleading while I opened the bottom drawer of one of the file cabinets and felt around for the cell keys that were attached in a magnetic box. Their arguments for release continued even after I'd locked them in.

"You might as well have a seat. You're going to be there for a while." I didn't tell them I'd let them out in time for supper. The door separating the cell from the rest of the cramped office stayed open. No need to make them feel like they were in a coffin.

May was waiting by the office door. She fidgeted in her pointy-toed boots that were worn thin as a murderer's alibi. Her plaid men's Western shirt, probably bought from JCPenney in the eighties, was faded but made of such sturdy polyester it'd outlive me by decades. She hitched a thumb toward the hall and slipped out the door.

"I'll be right back," I called to Newt and Earl, not sure if they heard me over their complaints.

I assumed May needed a cigarette as she scurried down the hall and skidded a left to the front. She touched the lighter to the end of her cigarette and inhaled with gusto before I'd even stepped into the sunshine. I positioned myself upwind but still caught the whiff of acrid smoke to mask the lilacs blooming across the street.

She took another puff and let it filter out her nostrils before she spoke, her voice as crackly as cellophane. "Somethin's up with those two igits."

"I agree." Keeping the law was my job. Although I'd only been elected sheriff a little over two years ago, I'd been at this for quite a while. While Ted held the position for eight years before me, I'd helped him investigate what few problems came up. Thefts, cattle rustling, domestic disputes. The Sandhills wasn't normally a hotbed of crime, but I'd handled three murders and some dicey situations in my time. Did I need to get involved with two bachelor brothers and their disputes? "Whatever it is, locking them up for the afternoon ought to knock it out of them."

May scowled at me. "I didn't take you for the do-nothin' that old cow talks you up to be."

I considered who "that old cow" might be, but May didn't have the patience to wait for me.

She flicked her ash onto the greening grass of the courthouse lawn. "Didn't think you missed the fact that Dahlia Conner is bad-mouthin' you every chance she gets."

Oh, that. I dismissed it. "She's never liked me."

May jabbed a shortened cigarette in my direction. "And believe you me when I say I lose no love on that old biddy. But she's got a knack for causin' trouble, and I hate to see you not take her serious and then we end up with that pampered cupcake for sheriff again."

That would be Ted, Dahlia's pride and joy. "Thanks for the advice." I tried to sound appreciative and hoped that would shut her down. I figured folks in Grand County knew to give Dahlia the same consideration as rain on a river.

She dropped the cigarette to the sidewalk and ground it out. "We can talk about how you're gonna deal with that ol' tub-thumper on our way out there."

I'd been making a note to pick up the butt she'd dropped here and the one by the back door, but she startled me. "What? Where?"

Both hands landed firmly on her hips, and she snapped an annoyed expression my way. "Maybe Dahlia's right after all, and you're getting fuzzy-headed." She pointed at me. "I wouldn't have to spell it out for your sister. That Diane got the big serving of brains in your family, but I thought maybe you picked up a crumb or two. Now I'm not so sure."

May had a quirky way of showing affection. I didn't take it personally. Besides, there was no denying my sister Diane was sharp. "You're going to have to explain to me what you're thinking."

She patted the pocket of her plaid shirt, where she kept her pack of cigs.

"I told you. Somethin's up with those numbskulls, and we're gonna figure out what it is."

"You mean go to their house?"

She eased the pack out of the pocket. "Well, the explanation for their fool behavior isn't gonna appear here, is it?"

"Why don't we just ask them?"

She slapped the pack into her palm, and a cigarette shot out. "I already tried that. I shouldn't have to walk you through this investigation, but here it is. Those boys is always on the fight. But they don't mean nothin' by it. The way I heard it, they dialed it up and were out for blood last night at the Long Branch. Those shenanigans at Dutch's ain't like them. I seen those two fools act like this once before."

"When was that?"

"Right before they went to the war. And if things hadn't changed by the time they came home, I ain't sure they wouldn't've killed each other back then. But that situation worked itself out, and they got closer because of it." She shoved the cigarette in her mouth and cupped her hand around her lighter out of habit, even if the breeze on this perfect day wasn't enough to bother the flame.

I couldn't imagine a young Newt and Earl and a time when they weren't like part of the same unit. Maybe a clanking, clanging machine at times, but one that kept running. "What made them fight back then?"

May gave me a look that told me what a dumb question I'd asked. "What else? A split tail."

Well. Interesting phrasing aside, I tried to think of Newt and Earl being in love. It was an image hard to conjure. "Wonder what it could be this time?"

"They ain't dead, yet. Maybe it's the same thing. I ain't embroidering it none to say they pert near killed each other." She didn't wait for me to consider it. With the cigarette firmly in her teeth, she flicked both hands at me and spoke around it. "Go get your dad's rig. I'll wait here for you."

I wasn't sure what going out to the Johnsons' place would accomplish. They lived in a two-story clapboard house their mother had left them long ago. It sat on a few acres five miles west of town. "I need to have someone keep an eye on them in the cell."

She clamped two fingers onto her cigarette and pulled it from her mouth, giving the smoke a moment in her lungs before she blew it out. "Then get after it. Better put Ethel in charge. That Betty would let them talk her into unlocking the cell."

I hated to admit it, but May was right. Betty Paxton, the county treasurer, was a soft touch, which might explain why she supported me. As opposed to Ethel Bender, the clerk-assessor, who threw her support behind Ted in the last election and carried his banner still. Sheriff preference wasn't the only thing the two officials battled over. In fact, they only agreed on their mutual dislike of each other. It kept things interesting in the courthouse.

I tromped back inside and almost ran into Verla Hampton. Married to the Baptist minister, Verla helped round out their income by working at the bank. It was impossible not to like Verla, with her always crisp attire, neat makeup, and perpetual good nature.

"Oh, Kate. I was on my way to your office."

Not another problem. "What do you need?"

I must have signaled my wariness because she touched my arm. "Oh, no. I'm not in any trouble. I heard Newt and Earl are here, and I forgot to have them sign something when they were in."

It surprised me Newt and Earl used a bank. I assumed they kept whatever dollars they managed to save stashed in a mattress. "Sure. Come on back."

I led her to the office and the cell.

She hesitated a moment, the smile slipping from her face before she forced it back on with false cheer. "Oh, well. Here you are." Her chirpy laugh was strangled.

Newt clasped the bars. "Did you come to bail us out?"

Earl jumped up from the cot. "We didn't get a phone call or nothing."

If Verla had been wearing pearls, she would have clutched them. "W-w-well, I'm just not used to having people fill out the bank card forms, and I completely forgot to have you sign the papers. I know you've already used it, but I won't tell if you don't." She glanced back at me with a nervous chuckle. "I don't think it's illegal if they go ahead and sign it now."

I held my hand up to indicate to go on.

She rustled a sheet of paper and fumbled with a pen. "I just, uh, have this pen here." She handed the page to Earl, and he took his time to read it as if seeing it for the first time.

We stood awkwardly, Verla trying her best not to notice her customers were prisoners.

Earl pantomimed Newt turning and bending over to make a desk, and he signed the paper and shoved it and the pen at Newt.

He started to read the paper, but Earl said, "Just sign the derned thing. You read it all yesterday." Earl leaned over so Newt could use his back.

Newt scribbled his name and slipped the paper through the bars.

Verla thanked them and scurried out, then down the stairs, and we heard the door open and close.

Newt and Earl stared at me without saying anything.

Okay. I walked down the hall and into Ethel's office. Brittany Ostrander rose from the assistant's desk behind the tall front counter. One of Jeremy's sometimes flings, Brittany treated me with all the friendliness of someone who hoped to join the family. I'd tried to warn her about the unlikelihood of that happening, but she remained hopeful. She flashed a smile to rival the sunshine bursting through the large window behind her.

"I thought you'd be at Robert and Sarah's." She walked around the desk to meet me at the counter. With her long blond hair and pretty face, I could see why my brother found her attractive. "Jeremy said he'd be there most of the day."

How had the branding gone after I left? Maybe Garrett had erupted again and taken off for Arizona. I'd get all the news later. "I got a call, so had to leave. I need to talk to Ethel. Is she in?" Of course she was in. She was always in.

Ethel spent her days in the vault. The space was exactly as the name suggested. A metal door about a foot thick with a dial for the combination lock and lever on the outside that looked like it belonged in any bank. It stood ajar all day, and Ethel holed up at her desk inside the room the size of a single-car garage. No windows, not great lighting, it smelled of old banana peels and coffee. Ethel ate her lunch there most days among the decaying volumes of land transactions and maps dating back to the beginning of Grand County more than 150 years ago. Since she spent her daylight hours like a troll, it's little surprise she often acted like one.

I wound around the front counter and back to Ethel's inner sanctum. I tried to sound cheerful, but not too perky because that would put her off. "Hi, Ethel. How's it going?"

She sat at her desk, bent close to her computer. I honestly didn't know how she filled her time, but it involved precise recording of land parcels, permits, assessing taxes, and generally seeking to know everything about everyone in Grand County to ensure they paid their fair share. She seemed convinced the citizenry was out to bilk the county.

Ethel sat back and blinked at me, her eyes small and dark behind large-framed glasses. Wiry gray hair kinked around her face in a perm that would gradually ease up to thin fluff before she repeated the process, as she'd been doing for decades. "Is Brittany not at her desk? No one is allowed back here."

I didn't want to get the poor girl in trouble. "She tried to stop me. Just seemed easier to talk to you myself, and I hated to make you get up."

She scowled at me. Between Ethel and May, I'd reached my daily quota of those kinds of looks from old ladies. "The Johnson brothers are in the holding cell, and I need to go on a call. They'll be fine, but I'd like someone to keep an eye on them from time to time. They might need a bathroom break while I'm gone."

Ethel flopped back, her chair groaning with her shapeless bulk. "They must be serious about their feud this time. That's probably why they were at the bank yesterday. Splitting up the assets."

Ethel must have a mole at the bank. I couldn't figure it'd be Verla. At any rate, Ethel didn't need to know about the credit card. I waved my hand and pretended she'd made a joke. "Oh, you. Can't imagine Newt and Earl would have many assets to fight over."

She raised her eyebrows at me but probably wanted to hold her information close, just as I did.

When she didn't answer, I said, "I just wanted them to cool off a bit. Maybe teach them to quit fighting in public."

Her face pinched even tighter, giving her the appearance of freshly punched bread dough. "Because you want to make a silly statement, this suddenly becomes my problem? I never had to watch the jail when Ted was sheriff. He handled the job like a professional."

If being a professional meant boinking your mistress in the sheriff's office, then I'd happily keep up my amateur status. "If you're too busy, that's fine. I'll ask Betty if she can do it."

Ethel fell into the unimaginative trap as if she didn't realize she'd been played. She huffed and slid open a desk drawer to pull out a packet of Sanka. It was Betty's day to make coffee, and Ethel complained Betty made it too weak. I agreed but had learned not to join the fray.

Ethel pushed herself from her desk to stand on her always swollen feet. She bit her words off like a plug of tobacco. "I'll take care of it. Betty's likely to let them out. You can't trust her."

I set the cell keys on her desk. "Appreciate it." I let the words hover behind me as I walked back into the office and waved goodbye to Brittany.

It only took a few minutes to clamber down the back stairs and jog to Dad's Dodge still parked in front of Dutch's. I backed out and circled to the courthouse.

May crushed her cigarette and left the butt on the sidewalk with three others before joining me in the cab. She glanced out the window into the pickup bed. "Where's that hound of yours?"

Poupon and May had formed an unlikely friendship when I'd left him at her place during the trouble with Mom. Maybe May had been so fed up with Mom and my sister Louise by then, she'd taken to a dog with napping as his main hobby.

"He's out at Robert's branding with Dad." I maneuvered down Main Street, waiting while Doris Cleveland backed her twenty-five-year-old Lincoln out from in front of Dutch's without looking, swung into the oncoming lane, and eased into a slot in front of the post office directly across the street.

May muttered under her breath, then latched onto my mention of Dad. "Hank's been having his share of activity these days."

This wasn't a topic I wanted in on, and I kept my mouth shut.

But May obviously wanted a discussion. "You need to keep an eye out. That Wanda Jenkins has chewed through a husband or two already. And

Deenie Hayward had a case of crabs back in the eighties, and I'm not sure she's not still contagious the way she gets around."

Deenie Hayward? She lived up north in Choker County. I hadn't heard about her and Dad.

May shouted, "Where the hell are you going?"

I slammed on the brakes, and my heart banged into my chest.

8

When I could speak, I said, "To the Johnsons'. Isn't that what you wanted?"

May grabbed the door handle. "I gotta get my rig. I ain't riding out there with you and have to come back to town."

It took me another circle around the block to drop May off at her little Chevy pickup that was parked in front of the post office. I sped out of town as she hauled herself into the cab.

May caught up to me as I slowed to turn off the highway five miles from town. I rolled down the pickup window. With a day this spectacular, it seemed necessary. New growth pushed aside the dead brown from last winter, giving the hills the look of yards of satin tossed over an unmade bed. After another mile, I turned from a maintained wide gravel road onto a rutted trail and wondered how Newt and Earl managed to keep their ancient Monte Carlos running when they traveled this nightmare every day.

Newt and Earl didn't have wives, children, or any family I knew of. They had each other and their Monte Carlos. They'd acquired them on high school graduation in the early seventies. Earl's was an old gold and Newt's a faded turquois. Like a well-loved grandmother, the cars showed signs of age but were pampered and honored.

A curlew dipped and shrieked. Maybe my favorite birds, with their long bills and ungainly demeanor, they arrived with the first inkling of spring. This one had lingered longer than they usually did, and that made me grateful. A kingfisher flicked in the rut in front of the pickup, wasting his time trying to deter me from a nest I had no intention of robbing. A meadowlark's trill filtered through the window, and my thoughts wandered back to the branding and the fun they must be having.

By now, assuming they'd succeeded in gathering up the herd and hadn't had any more hiccups, they'd be finishing up dinner. The women, whether they'd been in the pen or the kitchen that morning, would be washing dishes, spooning leftovers in repurposed cottage cheese containers, and straightening up. The remaining branding help would be loading horses and heading home, lounging in the yard with another beer, or, like Dad and a few other traditionalists, gathering around a poker table for a few hours of cards. Even though Sarah would have plenty of help, I wished I could be a part of it.

Sheriffing in a county with a population of five thousand didn't keep me occupied forty hours a week. I often had time to help out my family or work in my garden, as long as I was on call most of the time. The big drawback was the uncertainty. My plans were subject to last-minute scuttling. I hated missing out on the good times or not being reliable when my family needed me.

Speaking of family, I pulled out my phone and dialed my sister Diane. Her face appeared on the screen. It was an image I'd captured on our trip to Chicago last fall before she'd had her coffee or shower. I loved her messy hair and natural face. I'd even caught a rare softness to her. It was atypical of Diane's professional persona and more like the sister I'd shared a bed with in the crowded upstairs bedroom.

An important banking executive in Denver, there were years when Diane didn't have much time for me. Then we'd had a major falling-out, and I could have had a severed artery and she wouldn't have offered me a Band-Aid. Nowadays, if she didn't take my call, it meant she was truly busy but that she'd call me back as soon as possible. Having that security in my sister meant a lot to me.

As usual, she didn't wait for a greeting but galloped full speed. "Okay, so listen. Louise keeps calling me about Dad." Middle of the day, Diane had little time to mess around with pleasantries.

Sure, we could talk about her stuff first. "Tell her to quit."

"Wait. Let me look at that again." I understood she spoke to someone in her office, though she hadn't taken the phone from her face. "Okay. But change that to a subtler color of red. We want them to notice it, not keel over from a heart attack. I told her it's not our business, but her calls are like bamboo under my fingernails."

I walked back in her monologue to see where I came in again. Bamboo under the fingernails obviously referred to Louise, making the last sentence mine. But before I could respond, she continued. "Talk to him. Ask him to be more discreet because if he isn't, Louise is going to end up in the loony bin."

I watched a wren fly alongside the truck, stopping to flit on the barbed wire every few feet before taking off again. Just for fun, I flipped the table on Diane. "I hear you're acting weird. And Louise is worried about you. I told her you're in love."

A sharp intake of breath from her made my mouth open wide. "Oh my god. You are."

A quick clack had to be her heels on the tile floor of her office hallway. "Don't be an idiot. Who has time for that? I've got a career and two kids. I'm a single mother, for fuck's sake."

Truly tickled for her, I was back to being ten years old and taunting her. "You've got a boyfriend."

A door opened and banged closed. "I swear if you breathe a word to Louise, I'll take Poupon back."

"Statute of limitations is up on him. He's mine. So, tell me about your new sweetie." I couldn't help teasing.

"I'll tell Louise you're going to talk to Dad if you promise not to tell her about this." A knock on a door came from her end.

"How can I make that deal when I don't know what *this* is?"

A woman spoke to Diane. "*Fine.*" Whether that was for me or the woman, I didn't know.

The door closed again, and Diane said, "I'll tell you about it, but I'm busy now. I'll call you later. But here's the thing. If I can do this, you can, too. And it's time for you to get back out there."

I opened my mouth to answer, but the line went dead. I didn't even get to remind her to pick up the stroller for Zoe's baby shower. Diane's husband, and the cause of the rift between us, had died two years ago. I had never seen anything rough her up as much as his death. But here she was, taking another shot at love. Duly noted, big sister.

About a mile in from the gravel turn-off, I was startled to see a truck lumbering toward me. I pulled off to the weeds, and May did the same. The young woman driver waved, and the big blue Amazon smile passed and continued down the road, leaving a trail of dust floating behind. Newt and Earl didn't even own a smart phone as far as I knew. It surprised me they'd be ordering things online. But the boys were full of surprises lately.

Around a bend, a tractor's carcass with flecked red paint perched at a wacky angle half-buried in sand, like a boat sinking into the ocean. Spikes from prairie grasses that had already grown impressively long poked up through the axle. In a few more yards, a pile of rusted fifty-five-gallon barrels scattered on the other side of the road.

A little farther down, a wire fence blocked my way. It would've been convenient for us all if the Amazon driver had left it open, but I applauded her respect to close it. When I got out to open it, May wandered up from her idling pickup.

"This is a crime," May said.

Her croaking voice startled me into noticing another pile of unidentified junk. "What?"

May coughed, a gurgle giving it an ominous encore. "The trash those boys toss everywhere. Blanche would be rolling in her grave."

Blanche, Newt and Earl's mother, had passed long before I was born. It seemed to me that Newt and Earl had always been here—never born, never aging, never dying. Constantly hovering on the periphery, knowing more about everyone than they should, since they dug through people's trash. Now I gave a thought to Blanche.

May grumbled, "Not that the exercise wouldn't do her good, mind you."

"Blanche?"

May gave me a "catch up" sigh, her frown deepening the crannies on her face. "Yes, Blanche. Rolling over in her grave for exercise. She was a sweetheart, but she could go bear hunting with a stick. Could have used a better diet and some moving around." Another cough. May had once told me she was allergic to oxygen. She sure sounded as if it could be true. "But she liked to keep things neat. She would hate to see the place in such bad shape."

I paused to let a meadowlark finish his signature riff. "How did Newt and Earl get into the junk business, then?"

May looked surprised. "Hank never told you about them? Well, that's neglectful."

I waited for her to cough again and pat the cigarette pack in her pocket. "Blanche had this way of making people want to look after her. She had a big heart, and there wasn't anything she wouldn't do for you. Like I said, she wasn't a looker. But Skeet Johnson sure loved her. They got married and had them two boys right away. And let me tell you, Newt and Earl haven't changed a whit since they come out of the womb. Fightin' little boneheads then and now."

I raised an eyebrow at May. "I hope those 'boneheads' learn a lesson sitting in the jail."

She responded with a blank look, ignoring my interruption. "Blanche liked to cook and bake and clean her house. Kept it tidy. They was a happy family—well, as long as the boys was outside playin' in the dirt. And then Skeet got all wrapped up in the PTO of a tractor."

She paused and stared out at the hills. "It was a mess, I'm tellin' you. I was the first one to get here since Blanche called me and couldn't do a damn thing else." A lump traveled down her sinewy neck that looked a lot like a chicken leg. It surprised me to see emotion after all these years. "So, then Blanche had a little Social Security to live on. I went ahead and bought their ranch and gave Blanche that house. But she wasn't much for handling money or repairs or anything, really. She baked her cakes and tidied her house and them boys ran wild."

Maybe May Keller had dispatched her husband, as *they* said, but you couldn't deny she hid a soft spot under all that mummified skin. "That was good of you to buy the ranch and let them stay."

She blew out a dismissive breath. "It joined my place. Made sense."

"Maybe, but it was still nice."

With an expression that could have been gas, she let it all pass without another comment. "Then Blanche kind of quit. Don't know how else to put it. She got weak and hurt everywhere, and the docs never could find what was wrong. I supposed Newt and Earl were sixteen and seventeen when she passed. Not out of school, anyway. Don't even ask me how they kept the authorities from comin' in and cartin' them off like they do. Maybe the government never found out they was orphans. Don't know. But they needed to earn a living, and junking is what they did. Though I think they continued to get some benefits from Blanche somehow, and then, of course, they had money from the goings-on in Vietnam."

I hadn't heard about that. "What happened?"

She patted her cigarettes again. "Some settlement about getting poisoned. Whatever the damage, it didn't seem to affect those two knuckleheads. I don't think they was even in the place where it happened. Regular gov-mint SNAFU."

We started to mosey back to our pickups. May finished the tale. "They went off to war and come back, and that's all there is to Newt and Earl."

"But before they went into the army, they had a big fight?"

"Over some silly gal not worth a second thought. But they were determined one would get her, and they set to dueling, maybe to the death if they hadn't been drafted."

I stopped at my vehicle. "And you and Blanche were friends?"

May let out a pshaw. "Don't know about that. She was younger'n me by quite a ways. But we was neighbors, so I kept an eye on her. Then she asked me to watch out for her boys when she was feeling poorly. I ain't no mother. But I do what I can."

We drove around another hill, and the two-story house came into view across a pasture.

The closer we got to the house, the slower May drove. She stuck her head nearly out of her window and looked behind us. Then she leaned to her right and looked out the passenger side.

The house needed paint, but it looked neat. Three folding chairs sat on a swept front porch. The lawn had been recently mowed. A barn stood off to the side, and several bare patches radiated around it, like maybe something had been sitting in those spots and been removed not long ago.

While piles of what I'd call junk still littered the pasture stretching out from the barnyard and house, closer in, everything looked spiffed up. Of course, Newt and Earl's matching Monte Carlos were still parked in Hodgekiss, so I was surprised to see a tangerine Ford Mustang, covered in mud and dust, parked at the edge of the lawn.

Not only was the neat appearance of their place startling, but the Mustang also made me wonder. The way Newt and Earl loved their Monte Carlos, I couldn't feature either brother committing the infidelity of driving a different vehicle. And this one looked too sporty for them.

I parked Dad's pickup, and May slid to a stop next to me, barely keeping her tires off the grass. She hopped out of her old Chevy and planted her hands on her hips and circled the Mustang. A cigarette, more ash than anything, dangled from her mouth. "What on God's green earth is this?"

I started with the easiest explanation. "Newt and Earl got a new car?"

May winced as if my stupidity pained her. "Try again." She perked her head up and surveyed the whole place. "There's something fishy goin' on here. Look it. Where's all their treasures?" She said the last word to sound exactly like Newt.

"It's been years since I've been here. I couldn't speak to that." My glance had settled on a stack of cardboard just outside the front door. It looked like boxes someone had broken down. Probably from a delivery. If they came from the truck we'd passed, it meant someone was here. If it was from an earlier order, it meant Newt and Earl were on a buying spree. Either way, it didn't feel right.

I turned to say as much to May but stopped when her mouth dropped open and her hands fell to her sides.

That made me spin back to the house. I was pretty sure my expression matched hers.

9

A woman stood on the front porch. The jumper she wore had a loose bodice that gathered at her waist and billowed out to her knees in a soft swirl of pink and blue flowers. She wore a blue T-shirt underneath. Flat canvas shoes completed the outfit part hippie, part polygamist cult. Her brown hair was pulled up into a neat bun, leaving her bangs. It seemed like a strangely childish look for a woman who appeared to be in her late sixties.

She gave a hesitant smile. "H-h-hello."

I walked toward the three steps leading to the porch.

May focused on the woman like a dog stalking a bunny. "Who, in everything that's holy, are you?"

Good question. If Newt and Earl had a sister, I'd never heard about her.

One of the woman's hands fluttered over her chest. "Why, it's Miz Keller. It's awfully nice to see you again."

May's eyes glittered with fury. "That's what I thought. You're Ramona Hinze, ain't you?"

A large lump that I figured was fear traveled down Ramona's throat. Her chin trembled. "It's Blakey now. I'm m-m...I was married."

Bright sunshine lit the porch and the three chairs lined up toward the railing. They'd take in the sunset later on, but right now, it would be a grand place to watch the clouds puff and glide. Shirtsleeves would give way to jackets by sunset, but the day was about perfect.

May stomped past me and up the steps and didn't stop until she'd backed Ramona to the door. "You got no business coming back here. Them boys were done with you a long time ago."

I hurried to insert myself between the two and force May back a few steps. "You two know each other?" I'd never heard of a Ramona Hinze. Didn't know any Hinzes in the Sandhills. I couldn't say I knew everyone who lived in this four-county area that covered nearly a quarter of Nebraska, but those I hadn't known or heard of wouldn't fit in a teacup.

Ramona's little-girl voice squeaked. "Miz Keller used to sell me bucket calves."

May's face scrunched up, making her look even more like a dried apple doll. The scary type. "One year. That's all it took before you messed up them two boys and disappeared."

"Oh." Ramona sounded like she'd come to the end of her courage. She opened the screen door and slipped into the house.

I turned to May. "Want to tell me what that's about?"

May glared at the door as if trying to see into the dark space beyond the screen. "That little twit. I would've died happy to never set eyes on her again."

That seemed extreme, even for May. "She seems harmless. How do you know her?"

May spun around and pounded to the end of the porch facing the barn, making way more noise than her flyaway frame should. "I told you about Blanche Johnson. She wasn't no match for those two hellions God gave her. They needed a man around, and I was as close as they got after their daddy passed away."

At this rate, by the time May recounted the history, Newt and Earl would be dust in the jail cell. "What about Ramona Hinze?"

May flicked her head toward me and spit her words. "I'm gettin' to it. But you want the *Reader's Digest* version, okay. That floozie in there..." She pointed to the house while I tried not to laugh at the woman in the prairie dress being called a floozie. "She come on the scene when they was in high school. They both fell for her."

Seeing Newt and Earl as teens took a vivid imagination to erase the wrinkles and dirt, but it was possible they might have been handsome. Ish. And Ramona. It's true that youth is its own beauty, so she'd probably been cute.

"She had them wrapped up in fighting over which one would marry her. She'd play one, then the other. It's no wonder they had the guns out yesterday and the Miracle Whip bombs in Dutch's. It's just the kind of tomfoolery they did back then. Now she's back, looking like a walking couch."

I had to admit the dress, with all its fabric and flowers, did resemble the chintz furniture in May's house.

The story of the old drama wasn't finished. "If they were in love with her, why didn't one of them marry her?"

May zeroed in on the doorway again. "Because they went off to Vietnam, and when they come back, she was long gone. And good riddance, too."

I let my gaze follow May's to the house. "So why come back now?"

May's boots thudded across the porch. "That's what I'm gonna find out. Right before I send her packing."

"Whoa." I grabbed May's arm as she reached for the screen door.

She pulled back the fist of her other arm and swung—on reflex, I was sure.

But I'd been raised with a mess of brothers and sisters, and I could duck and weave better than most. Which I did and avoided contact with May's fist.

We both stood back and held a breath. Then May's face cracked in humor, her cigarette-yellow teeth on full display. "Nice moves, girlie. There's the fire I like to see. Let that out a bit more and you won't need to worry about losing the election."

I hadn't been worried about the election until May kept bringing it up. The primary was still a year out and the election another six months from then. Aside from Dahlia, who was always focused on when Ted could return from exile, I didn't suppose anyone else in Grand County thought about it.

May wasn't helping out on any fronts now. I said, "Why don't you let me take it from here? I'll talk to Ramona, and if everything is okay, let Newt and Earl out of jail."

May considered me and then the dark doorway. She inhaled, and out came a series of gurgling coughs that lasted a full thirty seconds. "I'm gonna give you this one shot. But if she don't skedaddle out of the hills by tomorrow, I'm taking matters into my own hands."

She pounded down the stairs and had a cigarette lit before she climbed into her pickup. Gravel and dirt sprayed across the lawn as she peeled away.

Before I knocked, the screen door creaked open. Ramona peeked her head out, eyes trained on the dust trail disappearing behind May's pickup. "Is she gone?"

"Coast is clear," I said.

She stepped fully out of the house. This close, I could see lines on her face and crepey skin on her arms and neck. "She's always scared me."

I tried for a reassuring smile. "She scares everyone." I didn't repeat the legend about May's husband, who had disappeared decades ago and who might or might not be buried somewhere in one of her pastures.

Might as well get to the bottom of this weird situation. "So, you're an old friend of Newt and Earl's?"

Ramona gave the road one last look as if to make sure May wasn't on her way back. Everything about her seemed cushioned and round. Her face had almost a cherub look. "Why don't you come inside? I made lemonade for the boys. They were only going to town for a few groceries, and I thought they'd be home by now."

I let her go in first and trailed her. "I'm sure they'll be along soon." Only if I didn't hang out here long.

Whatever I expected inside the house, this sunny, immaculate room wasn't it. The front door opened into a small foyer with stairs leading up from the right. Beyond the front door, a living room with several large windows looked welcoming and homey. The glass panes sparkled, and not a speck of dust marred the old but polished dark wood furniture.

Ramona stopped and clasped her hands as if nervous about my assessment.

"This is really nice," I said, since she seemed to expect something.

She broke out in a radiant smile that made me want to mirror it back at her. "I'm so glad to hear you say that. The boys have put a lot of elbow grease into this room. If it wouldn't be too much to ask, would you mind mentioning it to them when they get here? We've got the whole upstairs to whip into shape, and I know the encouragement will help."

Interesting. "You've been helping Newt and Earl clean up the place?"

She indicated I should walk toward the back of the house and what I assumed would be the kitchen. "Oh, well. They kind of let it go over the years, and they needed a little nudge. You know how it gets when you live someplace a long time. You stop seeing it. I only brought a new set of eyes."

I stepped into the kitchen. Like most houses built in the early part of last century, it was spacious enough for a big dining table. This one contained neat piles of papers at one end, leaving the other open for eating. Three flowered placemats centered in front of chairs, with a lazy Susan holding a strawberry-shaped creamer, sugar bowl, salt and pepper shakers, and napkin holder placed in the middle.

The counters reminded me of the combination of the brothers' cars. Gold flecks sparkled in the turquoise Formica. The backsplash up to the old painted cabinets was a yellow melamine, easy to wipe clean, even from canned spaghetti sauce. I know because Grandma Ardith's apartment at the old folks' home had the same stuff on her kitchen walls. The floor, though scrubbed clean, was the type of roll-on vinyl popular in the seventies, with a forest green and yellow pattern. Everything in the kitchen was sparkling, if slightly off.

Ramona giggled, behaving like a much younger woman. "I know. They tell me Blanche was color-blind and didn't realize nothing blended together. It'll take me a little bit to convince the boys it's time to update it. But they'll get there."

I tried to sound casual. "You're planning on staying for a while?"

She pointed to a chair at the table. "Please have a seat. I baked some ginger cookies yesterday. Newt loves them with lemonade." She opened the fridge, moving with confidence and looking perfectly domestic in her dress and canvas shoes. "Tomorrow I'll make chocolate cupcakes for Earl. They're his favorite, and I don't want him to feel left out."

I noticed she ignored my question but couldn't say whether it was on purpose or she'd only wanted to tell me about the treats. I pushed a little more. "I imagine they enjoy having someone cook for them."

She tipped her head down, and her cheeks pinked. Maybe she was too old to act so coquettish, but somehow it worked. She set a glass of lemonade in front of me, along with a plate of cookies. The dish looked like what Grandma Ardith would call her good china, the set she'd collected piece by piece from the grocery store promotion. This one had a wreath of yellow roses decorating the rim. "To be honest, I think my being here is good for them."

I sipped the cold drink, the tart and sweet mixed perfectly. "How so?"

She folded her pudgy arms on the table and seemed to enjoy watching me select a cookie. "Do you know they didn't have a vegetable in the house? Not even a potato, which I don't consider a vegetable. Not even anything frozen. And the food they did have was mostly canned stew or corned beef hash and boxes of macaroni and cheese. I don't know how they've survived all this time."

The cookies had just the right crisp with a soft inside. Since I couldn't enjoy the branding dinner at Robert and Sarah's, I helped myself to another. "Looks like you've done some good work with Newt and Earl."

She colored again and looked at her hands folded on the table. With her housedress and softness, she made me think of the perfect kind of grandma who gives the best hugs. "Well, they had some clothes in their closets, and they needed a little urging to take baths and wear them."

I laughed. "Probably more than a little, huh? Did you burn the camo when you finally pried them out of it?"

She lowered her rounded chin, and her eyes twinkled to share insider information. "It took several washings on hot to get them halfway clean again. I didn't throw them away, but I hid them in a tall cabinet in the mud room." She gave me a mischievous and cute wrinkle of her nose. "Where I keep the cleaning supplies, so I doubt they'll find them anytime soon."

We both laughed, then I went for casually curious. "So, how do you know Newt and Earl?"

She leaned back, a serious look falling over her full features that always seemed as if she couldn't wait to smile. "My family lived here a long time ago. I hate to say it, but it was a hard time. Newt and Earl were very good to me back then. I really wanted to see them again. It's been a lot of years."

"What do you mean by a hard time?" Just two women sharing stories over cookies and lemonade.

She stared at her doughy hands folded on the table. "I don't like to talk about it." She pulled her head up and looked at me, pasting on a smile that turned both cheeks into little pink roses. "But here I am. And isn't this a beautiful day? I ordered some gladiolas bulbs that were just delivered, and I'll have the boys plant them when they get back from town. I think they'll be perfect lining the front porch. Don't you?"

I tipped my head toward the porch and the stack of cardboard. "Looks like there have been a lot of deliveries lately."

Her eyes sparkled. "Long overdue, I'd say. I don't think they've updated a thing in the forty-five years since I was here. You probably noticed there are no drapes in the living room. I had the boys take them down, and the new ones arrived today, same as the bulbs. It's supposed to rain tomorrow." She stopped, and her faced clouded as if she couldn't touch a thought she reached for.

"Rain?" I nudged.

She focused on me, and it took a second for her to come back. "Oh. Yes. Rain tomorrow. It'll be a good time to work indoors, and I'll have Newt and Earl hang the drapes."

"It's really nice of you to help them make improvements. Must be expensive." May had suspicions about Ramona's motives; maybe she'd reveal something here.

Ramona leaned closer and lowered her voice, as if someone might overhear. "I know it doesn't seem like they have any money, but they haven't spent anything in years. There's money for a few things. And they deserve to have them. They need someone to help them, that's all."

For some reason, I felt warm toward Ramona and didn't want to find nefarious intentions. "So, you have their permission to buy things for them?"

She waved me away. "In a way. I show them what to buy, and after they agree, I order it and have it delivered."

She didn't seem to be hiding anything, so I kept asking. "How do you order? I mean, they don't have an internet hookup or smart phones."

She gave me wide eyes and an "I know" kind of nod. "I guess they don't see the need for anything but that old TV that gets three channels. And two of those are the same network, just different time zones. Those silly boys didn't even have a credit card."

But they do now, thanks to you. "How do you shop?"

She jumped up and scurried out of the room, and I heard her steps going into the living room and back. She returned with her phone held aloft. "This. I can get a connection if I go up the hill."

She had access to a credit card and, by the looks of the boxes, was having a heyday spending. Interesting.

"Why did you decide to come visit now?"

I might have gone too far, because her face lost its glow, becoming strangely vacant. "You know, sometimes when your life gets confusing; you lose track of where you are and what you're doing. And it makes you feel better to simplify things."

This seemed a little sketchy to me. "You came back here after so long to find clarity?"

She lightly slapped the table and brightened. "That's right. Clarity."

Before I could get further down that path, my phone rang. I leaned forward to slip it out of my back pocket and held it to my ear. "Sheriff."

Ramona's mouth dropped open a moment, and she looked me up and down in surprise. Seemed like every time I identified myself as sheriff today, it was a shocker to someone.

The voice on the line started in with force. "This is Dick Fleenor. And I've got some trouble out here at the ranch."

I rose, scraping my chair on the old flooring. "What kind of trouble?"

"I'm out in the Brenner pasture, and I see some hooligan has cut the fence. I won't know if there's cattle missing until I get 'em rounded up and counted."

The Fleenors' ranch, the Bar Lazy L, was seven miles south of Frog Creek, the ranch I'd called home for almost eight years. In that time, I'd neighbored with the Fleenors, branding, cattle working, repairing shared fencing, and dropping off garden produce when one or the other of us got hailed out or the zucchinis threatened to take over the ranch. I knew the

Brenner pasture. It would take an hour or more to get there in Dad's trusty pickup.

"Okay. I'm on my way." I hung up and turned to Ramona. "Thanks for the treats. I've got to take off."

She scooted after me. "You're the sheriff? I never would have thought it."

Four years ago I wouldn't have thought it either. But now I was having to think about a reelection campaign. "It's my first term. I'm still learning the ropes."

"Well, good for you." She twisted her hands in front of her. "Um. Am I in trouble for using May Keller's internet?"

I must have looked confused, because she explained. "When I go up on the hill. I connect to hers. She doesn't have a password or anything. Is that why she brought you here?"

No one this far in the country bothered with a password for their connection; what would be the point? Her confession seemed sincere, not like someone who was swindling two old bachelors. "No. It's fine. Bake May a pie or something in return."

I walked out to the porch, and she followed. "It's been nice meeting you."

She waved at me. "I'll tell the boys you were here." That confused look dropped onto her face again. "Why did you say you stopped by?"

Had a gear slipped that she didn't remember the conversation a minute ago? "No particular reason. Just checking up on the Johnsons." I climbed into Dad's pickup, all the while eyeing the orange Mustang with the Arizona plates, wondering about the story behind it.

Ramona had followed me to the edge of the yard.

I rolled down my window and leaned out. "That's quite a car."

She cocked her head and studied it as if seeing it for the first time. Then her face brightened. "It reminds me of the movie *Thelma and Louise*. Have you seen it?"

A movie? I tried to remember. "Maybe a long time ago. Wasn't that where Brad Pitt had his big break?"

She gave a blank look. "Well, what I remember is that two best friends have a road trip in a convertible. They had such fun."

Fun. That wasn't exactly how I remembered it.

10

Knowing a trip to the Fleenors could end up taking me the rest of the day, I stopped at the courthouse and retrieved the cell keys from Ethel.

Ethel stuffed the keys into my palm. She offered up a disgusted twitch of her lips. "Brittany says Newt's got a shiner."

When you don't want to explain something, counter with a question. "Brittany was checking on them?"

Ethel *hmphed*. "She got them a pop from Dutch's."

"That was nice of her." I closed my fingers around the keys.

"That's what's wrong with the country these days. We've got to make sure everyone is comfortable and get them snacks and drinks. Even criminals. They won't learn if it's not painful."

"Newt and Earl aren't really criminals. And a few hours locked up will resonate with them, I'm sure."

Ethel's nostrils flared, giving her a comic look when coupled with her gray permed hair. "They shot a gun off in the Long Branch and fell to fighting in Dutch's. What do you call that?"

I didn't answer as I turned and walked out of her troll cave. Mostly because she was right.

Newt and Earl both jumped up and pressed against the bars when I entered the office.

Newt was the first to speak. "We learnt our lesson. Won't be fightin' in public no more."

Earl was fast on Newt's heels. "We'll be like Sunday school every day."

I looked them both over. The swelling on Newt's eye had gone down a bit. "I expect you to behave. And if you don't, I won't hesitate to tell Ramona about it."

Newt gasped. Earl stared at me with wide eyes. "You been out to the place?"

Newt whispered, "You didn't tell her we're convicts, did you? She's already mad at Earl for punching me in the face."

"She's mad at you, too, for startin' the whole thing."

"I ain't never!"

I held up my hand to stop them. "It's between us," I said to Newt. "What is she doing out there?"

Newt snapped his mouth closed, then opened it to speak. "She said she missed us. And we missed her, too, so it's working out good."

Earl's smile was uneasy. "She's here to take care of us. Not that we ain't been doing that for ourselves, but it's nice to have a lady there."

I twirled the keys and watched them. "When did she get here, and how long is she going to stay?"

Newt and Earl exchanged a questioning look between them. Earl turned to me. "It's been a week almost. She ain't said when she's leaving but..."

Newt picked it up. "We told her she can stay as long as she wants. We like her."

They needed to give this some thought. "Do you know anything about her? Where she's been living? Is she married? Have a family?"

They took a second to confer wordlessly. Earl said, "We didn't ask too many questions."

Newt said, "'Cause we didn't want to spook her."

"She gets all twitchy when we ask 'cause I don't think she remembers everything," Earl said.

Newt went on. "It's like when we was young. We knew she had trouble, but she couldn't tell us what it was."

Earl said, "So we think maybe she's got trouble again. Maybe the same kind."

"Like with her dad." Newt's distorted face looked like he'd bit into a fuzzy caterpillar.

Earl bristled. "He was a bad man."

"Why are you keeping this a secret?" I asked.

They consulted each other soundlessly in that weird way they had, and finally Earl spoke. "We like her, and she likes us, and we didn't want anyone to mess that up."

Newt studied me as if debating if he could trust me, his swollen eye making him appear lopsided. "She said she killed her husband."

Killed her husband. That fell like a bowling ball in my stomach. How could someone so cuddly kill her husband?

Newt hurriedly added, "Now, we don't believe that for a minute."

"We think maybe there was a accident and she blames herself," Earl said.

"But she gets upset about it, and so we don't talk about it."

There was more to this situation, and I'd need to dig a little deeper into Ramona Hinze or Blakey to make sure Newt and Earl were safe. In the meantime, I gave them a stern scowl. "If you want Ramona to stick around, you're going to have to knock off this silly rivalry between the two of you. She says she's friends with both of you. So, you act like gentlemen, or I wouldn't blame her for leaving and going right back from where she came." Wherever that was.

They talked over each other with their reassurances, both saying versions of, "We'll be good."

I couldn't see a reason to keep the brothers and didn't think Ramona posed immediate danger. "I'm going to let you out. But I swear, if you cause any more problems, even so much as raise your voice, I'm going to charge you with disturbing the peace and you'll be in here for months."

They stepped back, clasped their hands in front of them, looking like little boys praying for forgiveness. Earl started, and Newt followed so close that it sounded like reverberation. "We're sorry. We won't let it happen again. Thank you."

They hurried from the office, still looking like schoolboys with their shirts tucked in and their hair washed for picture day.

As soon as they made their escape, practically running down the hallway and bursting out the front door, I pulled my phone from my pocket. Dick Fleenor was expecting me, but it felt important to check out Ramona Hinze. It was hard for me to think she was stringing the Johnson brothers along for a measly financial gain of drapes and flowers. But scam artists could be convincing.

If I'd had my cruiser instead of Dad's pickup, I could have radioed the communications center. As it was, I gave them a call and relayed the license plate number for the orange Mustang. It seemed like the most logical place to start. It would take them a few minutes to call back.

I fired up Bessy, my old desktop computer. She hissed and groaned a bit, but the screen popped on, always a small relief. At some point, I'd need to spring for a new computer, whether it was in my budget or not.

While I waited, I googled Garrett Haney in Scottsdale. His name came up in reference to a fancy-looking law firm: Dougherty, Fleishman, Haney and Associates. When I clicked on his name, a professional headshot showed a handsome, if serious face. He'd graduated from the University of Nebraska (Go Big Red) and the UN Law College with high distinction. He clerked for some judge in the Eighth Circuit Court of Appeals and even had admission to argue in front of the Supreme Court of the United States...twice. Apparently, he walked on water and sat at the right hand of God. It did not mention anything about ranching in Nebraska. No wonder Sarah found him so annoying.

The results returned for the Mustang, and I closed out Garrett's search.

A 2015 model, registered to Ramona Hinze from Tucson, Arizona. So far, so good. Why did I have a little prickle that I ought to take this a step further?

Feeling the clock ticking and imagining Dick Fleenor waiting for me in the Brenner pasture, I still decided to take a bit more time to follow through.

Maybe if I were a detective on *CSI*, I'd have contacts all over the place. But I googled Tucson PD and called the number listed. I explained who I was and that I needed someone to help with feet on the ground. I was shunted to someone else, and when I asked to speak to a detective, I was transferred to yet another person. Apparently, no one wanted to deal with a sheriff from rural Nebraska.

The last number they routed me to was answered by a tired woman's voice. "Detective Matthews."

"Sheriff Kate Fox, from Grand County, Nebraska. I've got a favor to ask."

The sigh that greeted my statement was long and deep. I imagined she wanted to say that she had enough to do without helping out some hick from Nebraska. "Grand County, huh. Do you know Jeremy Fox?"

Taken aback, I paused a second. "I don't know if I should admit this or not, but he's my brother."

A hearty laugh greeted that. "Well, when you see him, tell him Kim Matthews from Las Vegas says hi."

So many questions. And yet, I probably didn't want to know the answers. "You're in Tucson, right?"

Again, a chortle that made me want to meet her and hang out. "Wild weekend about two years ago. A lot I forgot, but I do remember the part about Jeremy Fox from Grand County, Nebraska. What can I do for you?"

It's a fact that despite the Nebraska Sandhills' minuscule population, you'll run into Sandhillers everywhere. Or, as in this case, people with some Sandhills connection. "I'd like you to check out an address if you've got the time."

Kim Matthews gave a quick chuckle. "I don't have time to spit. But for Jeremy Fox's sister, I'll take the time. Whatcha got?"

I gave her the address. "It's from a registration off a 2015 Ford Mustang. There's probably nothing suspicious, so maybe I'm sending you to the house for nothing. But I'd like to be sure."

"No problem. Sometimes it's those icky hairs you get that mean you're on to something, even if it doesn't seem like it."

Now she had me laughing. "Icky hairs. I haven't heard that phrase before, but I know exactly what you mean. I appreciate the help." I sure wished I'd get an icky hair or two about the stolen statue.

"It's only 105 here today, so a perfect day for a joyride." Her voice held a smile, so I didn't take offense to her words.

Not wanting to go back to my house and switch vehicles or change into my sheriff browns, I climbed back into Dad's Dodge. About halfway to the Bar Lazy L, my phone rang again. "Sheriff."

"Hi, Kate. This is Merle Doak. I've got a situation out here."

The drizzle that began with a theft at the Creekside resort had suddenly turned into a full-on storm.

11

Merle and his wife, Cindy, ranched on the opposite corner of Grand County. I'd gone to high school with their two kids, who were off in cities somewhere, no doubt living their best lives.

The one-lane blacktop I drove down twisted around a sharp bend, and I struggled with Dad's truck's power steering, which apparently needed more Wheaties. "What's going on?"

Cindy spoke quickly in the background, her voice rising.

Merle stuttered as if trying to speak to me but also listen to her. "We have a few things missing from the house." He paused, then said into the phone, "Wait."

Cindy's rapid speaking continued. Merle sounded like he was trying to calm her down. "Okay. Okay. I'm talking to the sheriff. We'll get her out here." More of Cindy. Then Merle said, "Yes. I know."

I interrupted, eyes on the sunflower stalks in the pasture heavy with round pods waiting to burst into bloom. "I'm going on a call south of Hodgekiss. As soon as I finish here, I'll head up your way."

Merle sounded exasperated, and I assumed he still addressed Cindy. "I know. She's busy right now and will be here later."

This time I had no trouble understanding Cindy. "Later? We need her now."

I tried to speak loudly enough for Merle to hear above Cindy's complaint. Three-strand barb wire fences paralleled the narrow road and the county road crew—that would be Ryan Stumpf, the crew of one—had been out recently mowing the strip between the pavement and fence, making it look downright civilized. "Are you in any danger? Is someone there?"

He continued to address his wife. "I can't do anything about it. She's busy and will be here when she can. I see you're upset."

Actually, Merle might not see it all that well. He had only one eye. The other had been taken out in an unfortunate incident involving scissors and running. Really. "Merle." I shouted to get his attention.

He shouted right back. "What?" Then stuttered, "S-s-sorry, Sheriff."

I spoke slowly. "Are you in danger?"

He seemed exasperated. "Unless you count Cindy's head blowing off her neck, I guess not."

Allowing for the drive time from one corner of Grand County to the other, I assured him, "I'll try to be there in about two hours. In the meantime, take inventory of what's missing."

It took another fifteen minutes to maneuver Dad's Dodge down the sandy trail to the Brenner pasture. Not many grasshoppers sprang in the track road. Maybe they were saving up for when real summer hit.

A fence cut this thousand-acre parcel, separating a sweeping valley with the north section belonging to Frog Creek. A spattering of yellow and purple wildflowers pocked the lush sea of green, stretching into a valley that required a person to inhale deeply.

The Fleenors owned the sweeping southern half. What I wouldn't have given to tear out the fence and open up this whole pasture when I lived at Frog Creek, because a narrow lake nestled in the eastern edge surrounded by rough hills.

A few wispy clouds sauntered in the almost aqua sky as I drove past the clanking windmill where about twenty head of black heifers milled around.

When I managed Frog Creek for Ted's family, I'd coveted this part of the Brenner property. It still churned up my love of ranching. Miles from either ranch headquarters, only nature, deer and coyotes, and whatever cattle the rancher turned out to graze on the knee-high, sweet grass populated this valley that stretched for nearly a mile in both directions. Instead of the barbed wire fence dividing the expanse, I wanted to see it open and free.

The sun was like a smile from heaven, warming everything to a summer temperature, although it'd be chilly again once the sun sank. As always—or plenty of the time, anyway—a nice soaking rain would help out. Since the Sandhills are basically the world's biggest sponge, it takes frequent showers to keep the grass growing. Around here, drought is always the Grim Reaper hovering in the shadows.

A movement in a sand bank a few feet from the road caught my eye, and I slowed, then stopped and put the Dodge in park to watch a mama badger shamble to a burrow a few feet off the road with a cub clenched in her teeth. Even though I knew badgers could be vicious, I admired her fluffy coat of brown and black, with the prominent white stripe running from nose to tail. She waddled along low to the ground but didn't waste time as she made tracks to her burrow. She stuffed the little guy in the sandy hole and wriggled in after him.

Who had taken off with Mom's bronze from the golf course? With May Keller breathing down my back about Ramona, I probably needed to do something about Newt and Earl. Dad's love life weighed on me, and now not one, but two more crimes called for my attention. Still, I took this three-minute interlude as a gift. Oh man, I loved living on the ranch and not needing to deal with other people and their thorny problems.

Ranching required vigilance, resilience, strength, and foresight. You didn't get much time off. You were subject to the weather and its unpredictability every day. Rain washed out roads and mildewed hay on the ground, blizzards scattered and even killed livestock, wind rattled through your brain until you were nearly mad, cold burrowed so deeply into your bones only long, hot showers saved you, and heat so intense you'd cry if your tears hadn't dehydrated. Cattle got sick, struck by lightning, threatened by coyotes. Drought years and flood years, both with enough stress a good night's sleep was nearly impossible. Operating loans that depended on the whim of cattle buyers and futures markets. Whyever would anyone want to be a rancher?

And yet, I hesitated one second longer to see a flick of sand fly from the badger hole, ranching had a rhythm and peace I didn't get being sheriff.

I found Dick Fleenor in a low, sandy spot about a half mile from the windmill. Potbellied, in his early sixties, he wore a threadbare long-sleeved shirt and dusty jeans held up with rainbow suspenders I guessed one of his kids gave him. A greasy Nutrena feed cap was pulled low over his face. His rusty old Ford was loaded with barbed wire, posthole diggers, shovels, a box of wire clamps, a few fence posts, and wire stretchers. A large plastic canister of water perched among the rest of the supplies, and from the size of the sweat stains on Dick's shirt, it looked like he'd been at this for a while.

He watched me stop and get out. "How do, Kate. I don't know how long this fence's been cut. I haven't been out this way for a bit. Gonna kick the heifers in here for the summer, and Sid generally puts out pairs on his side. Thought I best get the fence shored up before we end up with bulls jumping back and forth."

Whoever had done the damage cut through all three wires. There was no sign of any tire tracks crossing the fence line. A few hoof prints scuffed the damp sand. "Looks like maybe a heifer or two strayed across," I said.

Dick lifted his gaze to the north, as if searching. "Yup. It'll take a day to round up that pasture with all them hills. I counted nineteen at the windmill on my way here. I got thirty-two out here now. I got it leased to Clevelands for a hundred head next month. I don't have the time or the help to deal with this kind of foolishness."

Dick and his wife, Eunice, had one part-time hired man, a kid a few years out of high school who wanted to spend summer weekends rodeoing and had no inclination toward college. Like so many of the midsized ranches around, the Fleenors ran their ranch on a shoestring, without the means or the manpower to do more than get by. The youth drain in our region had been going on for years. It seemed like the families who owned the ranches sent their kids off to college and jobs out there in the big world. Many of the kids who wanted to stick around didn't have the means to buy in. So, the older folks hung on to their land and kept working even if they wanted to slow down.

I picked up one loose wire. "Did you tick anyone off lately?"

Dick brought his attention square on me, clearly not happy with my question. "What do you mean? I got no beef with anybody. I work out here, go to the Elks once in a while, but don't get in trouble. And Eunice, everybody loves her."

Eunice almost single-handedly ran the rescue unit in Hodgekiss. She was a smart and efficient EMT. Not the warmest or cuddliest woman, but Dick was right, people loved her. "I know. I guess maybe hunters last fall?"

He tilted his head and frowned. "Are you asking me? I turned the windmill on in May and did a quick check of the fences then. It was loose but not cut like this."

He might have mentioned the timeline before he expected a theory. "I'm not sure I can do much to help. I'll keep an eye out. I appreciate you calling."

His forehead wrinkled, making his cap bounce. "I thought maybe you'd have some fingerprinting thing or tire cast like they have on TV. If it's kids, we need to get 'em stopped so they don't do it again."

CSI and *Forensic Files* to the rescue again. "We're not really equipped for that kind of investigation. If you come up with cattle missing, it'll be more a case of rustling, and we'll watch for the brand."

He seemed disappointed. "Sure, Kate. I'll let you know."

Feeling guilty I couldn't solve the crime and bring him satisfaction, I helped him stretch the wires and repair the fence. It might salvage his vote for the next election. And I hated myself for thinking it. Helping him out was neighborly and the right thing to do.

This thing with Dahlia was working on me. I wasn't married to Ted anymore. Dahlia and her opinions weren't my problem. She didn't carry the gravitas to sway public opinion—I didn't think so, anyway. But the way I worried it, maybe I did credit Dahlia with some weight.

I gave Merle a call when I made it back on the road. Since I didn't hear Cindy in the background, I assumed she'd calmed down a bit. I had to pass my turnoff on the way to the Doaks, so I stopped off to get my cruiser and change into my uniform.

From the seat of Dad's pickup, I surveyed my house. A tiny bungalow with a front porch. Not much, but mine. My yard needed mowing already. And I ought to get the carrot seeds and onion sets in the garden. Maybe I'd get time tomorrow to finish up those chores. Robert and Sarah could probably use some help moving pairs out to pasture and putting things to rights after the branding.

A terra-cotta planter with a profusion of geraniums sat on the concrete step to my front porch. Had someone brought me a gift?

I hated that my heart skipped a beat and a vision of Glenn Baxter flashed in my head. Not the image of him from the first time we met, pale and weak. Nor the Baxter occasionally sighted on TV even though he tried to stay out of the limelight. Not even the man I'd spotted across a busy Chicago street as he exited his skyscraper office over a year and a half ago. The film that ran through my mind was both excruciating and precious. I never wanted to remember it and yet was terrified I'd forget. Baxter's naked body next to mine in a remote cabin on a mountain in Wyoming.

The memory hit before I had a chance to guard against it. The vision of him always came at me when I didn't expect it and sucked the air from my lungs. It left me feeling as if I had glass shards in my blood. In that instant, my heart soared and crashed, leaving me devastated all over again. The flowers taunted me. They'd never be from Baxter. He'd never sent me flowers before, and if he had, they wouldn't have been geraniums. He'd forgotten me by now, almost two years later.

I needed to do the same.

I convinced myself curiosity, not hope, drove me from the pickup to the front steps. Maybe I had a secret admirer. Diane had a new relationship; maybe she was right, and I ought to think about romance. The idea curdled in my gut like mayonnaise left in the sun.

What if Josh Stevens sent me the flowers, hoping we'd get back together? I'm not sure I had the strength to turn him down again. He was too nice for me and should be with a woman who truly loved him. But the thought of me being alone forever might overcome my ethics.

My old boots scuffed along the emerald-green yard, already riddled with dandelions, before I clacked onto the cracked walkway to my porch. I'd never been a fan of geraniums. Grandma Ardith used to line pots of them in the windows of her kitchen, and they always seemed old and dusty. These bright red blooms looked fresh and cheery, though. A small card was propped among the buds, and I reached for it and pried it open.

Hank: Roses are red, violets are blue, these flowers are from me, as a reminder for you. A little swirly heart highlighted the puke-worthy poem. All of it written in purple ink by a decidedly feminine hand.

I started to talk to Poupon, then realized he wasn't around to hear, and shut my mouth. I guess I didn't have anything important to say about Dad's love life anyway. Except maybe, "Ew." And then, "Glad it's your problem and not mine."

I had a moment of the willies thinking about someone dropping by my house while I wasn't here. It's true Sandhillers didn't lock their houses, but it's also true that no one except family would invade your privacy. Mostly.

I thought of the Doaks. If someone had stolen things from their home, they must be creeped out as well as fuming. I hurried to change my clothes and get on the road.

12

The sun was giving serious thought to giving up for the day by the time I reached the Doaks' ranch. They didn't live far from the highway, but the twenty-mile drive had taken some time because I got behind the Merri-hews' cattle drive. They needed to take the cattle four miles from one pasture to another. They hadn't intended to shut down the highway, but a fence had broken, and the herd streamed through. It took a while to chase the cows from the highway through a gate a mile up the road.

Cindy and Merle stepped out of their ten-year-old modular home onto the redwood deck. In their fifties, Merle's lean frame contrasted Cindy's widening figure. He was nearly bald, and since he wore a hat outside most of the time, his forehead had a freckled, pink look compared to the tanned lower part. A black eye-patch might give the impression of a Halloween costume, but he'd worn it forever, so we hardly noticed.

Their yard and outbuildings looked cared for, if a little worn and needing paint. Even the light breeze from earlier had died away, leaving a quiet so smooth a blackbird's call sounded like a trumpet blast. Pending evening gave the air a softer scent, as if hinting of a coming rain, though no prospective clouds floated overhead.

I approached a scowling Cindy. "Sorry it took so long to get here."

She inhaled slowly and let it all out in a huff of annoyance. Her eyes seemed too small for her rounded face, a hazel that looked hard against her pale complexion. "I guess it doesn't matter much. My teaspoons are gone, and they're not getting any goner."

"Teaspoons?"

Merle stepped back on the deck to invite me up. The skin on his face drooped as if starting to melt. "That's right. She's got this collection from all the places we've been. Probably, what?" He nodded at Cindy. "Twenty?"

The Hodgekiss Longhorns T-shirt she wore hung over her jeans. She flattened her mouth in annoyance, and her eyes glittered. A look that would make a freight train take a dirt road. "Thirteen. But they mean a lot to me. It's the memories they recall."

Merle held the screen door open, and I walked inside. A five-by-five area of beige patterned vinyl flooring ended in wall-to-wall brown carpet, perfect for not showing dirt. Cindy led me to the kitchen, where she had coffee made.

As Dad always said, a good Sandhiller always provides refreshments, usually coffee. I hadn't eaten since Ramona's cookies before noon and feared coffee would burn through my stomach. I didn't need to worry. What ended up in the cup only hinted at coffee, which was probably for the best if I wanted to sleep tonight.

"When did you notice things went missing?" I asked.

Merle said, "Hardys were branding this morning. I went early, of course, and Cindy came over to help with the meal. You know, they always do a good dinner."

Cindy seemed impatient with his meandering and jumped in. "I noticed the spoons were gone as soon as I got home. Somewhere around one."

I'd call Bill Hardy for a list of everyone at the branding. It would eliminate some and maybe highlight neighbors who hadn't shown up or someone who'd arrived later than Cindy.

Cindy showed me the empty wooden printer's case that had displayed her spoons hanging on her dining room wall. "We went through everything else and found out they took the sword."

When she didn't give more details, I turned to Merle. "Sword?"

He dipped his bald head in a sheepish way and his face drooped even more, but he didn't answer.

Cindy leaned closer, and her voice took on a reverent tone. "I couldn't guess what it's worth. It's an army sword. It belonged to Merle's great-great granddad when he fought in the Civil War."

Theft of a valuable antique was serious. "Do you have any pictures of the sword? I hope it was insured."

Merle rubbed his chin and focused his eye on the wall behind me while Cindy mumbled about wondering if they had any photos of the family heirloom. He cleared his throat. "That sword. It's not really authentic."

Cindy's little eyes opened wide enough for me to notice they were more green than hazel. "What?"

Merle's head sank into his shoulders, as if his neck lost its bones. "My granddad's dad, Jess Doak, fought in the Civil War, and I've seen a picture where he had a sword. I thought it'd be fun for the grandkids to have something to look at. I found that old sword on eBay and paid fifty bucks for it. I can't think it's a real antique."

Cindy swatted his arm. "You old faker. You can't lie to the kids like that."

Merle lifted his head, fueled with defiance. "It made history more alive for 'em. They don't know the difference."

Cindy folded her arms in a huff and addressed me. "The spoons and the sword. The point is, someone came into our house and stole our stuff. Now maybe it don't seem valuable to you, but it means something to us."

I scanned the room. They had a good-sized TV, bigger than I owned. A closed laptop sat on a desk shoved into the corner of the living room, and an iPad rested on the coffee table. "Did you check your jewelry?"

Cindy and Merle gave each other a shocked look, and Cindy rushed across the living room to the hallway. Her heavy footsteps rumbled through the house. In a few seconds, she reemerged with her fist held in triumph. "They didn't get Mom's wedding rings. And your granddad's pocket watch is still here." She opened her palm to show us. She made a fist and held it up like a threat. "You better not tell me you bought this on eBay."

With a straight, if saggy, face, he said, "Nope. Picked it up at an estate sale."

Cindy's face fired up in a way I was sure kept even the most fidgety toddler still in a church pew. "Merle Stanley Doak!"

When he brightened, all his loose skin lifted and he looked years younger. "Joking. Look at the engraving."

She spared an annoyed glance at him, then flicked open the watch lid. "*To TD. Love, ED.*" She looked up at Merle. Her eyes smiled even if the rest of her face didn't, and I felt relieved. "I guess I'll let you live."

A tiny spark of amusement and affection passed between them. Just enough for me to understand their deep attachment to each other. Not showy, but solid, strong, and shared.

Exactly as I'd thought of Mom and Dad before that straw house had been blown to smithereens by lies.

Merle turned to me. "Anything you can do? Take fingerprints or DNA samples or anything?"

These people had to quit watching so many police procedurals. "Not really equipped for that kind of an investigation." Especially since there was no real dollar value to their loss. "Can you think of anyone who might want to pull a prank on you? Or anyone who might be mad at you?"

They stared at each other for a few seconds before Cindy said, "Nope."

I wished I could give them more. "I'll ask around. Talk to a few people. I'll try to figure this out."

Years before, there had been a string of calves that went missing. Ted and I had followed the clues that led us to Boon Dempsey's son. The one who suffered brain damage in a four-wheeler accident. Boon replaced all the stolen cattle, and no one pressed charges. Maybe something like that had happened here. Someone's grandson visiting or an elderly person who went wandering, perhaps.

Merle and Cindy walked me out the front door and down the deck to my cruiser. Neither of them looked happy.

Dusk draped a blanket on the day, giving everything that drowsy, done kind of feel. The air tinged with the sharpening chill of night. Sound seemed to carry as our feet crunched on the dirt driveway.

I opened the cruiser door and paused. "I know it's disturbing that someone snuck into your house when you were gone. It's strange they took things that were meaningful to you but left the electronics and jewelry, things they could sell. Maybe someone is trying to make a point and we can recover your things soon."

Merle draped his arm around Cindy's shoulder. In the growing darkness I still saw disappointment plainly on their faces. "Hope so," Merle said, but he didn't sound hopeful at all.

Worn out and hungrier than a polar bear on an ice floe, I figured my day was done and contemplated the deliciousness of a frozen pizza I'd hoped Dad hadn't discovered and eaten.

But before I got to the highway, my phone rang again.

13

The 520 area code baffled me until I recognized it as Tucson and answered right away. Kim Matthews said hello and got right to business. "It's an older section of town. Some of the neighbors have been there for years. The house belongs, well, belonged to an Erma Rodriguez."

It took a quick calculation to realize Tucson's time zone was an hour earlier. "Not Ramona Hinze?" Stupid question.

"Ramona Rodriguez is Erma's wayward daughter. Erma moved here maybe forty years ago. At least, that's what the next-door neighbor told me. This lady, man, she liked to talk. Told me Erma was single when she moved in and then married Domingo Rodriguez. She said Erma's first husband was some kind of bad news, but Domingo was a sweetheart. Anyway, the daughter, Rami, wasn't around much. For the last five years or so, Erma's been in a nursing home. She died two or three weeks ago."

If this Erma was Ramona's mother, that would make her pretty old. It made sense she'd be in a nursing home. And it also explained why Ramona would choose to travel now, since it might be the first time in a long time she'd felt she could leave her mother. Newt and Earl had said Ramona's father was a bad guy, so maybe that was the same one the neighbor called Erma's first husband.

"The neighbor said Erma's daughter had a fancy car she kept at her mother's place. An orange Mustang. So, there's our connection."

It all seemed on the up and up. Ramona kept her second car at her mother's, and now that her mother had passed, she'd picked it up and taken a road trip to see old friends. "Thanks for taking the time, Kim. If there's anything I can do for you, let me know."

She let out that hardy guffaw. "Tell that delinquent of a brother of yours that if he needs a dose of sunshine and a fun weekend, he knows where he can find me."

Why not? "Will do."

I finished the rest of my drive home with the windows open, the night air blowing through, whipping visions of a pizza into a froth.

I pulled up to my house in darkness lit only by a rising half-moon. Frogs on Stryker Lake thundered in a way that made me skeptical they were only the size of my fist. Strength in numbers, I guessed. I hadn't grabbed my jacket when I'd changed earlier, and I hurried across the yard and up the porch steps. The screen door creaked open, and another step brought me to my front door.

The house was dark, and it seemed early for Dad to be in bed. But we'd risen hours before dawn, and I was beat. He might have called it an early night. Or maybe he was still out at Robert and Sarah's with a long-running poker game. In that case, Sarah would be livid.

I slipped inside, shut the door, and reached for a small lamp on an end table, trying not to make a lot of noise and light in case Dad was asleep.

Poupon blinked his eyes and raised his head from the couch pillow where he'd been resting it, so that meant Dad had made it home from the branding. I tugged his collar and whispered, "No dogs on the furniture."

He dropped his front legs to the floor and walked his back legs off one at a time, obviously making a point of the unfair treatment.

The pot of geraniums sat on the dining table. I tiptoed toward the kitchen. The door to Dad's bedroom was open, so I glanced in. No need to be quiet. He wasn't home. I flipped on the kitchen light and slid open the drawer of my freezer. "Hallelujah!" The pizza seemed to shimmer with a holy glow.

As I reached to turn on the oven, a note on the counter stopped me. Dad had scribbled in his tight hand, "Don't wait up."

With no one to hear me discussing my father's love life with my dog, I said, "Don't that beat all."

While the pizza cooked, I paced my small house. The majority of my days as sheriff would be listed as uneventful. Occasionally, I'd had to deal with a major situation, and I could focus on that. But today had been like an ambush in a slot canyon, with problems flying at me from every direction. The robbery at Creekside, Ramona upturning Newt's and Earl's—and May's—lives, fence cut at Bar Lazy L, and Doaks' break-in. Not to mention the branding and Garrett Haney's overreaction. Plus, Dad's crazy behavior. I needed to make some plan for how to handle all of this tomorrow.

Exactly fifteen minutes later—two to heat the oven, twelve to cook the pizza, and one to carry it onto the porch and open a beer—I fanned the roof of my mouth from burning it on the first bite, and my phone rang…again.

Maybe it would give my pizza time to cool off before singeing the rest of my mouth. "Hi, Diane." And before she could start, I jumped in. "Did you get the stroller for Olivia?"

She paused. "Who's Olivia?"

Guess that was a big no. "Zoe's baby. Carly ordered the stroller. You need to pick it up and bring it for the shower." I hoped I wouldn't have to remind her who Zoe was, since Diane was her godmother. Zoe's wedding two years ago had been instrumental in helping me find Carly.

Road noise sounded in the background, albeit subdued, because Diane's luxury vehicle didn't tolerate much racket. "Zoe. Yeah. I'll get it. So, that's not why I called."

Obviously, but I felt victorious because I'd gotten my topic in first. "Shoot."

A blinker ticked while she started. "What the hell is going on at Creekside?" Diane was a board member, of course. She often brought groups of clients or potential investors to the club, including them in whatever it was she did to make her extraordinary income. I supposed she leveraged her hometown connections to some advantage.

"Did you know they had one of Mom's pieces? Or that she sold her stuff for so much?" I asked. "What do you suppose she did with all the money she made?"

Diane snorted in irritation. "If she didn't hide it in the walls of her studio, she probably stashed it in offshore accounts so she can be on the lam in luxury."

Sure. She and the love of her life, Marty. The father of three of her children. I slammed my mind shut on that thought. Even I admitted I stuck my head in the sand on this issue, but I preferred it that way

"You son of a bitch! Ever heard of a blinker?" I assumed that bit wasn't for me. "Mom's money is not the point. Woody called an emergency Zoom today for the board."

I chuckled silently to think of the pompous Sherwood Temple called Woody.

"I don't think he made the connection that you're my sister, and I didn't enlighten him. He wants authorization for a private investigator because the local law enforcement person apparently showed up smelling like a barnyard and wearing clothes not fit for the homeless. There was no real investigation started, according to him."

I chuckled before taking a huge bite of pizza, now cool to nonlethal temperature. Mumbling around the mouthful, I said, "I interviewed the staff. A private investigator will be a waste of money—"

"That's what I said. I told him local law enforcement has the connections and can notice what's out of the ordinary."

Another bite, another garbled reply. "Exactly."

"Jesus, Kate, are you underwater?"

I started to explain I was eating, but she didn't pause.

"So, you need to figure this out. Woody isn't the kind of guy to let things ride. If you don't retrieve that statue, he's likely to make life really hard for you."

Not taking another bite, I sounded clearer. "I'm working on it. But really, what can Sherwood Temple do to me? I don't think he's ever been to town."

The unmistakable sound of her garage door opening signaled the imminent end of our call. "Aren't you subject to recall?"

14

I jerked awake to loud pounding on the front doorframe a millisecond before the door burst open and May Keller's smoke-roughed voice called out. "Get yer butt out of bed. Half the day's gone."

I rolled over and lifted my phone from the bedside table. Six a.m. Maybe the sun had poked its head above the flattest bit of the east forty, but it hardly counted as late. "Hang on."

I doubted she heard me.

She lowered her voice to a singsong rumble as I imagined she bent over the couch where Poupon no doubt lay. It must be a scene straight out of *Sleeping Beauty*. "How's my best boy? Yes, you are. My best boy."

Poupon was a bit of nonsense, foisted on me by Diane, because she couldn't be bothered with a ridiculous dog that stood thigh-high, required expensive grooming, and who wasn't adored enough by her two kids that they'd walk him or play with him. Not that he'd appreciate either of those activities. In the two years he'd been with me, he showed me little respect or affection, except he preferred to keep me in his sights.

But he'd somehow charmed the two brittlest biddies in the whole county. Ethel Bender saved all her bones and meat scraps for his pleasure. And May seemed to transform into a fairy godmother when she saw him.

I pushed myself out of bed and pulled on a pair of gym shorts and T-shirt. "Coffee?" I asked on my route to the kitchen and bathroom after that.

"Make it strong or don't bother," she said from where she sat on the couch with Poupon's head in her lap.

Curious about why she blasted into my house this early, I felt it was wiser to take care of pressing business and get my coffee before I got dragged down her badger hole. I was sure it had something to do with Ramona Hinze Blakey.

As the fog lifted from my head and I waited for the drip that would sustain life, I folded my arms against the morning chill and stood on one leg, warming my off foot on my standing one. The window in the back door off the kitchen revealed my lawn, getting longer and thicker. If I didn't get after it today it'd be a jungle, plugging up the mower and turning a normally pleasant task into an onerous chore. The Wall O' Water teepees around my precious tomato plants stood in my garden. They'd moved up my harvest by a month at least, and now I had little green fruit dangling from the vines. Nothing in the world compared to homegrown tomatoes fresh out of the garden.

"How's that java comin'?" May hollered from the living room.

Catching the last of the drops with one cup while I poured another, I hurried up the job and took both cups into the living room. I handed her one, then tugged on Poupon's collar.

May got up and followed us as I urged Poupon to the front door and then held the porch screen open for him to descend the steps onto the grass like Madonna making her way down a winding staircase.

In her faded Levi's and what looked to be the same shirt she wore yesterday, May settled in a metal Griffith porch chair.

We watched a few ducks floating in the early sunshine sparkling off Stryker Lake. The air smelled fresh and green, the blackbirds making sure we heard their excitement that summer was only beginning.

May's voice stroked the air in a quiet way, as if she, too, felt the sacred promise of morning. "I've always loved this time of day on this porch. I used to come out here pert near every sunrise when I lived here, snow or shine."

A few fish jumped, the splash almost loud in the morning stillness.

"Me, too." I sipped my hot coffee. Stronger than I normally made it, but in tribute to May.

So much for our quiet moment of connection. "Bull hockey. If this morning is any clue, I'd say you sleep more sunrises away than enjoy them here. Which is a damned pity."

She was wrong about that. Me and chickens, we liked the new day. "I'm happy to see you first thing, of course," I said, with a slight sarcasm she might not have registered. "But doubt you came just for my coffee."

She raised her cup. "Good joe. Got more?"

I nodded, and she jumped to her feet. She opened the porch screen door, and Poupon sauntered in, having his fill of sniffing and peeing in the dewy grass. I stayed sitting, sure May'd get to her mission in her own good time.

She hollered from inside. "I thought we'd get over to the boys' place early. Before they took off again. We can't whisk that hussy out of there when they're gone. That's likely to send 'em into orbit."

Pretty much what I thought. May had an agenda that had nothing to do with legality.

Poupon sat by my chair, and I dropped a hand onto his soft curls. I'd let his big-city grooming fall away a long time ago. Now he got a clip twice a year and we had nothing to do with balls on his joints. He was a country dog now and not out to impress anyone.

May's pointy-toed boots clacked onto the porch, and she offered Poupon what looked like a piece of bread. "You know you ain't got much in that kitchen in the way of real food."

I was aware. "Was hoping to hit Dutch's today."

She stood next to my chair. "Okay, that's probably enough lounging around. Let's get going."

I guessed she'd guzzled her second cup in the kitchen. I stood up. "We're not going to Newt and Earl's. I checked out the registration from the car."

She started in. "That swanky hotrod? I bet she stole that. But I'm willing to drive her to the bus station in Ogallala. You can impound that car and get it back to its owner."

I brushed past her into the house. "It's registered to her. It seems legit. If she wants to visit old friends and help them out, who are we to interfere?"

"Help herself out to their hard-earned dough, more like." She stomped after me.

I poured another cup of coffee and didn't answer as she continued to rail at my back about how that *accursed skirt* had been nothing but a problem her whole life. Erma's neighbor in Tucson had hinted about the daughter being trouble. If Ramona Hinze was trouble, I'd yet to catch hint of it.

I made it back to the porch and turned to May, trying to form an argument she'd accept when the rumble of Dad's old Dodge stopped me.

May heard it too, and her wrinkles rearranged themselves from angry crevices to mischievous laugh lines. With an amused expression, she watched Dad pull up and let out a cackle. "Oh, that devil. What's he been up to?"

Should I make an excuse? Say he stayed with Robert after the branding? No. Let him suffer the consequences of his actions.

The laughter died from May's face. "Unless he was with that Wanda Jenkins. I told you she's a bad one."

This seemed like a perfect object lesson, and I didn't waste my chance. "I wonder if something's bothering you lately. First, you're upset about Newt and Earl having a woman friend. Now you're getting bothered by Dad dating. Do you think maybe it's time you take a long weekend?" I tried to imply air quotes around *long weekend*.

She opened her mouth, then slammed it shut. Behind the folds of sagging flesh, her eyes flashed at me. "Don't you use my own advice against me. I told you about taking yourself to the city so you could get out and get you some without hurting your reputation. I only now regret I didn't have the same talk with that fool father of yours."

Dad dropped out of his pickup. He didn't exactly have a spring to his step. He looked old and tired, his graying hair a mess and his shirt buttons done, but off by one. He walked toward the house as if every step jolted a brain not quite tethered in place. I didn't think he even registered May's pickup out front.

He paused at the porch, seeing May for the first time. He raised eyebrows to me in question.

"She stopped by to talk about Newt and Earl's houseguest."

Dad considered that. "She's got them taking showers and smelling better. I'd say congratulations are in order."

May stepped closer to him. "They may smell better, but you sure as hell don't."

Dad cocked his head to one side and studied May. "I appreciate you've lived your life as you see fit. No one can argue you haven't been a success, running a big ranch and helping others in need. But maybe it's okay for you to let other people make their own mistakes. Everyone has their own journey and things to learn."

It might have been the politest go-to-hell I'd ever heard.

May didn't seem to know what to make of it. Compliment or insult? "You get up in the morning and do what you got to."

Dad nodded with a serious face. "That's right. Excuse me now, though, I'll probably get called into work in a few hours, and I need to hit the rack."

It looked like wheels turned in May's head, and she watched Dad make his way into the house. "Yep. Well. Guess I got work to get after. Can't be having a coffee klatch with you all day long."

I walked her to her pickup, as you must in the Sandhills. And watched her drive away, giving one last wave. By the time I got back into the house, Dad was snoring.

I stood outside his bedroom door, thinking about what he'd said to May. Echoes of Mom laced his words, and I winced. My feelings about Mom balanced on some crazy teeter-totter, and I never knew how I'd react to thoughts of her.

For most of my life she'd been a loving, if idiosyncratic mother. Whether she was bipolar or some other label from the *DSM*, she retreated into her art and disappeared from our lives for days at a time. But when she reappeared, I valued her outlook on life, all 1970s new age-y and full of peace and love. But less than two years ago, I'd learned secrets from her youth that had forever shattered our family. Everything I'd taken for bedrock of family had been torpedoed. I kept delaying sorting out the rage from the empathy, the love from the disdain.

I didn't think long because my phone rang from where I'd left it in my bedroom. I lunged into the room and snatched it up, answering without looking at the caller ID.

My sister Louise started in. "Do you know where he spent the night? We're never going to live this one down."

"Not our business," I said, my voice low as I slipped outside and onto my lawn. The thick grass poked between my toes, leaving a film of cold dew. The chill was nothing like winter frost, and I enjoyed the promise of summer.

A noise that I figured was a skillet banging onto a stove burner answered me. "Not our business? I've got kids in school here. They're going to have to hear all the gossip and deal with their grandfather's infidelity."

If we were going to talk about parents' infidelity, we really should start with Mom. Louise had a unique way of twisting situations in her mind. I didn't want to mess with that.

The sun sent diamonds across the surface of Stryker Lake, and I focused on them, hoping to distract myself from the image of Dad in bed with someone. Like most shallow Sandhills lakes, mine was surrounded by the prairie, with no trees to block my view of ducks bobbing, coyotes hunting, deer stopping in for a sip. "I doubt the exploits of an old man are a hot topic at school. Unless he was with one of their classmates."

"Gross!" Her reaction was what I was going for, and I allowed myself a chuckle.

"Mose and Zeke, you go back in there and put on clean clothes this time." A conversation with Louise always involved sidebars with her kids. This time, I imagine she was preparing the twins for a 4-H meeting, since hanging out on a typical summer day wouldn't require clean clothes. "Eggs will be done in two minutes, so you better hurry or you'll eat them cold." Without a break in tone or tenor, she switched back to me. "It's almost as bad. Deenie Hayward."

Despite my best efforts, I cringed. But I fought back to maturity. "He's a grown man and can choose how he spends his time." *But Deenie Hayward? He could do better.*

"Did you hear me? Deenie Hayward. She could be his daughter."

Technically, I supposed she could. Practically, he'd have had to start procreating pretty early. "She's not so bad." If you didn't mind giggly women who dressed like teenagers and drank too much.

"You're not thinking of the same Deenie Hayward, then. Last time I saw her, she was wearing three-inch wedgy sandals and a halter top, and it was snowing." Then, "I mean it. Those are not clean shirts, and now the eggs are done. Go back and change."

"I think you mean wedge." A brown pelican splashed down in his awkward glory, probably after one of those fish I saw jumping earlier. I much preferred contemplating his journey than I did thinking about Dad's love life.

Louise was on a tear. "I don't know how I can hold my head up with his behavior. I never expected this from him."

Honestly, I hadn't either. All our lives it was Dad who reminded us that everyone was watching and probably talking about it. He'd counseled us to be kind and respectful, to adhere to the Sandhills hospitality mores as if they were laws written on stone tablets. But Mom leaving with her secret and longtime lover seemed to snap something inside him, and he wasn't the same man.

"Don't know what to tell you," I said by way of ending the conversation.

"That's better. Eat your breakfast or we'll be late."

The voices of the twins complained and twisted together.

Then Louise said, "I warned you. It's a long time until dinner, and this is all you're getting until then."

"Tell Mose and Zeke hi. I've got to get ready for work."

"You do not," she shot back at me. "You're just trying to shut me up."

Bingo.

She hurried on. "But I'm not done. I called you because we want you to talk to Dad."

Oh no. "We?" A scaly snake of trepidation coiled in my gut.

"Michael and Susan and I agreed."

Well, garlic and anchovies. These family discussions never ended well for me. "What about Robert, Douglas, and Jeremy?"

She huffed in annoyance. "I didn't have time to call everyone."

I wandered back to my garden to check the progress of the tomatoes. Instead of Louise and her nonsense rolling off my back as usual, this morning it started to poke at me. "So you picked those who would agree with you."

"Every bite. I mean it." A pan clattered as it likely landed in the sink to wash. "He's living with you, so you have the perfect opportunity. It's all rebound and reaction. You know he's acting out in pain, and it's our responsibility as his family to help him through this terrible time." The more she talked, the more passionate she became, sounding as if she was near tears.

Louise took family seriously, and I felt bad that whatever we did affected her so deeply. But that didn't mean I was on a crusade to make her feel better. "I'm not going to talk to him. He's got every right to do what he wants."

"You're a chicken."

I'd show her chicken. "Get Diane to talk to him." Asking Diane to stick her nose into this would be like laying your head in a lion's mouth.

Louise lowered her voice. No need since the twins wouldn't care about family gossip. "I'm worried about Diane."

Kind of interested to see how wrong Louise would get Diane's new situation, I was more relieved to get off the topic of Dad and me. "Why?"

Still in that conspiratorial tone, she said, "She hasn't been home in a long time."

"Have you forgotten she's an executive in a big financial company? And a single mother. She's busy." My inner little sister chanted, *Diane's got a boyfriend. Diane's got a boyfriend.*

Louise huffed again. "She's just." She paused. "I don't know. I feel like she's hiding something."

Diane had so many secrets buried in her closet she barely had room for all her designer shoes. It wouldn't be fair to discount Louise's feelings. But getting sucked into her machinations would be trouble. "Like Dad. Diane gets to have her own life."

"But we're family, and we need to be there for each other."

Here's a lesson I'd love for Louise to learn. "Being there doesn't mean interfering."

She was steaming up. "You're one to talk." Then a curt, "Boys, get in the car."

I started for the house, my own temper rising along with hers. "I don't know what you're talking about."

"Let me remind you. You spent almost two years tracking down Carly. She obviously didn't want to be found, but that didn't stop you. You investigated our own mother, for heaven's sake. How did that bit of interference work out for all of us? And now, when I'm only asking you to fix what you broke, you all the sudden decide you don't want to interfere."

Whoa. I stood in the middle of my wet lawn, the sun warming the hills and coercing the grass to grow and tried to unpack what she'd said. It took some doing to keep the hot lava of indignation roiling in my belly and not spew it all over Louise.

I weighted my words with all the offense I felt. "What happened with Mom is not my fault."

Louise wasn't backing down, and her voice sharpened like broken glass. "If you hadn't investigated, she never would have run. And you let her get away." She raised her voice, "Boys! I said car. Now!"

She did not just blame me for Mom's flight. That was some messed-up logic. Mom had fled from her crimes forty years ago, and she'd done it again less than two years ago. If I started to reason with Louise now, I'd explode. Even though the tether frayed on my control, losing my temper was sure to ruin my day, and possibly our relationship. And if I kept it up now, she might take it out on the twins. "I've got to go."

"You need to talk to—"

I hung up and stomped to the house. Did my other brothers and sisters feel like I'd blown up our family?

15

Since I needed to stop at Dutch's before I could rustle up any kind of decent breakfast, I headed to the Long Branch for a cinnamon roll before I tackled the day. After starting out with a faceful of May Keller and, on the heels of that, bashing antlers with Louise, I thought I deserved a little sweetness for balance.

I walked into the busy place to the smell of bacon and coffee, with the hint of maple syrup. Overheated, the Long Branch was as familiar as a hug from a friend. The restaurant side of the Long Branch had the shape and size of a railroad car since it split the east side of the building with the kitchen in the back. A half dozen fiberglass booths lined the windows facing the street and had an excellent view of the highway. A few four-top tables were butted against the wall on the other side.

Dick and Eunice Fleenor sat at one of the back tables across from the Clevelands. They looked all spiffed up, as if the four of them had plans for the day.

I stopped at the service window below the circular clip where orders fluttered from the kitchen fan. I waved at Twyla as she heaped bacon and eggs onto a plate.

She lifted her chin my way, eyes bleary and bloodshot. "Hey, kid."

"How about a roll?"

She didn't nod or speak, but her eyes showed acknowledgment.

I poured a cup of coffee and walked toward the back of the restaurant, nodding and saying good morning to the other customers, all of whom I had known my whole life.

When I said hello to the Fleenors and Clevelands, Dick seemed less than friendly. "What have you found out about the cut fence?" Four faces seemed to challenge me.

To my irritation, I felt my face flame at being put on the spot. "I'd love to have something to report. I'm not sure there's much I can do."

Their expressions didn't soften, and Dick said, "Dahlia said you haven't even talked to them about what they might know."

The fence did separate Bar Lazy L from Frog Creek, but the ranch house was several miles away. A sneaky criminal would hardly go out of his way to drive through their place. Furthermore, Dahlia spent most of her time in Broken Butte, only venturing out to Frog Creek occasionally, maybe for a conjugal visit with Sid, who'd had to resume managing the ranch when Dahlia fired me.

I'd always thought of Dick and Eunice as friends, but maybe their loyalty lay with Dahlia. "Did she have any information?"

Dick clucked his teeth. "So, I'm investigating for you?"

Eunice elbowed him. "Don't be a dick." She seemed to enjoy the play on his name, and at least she seemed to be on my side.

Dick reached for his thick diner mug of coffee. "Dahlia wondered why you hadn't bothered to track the cattle that went through there."

Because that's your job. "Well, Dick, there's no way of knowing when the fence was cut. Have you rounded up the pastures and checked to see if there are any missing?"

He took his time answering, so Eunice piped up. "They're all there. We counted yesterday. The bulk of them were on the hill east of the windmill."

"That's good news, at least." I gave a polite nod and slid into an empty booth.

I heard Dick grumble, "That's it? No cattle missing, so who cares someone was out vandalizing my property."

Eunice shot back at him. "For Pete's sake. She helped you fix the fence, now get over it."

After I'd nearly finished my coffee, Twyla plunked a heavy ceramic plate in front of me with a warm cinnamon roll filling it almost to the edges. It was slathered in cream cheese frosting, and a huge pat of butter melted on top. If I ever had to choose a last meal, this would be it.

She plopped down across from me with her own mug. This early, she'd be fighting off last night's hangover. With a thumb and forefinger, she massaged her temple. "I heard Hank had an overnight with Deenie Hayward."

I gave her a split-second evil eye before tucking into my roll. Then I closed both my eyes as the sweet frosting and spicy cinnamon combined with salty butter all in a heavenly swirl on my tongue.

Twyla's sandpaper voice penetrated my flavor stupor. "You don't have to act all offended. Deenie's okay. She's had some hard breaks, but she's got a good heart."

I opened my eyes. "It's not my business."

Twyla scoffed and raised her mug for a gulp. "I don't know what's up with Hank. He's been in here with Trudy Drake and Wanda Jenkins in the last few weeks. I swear he's trying to make up for lost time. Your mom had him all wrapped up for a long time."

I swallowed and cut off another bite. "They were married. That's what it means."

Twyla cackled. "Unless you're Ted Conner. Being married didn't tie him up much."

Thanks for the reminder. I shoved the bite in and tried to push out negative thoughts. Since I'd have all day to deal with whatever came my way, for a single moment all I wanted was to enjoy this one perfect bite.

"I gotta say." Twyla leaned in, and her voice sounded like whispering demons. She didn't smoke now, but years of the habit had made its mark, both in the lines around her mouth and in her rough voice. "I'm worried about him. I'm all for him having a good time. But he might get himself in trouble."

I focused on my roll. "We're talking about consenting adults in their sixties. No one's likely to get pregnant."

Her high-pitched cackle turned a few heads toward our table. She glared at people until they averted their attention. I figured the only reason

Twyla and Bud succeeded in their business was that it was the only eating and watering hole in town. She didn't spare much energy on customer service. "But someone's likely to get hurt just the same. These ol' gals he's romancing might take it wrong and lose their hearts. They're too old to suffer through that."

"They can make their own mistakes as they see fit." In went another bite and another feeble attempt to not care about people's personal lives.

"Here's what I think."

Uh-oh. I took a huge bite, hoping to get as much enjoyment as I could before she ruined it.

"You need to talk to Hank about this. He's living with you, so it's the perfect opportunity. Just remind him that he's an old man and shouldn't be toying with these lonely old ladies."

It wasn't like Twyla to agree with Louise, but this time it seemed she read the same script. I shook my head, my mouth full.

She nodded hers with vigor. "Oh yes. You're the one to do it. And really, it's kind of on you since you're the reason Marguerite took off in the first place."

What the hell kind of logic was this? It seemed like Twyla and Louise, and who knows who else, got together to find the most convoluted case they could make. Fighting seemed useless. I'd have to wait until they came to their senses and hope I didn't explode in frustration in the meantime.

The bite landed in the pit of my stomach along with the others in a sour pile of wrath. I pushed the plate away and stood up without saying anything. I fished a fiver out of my pocket and laid it next to the cash register on my way out.

Just as I reached for it, the front door whooshed open, and my stomach lurched again at who walked in.

16

Three whirling dervishes sped past me about waist height. My name and a hurricane of *hi* and *hey* and other grunts of greeting followed in their wake as Zeke, Mose, and Tony scrambled to a booth, nearly toppling Twyla, who carried my plate with the carcass of my roll.

She growled at them. "You hellions settle your butts down or I'll make you leave."

Zeke and Mose landed on one side of the booth, giggling but subdued. Tony's eyes widened in fear, and he looked behind me. I didn't blame him; I was half-afraid to look myself.

But I gathered my courage and pulled out a friendly face, turned around, and said, "Morning, Garrett. You're up early."

He dipped his chin to say hello, his face serious. The masculine version of Sarah, he was handsome instead of Sarah's pretty. Where her brown eyes always carried complete support and affection for me, even if her way of expressing it would make others wonder if she even liked me, Garrett's chill pushed me away. "Hi, Kate."

I turned to the boys. Tony had slipped into the booth opposite the twins, and they were engaged in a game of tabletop football with a sugar packet. Not a 4-H meeting but an outing with Tony Haney. And wouldn't

Louise be put out that they really didn't need to wait until noon to be fed again. "Looks like you've got your hands full."

Garrett watched them with a slight scowl, as if deciding whether they ought to be allowed to play at the table. "Yeah. Sarah's idea. She thought it would be good for Tony if I invite Mose and Zeke fishing."

I loved the wicked bend of Sarah's mind. She knew that "little dickens" didn't begin to describe the mischievous twins, and sending them with an unsuspecting Garrett would be his undoing. Couldn't happen to a more uptight guy. "That sounds like fun. Where are you heading?"

With only a quick glance at me, he returned his stern watch to the boys. "Thought we'd try Stryker Lake. It still has water in it, right?"

Had Sarah sent him there to get me in on a little torture, too? I wouldn't put it past her to land Garrett in my way just for fun. "Sure. I saw a few fish jumping this morning. Probably perch. Some carp."

He gifted me with a moment of focus. "This morning? You were fishing?"

Not feeling any warmth for him or the discussion, I made a move around him toward the door. "I live out there. Have fun."

He looked taken aback, almost offended by my abrupt departure. But then, why should he be? It wasn't as if he exuded amiability.

Poupon napped in the back of my cruiser. He opened one eye briefly before resuming his favorite activity. "You're about as friendly as Garrett Haney. But not as handsome." I gave a glancing thought to Ted's good looks. "But we know what hides behind handsome."

We drove to my parking place behind the courthouse, and I coaxed him from the back seat. Ethel lumbered from her office by the time we made it to the top of the stairs. Poupon put on the brakes before she even spoke.

"Hold up. I've got something for your dog."

Of course. He ate better than I did. I turned around and waited.

In her slippers, her ankles thick as telephone poles, she made her way to us and pulled out a sandwich bag from her cardigan pocket. "You're a good boy, aren't you?"

Poupon held his head high, and Ethel seemed to think it was out of respect for her instead of sheer opportunism. "What a good boy, sitting so pretty."

It looked like half of a hamburger patty, but Poupon gulped it down so quickly it was hard to tell.

Betty slipped from her office, hair dyed blond so often it was turning pink and spiked in back. She wore a wrap dress that would have looked cute on one of her granddaughters, whom I was sure picked it out for her. Betty clung hard to her cutting-edge style from thirty—maybe even forty—years ago. I was surprised she didn't wear blue eyeshadow. "Kate. It's good to see you. Coffee's made, if you can stand it."

Ethel pshawed. "Real coffee. Not hot water, like some people make." She turned away and shuffled back to her office, not exchanging another word with me.

Betty watched her go with a tsk. "I swear she's the most hateful person." She turned back to me. "Did you have Newt and Earl locked up yesterday? I thought I heard Brittany talking to them."

I wasn't about to blab about sheriff business, and Betty should know that. I opted for the safest subject I knew. "It's a pretty morning."

"It is that. Though we'll be in trouble if it doesn't start to rain soon."

"They say tomorrow." Enough of that so I could politely escape to my office.

"What about the coffee?" She sounded hopeful, like maybe I'd sit down and share a bit of gossip with her.

I gave her my most cheerful smile. "I had some at the Long Branch, and you know how Aunt Twyla's coffee is."

Betty gave me a knowing nod. "Almost as strong as this sludge. If you have more, you'll be jittery as a kitten at a dog show."

I unlocked my office, and Poupon made a beeline for my chair. I had enough to do today I doubted he'd have time to get too comfortable.

Leaning against the desk, I dialed my cell. The Hardys' phone rang six times, and my mind wandered a bit before I realized I was absently counting the rings without thinking about them answering. I'd probably waited too long, and they were working. If I'd been on the ranch on a day this nice, I'd have been out the door at daybreak. There would be plenty to do, of course, but I'd have loved simply experiencing the sunshine.

Myrna picked up as I was about to hang up.

Because it's the Sandhills and you're obligated to make some pleasantries, especially if you're running for elected office—*wish I'd quit thinking about that* —I started out with hello, then, "I hear you had a good branding yesterday."

Myrna spoke slowly, as if ready for a nap. She and her husband, Bill, were the stereotypical example of opposites attracting. He knew no strangers, announced all the rodeos and 4-H events, and was never at a loss for a corny joke. I didn't know who was harder to listen to. "Cindy said you'd be calling. I got together a list for you."

That would save some time if she'd already thought it through. "Great. Let's start with who showed up early." I spoke faster than usual, maybe to get her to speed up.

It didn't work. She started listing names much slower than it took me to write them, and I had time to tap my pen between each name. "Well, let's see. There was Phil and Deb Merrihew but not the kids. Which is good because they're not much help anyway and they eat their weight in roast beef. Then Rich Hamner came, but he didn't bring Janelle because she has that bronchitis again."

Her list, complete with commentary, continued until I figured I was caught in some unspecified ring of Dante's hell. She went from those arriving early, to the women who showed up to help with the meal. Thankfully, she left it up to me to fill in the family and hired help who'd stayed on their own ranches that day.

By the time I'd hung up, I figured it would be late enough to have missed the breakfast rush at Creekside and the staff might have some time. My only prayer right now was to keep asking questions and hope something someone said would fire up a string of clues to lead me to the statue.

Before I coaxed Poupon out of my chair, my cell phone rang. *Kim Matthews* popped up on my caller ID.

She started in after my greeting. "I have something you might be interested in."

I hadn't expected to hear from her again. "About Ramona Hinze?"

People talking and general confusion sounded in the background. I imagined she sat at a desk in a busy station. "Yeah. I saw a BOLO issued for Ramona Hinze. She's a patient at Verde Mesa Care Facility. She's gone missing. They haven't seen her in about a week."

Be on the lookout because she left a...care facility? Ramona looked perfectly fine to me. "That would track with about how long she's been here. Is she sick?"

Kim hesitated, and it seemed someone was talking to her. She sounded distracted. "I don't know. It's not a criminal warrant. I can do some checking if you want."

She obviously had pressing matters in her own precinct. "Thanks. But I'll check it out. If I need anything, I'll call you back."

Amid the growing clatter on the other end, she said, "Appreciate that. All hell's breaking loose here, and I've got to go."

She hung up before I could ask her for the contact information for the facility. But Google is everyone's best friend, especially a small-town sheriff. I found the number of Verde Mesa Care Facility in Tucson.

I tugged Poupon out of my chair, and he gave me a resentful glare before plodding to the expensive memory foam dog bed I'd provided for him.

As I was halfway through dialing, footsteps approached my office and Carly popped inside. She seemed to bring the whole prairie with her, sunshine, wildflowers, birds, and fresh grass in her smile and bouncy step. "What are you doing inside? It's a beautiful day."

I held up my phone. "Doing what they pay me for."

She flopped into the hard wooden conference chair I'd pilfered from the commissioner's room. "I had to run into town for wire splicers. Fixing fence. I thought maybe you'd want to help."

I chuckled. "That's a tempting offer. Digging postholes and stretching wire sounds like the most fun a girl could have."

She flicked her long blond braid over her shoulder, and her freckles danced on her nose. "You can sit in the pickup for all I care. I haven't had a chance to hang out with you since school got out and thought this would be fun."

It actually did sound perfect. I didn't mind fencing, and I missed Carly. "I've got to make a phone call and then drive out to Creekside Golf Club." I almost felt the warm sunshine and smelled the sand and sweet clover. We could grab some sandwich stuff and chips and escape for the day. Just the two of us and the peace of the hills. Disappointment settled like damp mist. "Maybe tomorrow."

She stood and made her way out. "It's gonna rain tomorrow."

Feeling like a gray cloud floated overhead, I finished punching in the number for Verde Mesa. A man answered, and I identified myself as a Nebraska county sheriff. He transferred me to a manager. "I'm Yvonne Cartwright. Can I help you?"

No reason to waste time. "The Tucson PD told me there is a BOLO for Ramona Hinze, and I think she's in my county."

Ms. Cartwright gave a startled, "Oh." Then asked, "In Nebraska?"

"Hodgekiss. It's a small town in the western part of the state."

She hesitated. "Does she have ties to anyone there?"

"Apparently, she went to high school here. There are two friends from her past that she hadn't seen for a while. I think they were surprised when she showed up."

"Have you seen Rami? Spoken to her?" Ms. Cartwright seemed very concerned.

Rami sounded like a strangely hip nickname for Ramona. "She appeared to be healthy and fine. As near as I can tell, she's been active and eating well." I had no idea what was wrong with Ramona and didn't think with HIPAA laws I'd be in my rights to ask.

Ms. Cartwright seemed to consider that. "What was her mood? Did she seem agitated?"

Unless you counted her reaction to May Keller's aggression, which I found appropriate, she was far from agitated. "Not at all. She seemed relaxed and happy."

"Hmm."

"Is there a problem?"

Ms. Cartwright sounded measured. "Not if she's taking her meds. Which it seems she is. But we should get her back here as soon as possible. I don't know how long her supply will last."

This didn't sound good. "What happens if she's not on her meds?"

Again, there was a pause. "Do you know what kind of clinic this is?"

Since Ramona was nearing seventy, I assumed it was what Grandma Ardith called an old folks' home. "Long-term care?"

She let out another hmm. "Well, yes. In some cases, it can be long term. We're a psychiatric-care facility. We mostly treat high-functioning patients with the goal of getting them ready to live on their own."

"And Ramona Hinze is your patient, and she somehow left too soon?" I didn't like what this meant for Newt and Earl. "You haven't said what happens if she's off her meds."

Ms. Cartwright spoke with slow and deliberate cadence, as if she thought carefully about every word she uttered. I understood how a person would train themselves to be cautious when they worked with mentally ill patients, but she was really jumping on my nerves. "Rami is a recent transfer. She's had some incidences of violence before she arrived here. But only when she neglected her medication."

"Violence? Could she hurt the people she's staying with?"

Again, a long pause. "It's possible, I suppose. Rami has demonstrated a strong desire to be healthy, and I'm sure she understands the importance of taking her meds. But she's not ready for the challenges of the big world at this point."

I didn't want to mess around with the possibility Ramona might hurt Newt or Earl. Even if it seemed impossible that sweet old lady had an ounce of violence in her, I wanted her far away from the Johnsons. "I'll collect her and take her to the North Platte hospital. They have a psychiatric ward and can keep her secure."

"That would be acceptable. We'll send a staff member to transport her home from there."

We made the arrangements and hung up.

This complicated my day. I needed to be at the golf course, and taking Ramona to North Platte would eat up several hours. I could ask Ted for help, but I'd rather smear my body with honey and crawl through a red ant pile.

Ramona would be okay for a few more hours with Newt and Earl.

"Let's go." I tugged Poupon's collar, and we clambered down the stairs. I loaded him in the back seat of my cruiser.

A voice hit me from the alley. "Hey, looks like you're taking off."

The sight of my younger brother Michael gave me a happy surprise. "Howdy, stranger. What brings you to town?"

Michael and his wife, Lauren, had a small acreage close to the county line to the east. Their parcel wasn't big enough to run cattle, but Michael and Lauren scrambled with any number of schemes to make money. There was the time they bred cattle dogs and broke even if they didn't account for their time. Lauren sold fresh cream and eggs until the milk cow died and a badger killed the chickens. They sold dietary supplements and Avon. Michael got his CDL and drove livestock trucks. They lived on their eternal optimism that someday one of their deals would pay off big-time.

Built hard and tight, he always reminded me of a speeding bullet, opposite of his twin, Douglas, who was the Foxes' perpetual teddy bear. Michael paced toward me, his face tinged with pink and a row of serious lines across his forehead. "Actually, it's you."

I held up my hand, ready to stop him. "I'm not having a discussion with Dad. His business is his own."

He halted inches from me, as if he'd intended to barrel through me and changed his mind at the last minute. "Except it's not. We're all family, and this is a small place. Everything we do affects all of us."

Horse feathers and hair cream. "Okay. That's stupid. First of all, we can't control what other people think. And secondly, we all only get one life, and we can live it as we see fit."

He planted his hands on his hips, so much like Louise in one of her snits. "So that's it, huh? You don't care that his running around acting like a bull let loose in a pen of heifers makes us a laughingstock? Why would you? You've got this job with a salary. But my business is making deals, and people don't want to make deals with someone whose family is insane."

Michael tended to take a drop and make it an ocean, but this was ridiculous. "You're all worked up over nothing."

His eyes popped wide. "Nothing? I had a horse sale fall through with Stewie Mesersmith because he said Mom was a communist and you'd let her get away with murder."

What? Mom did what she did long before I came along. Dad asked me to investigate her past. Diane let her escape from Chicago. Sometimes I felt like the Fox family dump where everyone chucked their garbage.

Michael was on a roll. "And Jeremy got in all that trouble, and he never served a day."

I held up my finger. "That's not true. Ted threw him in jail—"

Michael thrust out his chest as if he'd like to charge me, or maybe beat his fists into it to show his outrage. "It's like this whole family has gone bonkers."

Now I got it. Michael acted tough, but that was to hide his tender heart. He was torn apart about Mom and probably afraid the family was breaking. "Every family has some black sheep and goes through hard times, it's—"

His arm shot up and slashed the space between us. "It started with you. This stupid sheriff job. You just had to show everyone you're better than Ted. And now look at us."

The rusted, serrated edge of the knife sliced directly into my heart. I couldn't take a breath as I watched Michael whirl around and stomp away.

17

When I'd gathered air into my lungs, I collapsed into the cruiser and, not knowing what else to do, turned us toward the Creekside Golf Club. Maybe I let a few tears fall before I remembered all the fits and tantrums Michael had thrown over the years. He was an emotional volcano and spewed hot lava. When it cooled, he usually came back with an apology.

Just for reassurance, I called Douglas on my drive. He ran the University of Nebraska (Go Big Red) research ranch at the northern edge of Grand County.

Moos and shouts accompanied his greeting. "We're preg-checking heifers today, and I'm knee-deep in vaginas. Can you make it quick?"

"Michael just strafed me with all kinds of accusations that I ruined the family by being sheriff." There, how's that for tattling? "He says my job, and Dad's running around, is ruining his business."

It took Douglas a minute to respond, and I imagined he considered what I said while he attended to the work at the ranch. "He's super stressed right now. You know how he gets. Lauren took the girls to her folks' for a few days, and if she's not around to tie him down, he flies off the cliff."

That made me feel a little better. "You don't think I've ruined the family by being sheriff?"

He grunted at something on his end. "What I think doesn't matter. You get to live your own life. But I do wonder why you want to be sheriff. It wasn't something you ever talked about."

His words stopped me. "Do you—"

"Look, Kate. Come on out some evening this week, and we can talk. But I gotta go now." He hung up.

I glanced at Poupon asleep in the back. "I want to be sheriff. Of course I do."

He didn't answer, and I continued to the golf course.

I checked in with Sherwood Temple when I arrived, more to show him I could wear a clean and crisp sheriff uniform, complete with my utility belt, which I wouldn't need but thought might impress him.

It didn't, if his sour expression meant anything. Today he wore navy slacks and a pink polo. Must be casual Friday. "Have you worked your way through the members list?"

"Not yet."

He lifted an eyebrow as if to question why not.

Professional and confident, I didn't apologize. "We've had a few situations come up. I'd like to look around some more today and talk to staff again."

He opened his arms in an extravagant gesture and sarcastically said, "Please. Make yourself at home."

What a dipstick. After an hour or so interviewing a few new people but not getting any spark of inspiration, I headed out to see if any caddies were available to chat. Trying to stay discreet to keep Sherwood Temple's head from exploding, I exited the clubhouse through the back door and walked around the building on the tidy black tarmac. The temperature had to be in the mid-seventies, sunshine, an orchestra of birdsong. Smells of cut grass and whatever culinary extravaganza they planned for lunch made me wonder what it was like to be rich enough to spend your day in this kind of paradise.

I rounded the clubhouse and skirted a putting green when I got sucker-punched. There on the green, head down, hunched over his putter, was Ted. My steps stuttered, and my first thought was to hurry away before he spotted me. But then I thought better.

Ted's father, Sid, also hunkered over a ball, sizing up his path to a hole.

Across the way two other men made up the foursome. One I didn't know; the other was Dwayne Weber, a rodeo bucking-bull breeder. I might call Dwayne a thug, but mainly because he acted like one.

I stepped up to the green. "Hi, guys. Nice day for a little golf, huh?"

Ted muffed his shot, and it went wide. He spun toward me in irritation.

Sid snapped his head up and beamed at me. "Well, how do."

Dwayne frowned, walked to his cart, and plopped down. The other guy joined him.

Sid hurried over to me. "What are you doing all the way out here? I didn't think you golfed."

I leaned into his one-armed embrace. Sid and I had always been buddies. "I'm not a golfer. I had to come out to deal with a problem."

Ted sauntered over. "What kind of problem?"

I waved it away. "Sheriff business."

He scowled at me. "Right."

I ignored Ted. "The question is, what are you doing out here, Sid? Getting in some R and R before haying starts?"

He huffed an irritated breath. "I should be getting that swather ready to go. You remember how touchy it is. But Dahlia insisted I get out here. She said we owe Dwayne a day for some favor Kasey did for her." Kasey was Dwayne's wife, another piece of work.

Precisely the kind of interesting fact I was looking for. "I didn't know Dahlia and Kasey were good friends."

Sid shot me a comical face that said he'd stopped trying to figure Dahlia out years ago. "I'd love to visit, but I gotta see a man about a horse, and if I don't go now, we'll be late for our tee time." He strode away but turned back in a few yards. "It's good to see you, Katie. We really ought to catch a beer sometime."

"I'd love that," I said, and meant it.

I turned back to scowling Ted. As tight as Ted and Dahlia were, I suspected Sid and I being close made him a little jealous. "Are you following me?" he asked.

Truly surprised, I laughed. "Not at all. But I am surprised to see you out here instead of, I don't know, helping your aging father get his hay equipment ready." I didn't mention patrolling his own county because, like me, he wasn't kept hopping with crime on most days.

"I'd have helped him, but this is what he wanted to do today, so this is what I'm doing."

"Because Dahlia ordered it."

"Because Dad likes golf."

"And you and Sid are so tight with Dwayne."

He let out a breath laced with annoyance. "What's it to you?"

I stepped closer to Ted and stretched my neck to point my chin straight up into his face. "Dahlia is up to mischief. She's doing her best to make me look bad so you can run against me and have a shot of winning."

He held my gaze for an instant, then looked away and stepped back. "You're paranoid. But I have heard people grumbling about the job you're doing."

"You haven't."

He smirked at me, taking all the handsome out of his looks. "About your mother getting away. About Jeremy. And Dick Fleenor doesn't seem to be your biggest fan."

I'd had about enough of this from everyone. "For the record, I did not allow my mother to escape. I had every intention of arresting her. Did you want to see Mom in prison.? Did you want Jeremy to be punished?"

He lost all that nastiness in an instant. "You know I don't. We may not be married anymore, but I haven't stopped caring about your family."

That was one thing, anyway. But I wasn't done. "You need to get Dahlia to stop playing whatever games she's up to. For one thing, she's got me flying all over the county on wild goose chases, and if some real crime comes up, we're going to be in trouble. And since I don't know what's her meddling and what's true, I need to jump when I'm called."

Ted bristled. "Dahlia isn't—"

I stabbed a finger into his chest, knowing he'd hate it—and honestly, who wouldn't? "But she's going to make a mistake and end up embarrassed. Or worse."

Ted's mouth twisted. "You're crazy. I don't know what's wrong with you that you'd obsess about a job you don't even want."

"Who's to say I don't want this job?"

"You want to ranch. Wouldn't it be better if you don't run again? I can come back to Frog Creek and Dad wouldn't have to work so hard. You're so damned stubborn you're determined to make everyone as miserable as you are."

18

The drive back to town stretched into eternity. I tried to distract myself by rolling down the window to catch the trill of a meadowlark as I passed, or to admire the smell of sweet clover just starting to bloom. Usually, a drive through the vast emptiness of the rolling hills, with only the dark ribbon of road and barbed wire fences, acted like a soft caress on my nerves. But not today. Every time I tried to sort out my thoughts with Poupon, I got tongue-tied and shut my mouth. It was a bad sign when I couldn't even talk to my dog.

I called the Long Branch and ordered a BLT and chips and took it to my office. I needed to fill my belly and get myself under control. Because right then, I felt like everyone hated me.

With only a few bites left, the clack of boots on the polished hallway made me look up in dread. Who else wanted to rip into me today?

Carly popped around the doorway, a happy shine to her face and her standard buoyant cheeriness. "Oh man, wish I knew you were getting lunch from Twyla's. I ate a burrito at the gas station."

My heart rose from the bottom of my gut like she'd tied a balloon to it. "I thought you were fencing."

In her dusty boots and faded jeans, with her long braid and old concert T-shirt, she looked like a cute extra in a country music video. The sparkle had returned to her blue eyes after too long and all I wanted to do was be around her. "Decided to hang out and see what you're up to this afternoon."

I felt like kicking dirt. "I've got to run someone to North Platte. It's not going to be a fun mission."

She tilted her head. "I've got the day free. Why don't I ride shotgun and keep you company?"

Yes. Absolutely, yes. "You don't want to spend this gorgeous afternoon on the road."

"Not really," she said, and my stomach dropped again. "But I want to enjoy your sparkling personality. So, yeah, let's do it."

I didn't wait for her to change her mind. I snapped my fingers at Poupon. "Let's go." He opened his eyes, but he didn't jump up like a real partner would.

Carly chuckled. "A real go-getter, that one."

After I tugged him up, he shook while I hurried to the door and held it open.

Carly waited for me to lock my office. "What's the emergency?"

I started down the hallway with Poupon in tow and Carly beside me. "Not so much an emergency as a concern. Newt and Earl have a visitor from the past, and I'm not sure it's a good idea."

"I'm pretty handy in martial arts." She mimed a karate chop. "In case you need backup with such dangerous criminals."

I wondered how much of that was a joke. There was a lot I didn't know about Carly's activities when she went missing. We clumped down the stairs to the back door and out to my cruiser. Carly went around to the passenger side while I opened the door and let Poupon in. I climbed in and started it up. "This isn't going to be pleasant. Newt and Earl won't want to say goodbye to Ramona."

Carly's eyebrows shot up. "Ramona. They got themselves a girlfriend?"

We drove down Main Street. Only a smattering of cars and pickups filled the spaces in front of the bank and Dutch's. Spots in front of the post office remained empty. Barby Drake usually had the mail in the boxes by eight each morning, and gathering at the post office was Hodgekiss's version of an office water cooler. This was where little stories went to grow up into big scandals. In the early afternoon, the gossip had already made the rounds and the only people at the post office were those late getting their mail.

Thinking of Barby Drake made me think of Trudy Drake, and that wound me around to Dad and his romantic exploits. Not wanting to worry about that or get riled at Louise and Twyla pushing me to butt in where I knew I didn't need to be, or circling around to Michael's tirade, I turned the conversation to Carly. "How has it been at the ranch since you've been back?"

She inhaled as if thinking how to answer. "I love it. I'm really glad I decided to move into Granddad's place and not the house Dad built for Roxy."

There were long stretches I forgot Roxy's history. Currently, she was the woman who had an affair with Ted and was now married to him and the mother of his baby. Before that, she'd been married to Carly's father, the husband of my late sister, Glenda. It was always a punch to the gut to think Glenda had been here for such a short time and we'd all had to carry on when she was gone.

Glenda's husband and the love of her life had remarried two years after her death, and it felt like a betrayal. Although I didn't blame Brian for wanting a new beginning, I did blame him for his poor choice in partners. I mean, Roxy?

He'd built Roxy a garish monstrosity on the homeplace in sight of his father's old two-story ranch house. Sadly, Brian had died in a small plane crash not long after finishing the house. And when Carly's grandfather had been murdered just a few years later, it had sent Carly into a tailspin. She'd jumped the fence and been long gone before I even knew she'd vanished.

After almost two years, with the help of Glenn Baxter and his private investigator, I'd found her and brought her home. Since then, she'd been attending classes at the University of Nebraska in Lincoln (Go Big Red), without declaring a major yet. She'd decided to spend this summer on her grandfather's ranch, which she now owned.

She tapped the police scanner and studied the car's panel. "The house needs some work. What do you think of hiring Jeremy?"

I wanted to roll down my window to the summer smells of clover and growing things, but I didn't want to discourage Carly from talking. "He's got a job at Rocky L."

"Yeah. But he's going to quit. He doesn't like being tied down." She shifted in her seat to gaze out the window. I imagined she was taking inventory. If she was like me, she'd be calculating the quality and density of the grass and how that translated to nutrition and how many cow-and-calf pairs this pasture would accommodate.

Oh, Jeremy. At twenty-five, he didn't show much interest in the adult responsibilities of a savings account, long-term employment, or a lasting relationship. The Rocky L job could be a good one for him. A house on the place, a regular paycheck. Stability. None of that interested him much. "He's a decent carpenter. And he's done enough handy-man jobs to know how to repair most things."

"That's what I thought. And I like the idea of family being on the place," she said.

We rode in silence a minute or two before she started in again. "Which brings me to you."

Me? Uh-oh. We turned off the highway. "What do you mean?"

She stared ahead and bit at her lower lip before starting. "Rope says he wants to retire and move closer to Nat."

Rope was Carly's foreman on the Bar J. He'd hired on with her grandfather when both men were young, and Rope had raised his family there. His wife, Nat, had gotten into some trouble before I'd been elected sheriff and was in the women's prison in York.

I considered Carly's suggestion. "Jeremy's good at odd jobs, and he's reliable. But as foreman, he'd likely do what he's doing right now, getting antsy and wanting something new."

"I wasn't thinking of Jeremy for foreman."

When she didn't continue, it took me a second to get it.

Oh.

I didn't say anything.

19

She swiveled toward me, her blue eyes lighting with excitement. "You'd be perfect. You would do things the way I want them done. And when I'm finished with school and come back, we could run it together. I know we'd get along, and you aren't really suited for sheriffing, and I know you want to get back to ranching, and this is the best solution for you and for me and please say yes you know you want to."

The faster she talked, the more my heart raced. Everything she said rang true. I could picture us in her granddad's house. Coffee together in the morning, planning our day. Strategizing how to build the genetics in our herd, working with the seasons, spending our days outdoors.

Seemed everyone lately figured out I wasn't cut out to be sheriff. Here was a perfect opportunity to move on.

But was that really what either of us wanted? Shouldn't Carly be engaging in life before settling down? If she came back here right after college, what were her chances of finding a partner? Did she want a man in her life? Did she need one?

Maybe we'd both end up like May Keller. And honestly, that might not be so bad. May seemed plenty content with running her ranch and living on her own terms. She didn't seem to miss a husband and children. I'd never once heard her lament the lack of grandchildren.

I'd dreamed of a family with Ted. Living on Frog Creek and watching little ones toddle around the yard, teaching them to ride a pony, guiding them through all of life's joys and sorrows. But Ted had different plans, and now he was raising a child with Roxy.

I tried not to think about Baxter but had no better luck with that than I usually did. The same dull ache thudded into my heart like a cold sledgehammer. Even though the odds of us making it seemed insurmountable, our connection felt so deep and true, we were willing to try. And I truly believed we'd make it. And then I let in a specter of doubt and watched it drain the love from his eyes.

I'd proven no match for love. Hiding out on the Bar J seemed like a comfortable way to spend the rest of my life.

Maybe comfortable shouldn't be the goal for my life.

Carly deserved her chance to explore and find love, create a family. And having Carly's old-maid aunt living with her and managing the ranch together might keep Carly from venturing out on her own and finding her own life.

"This is a big thing to think about. I'm not sure it's the right solution for either of us." There. Mature and seasoned.

Carly sat back and gave me a skeptical smirk. "The timing seems about right for you."

A stab of worry hit between my eyes. "What do you mean?"

She watched me closely. "You know Dahlia's after your butt."

I scoffed. "Like I've been her favorite person all along?"

"Well, now she's all over town dissing you, saying you can't keep the law in Grand County."

"No one listens to her."

Carly obviously had another opinion, and she didn't hesitate to share. "They think they're not listening. But politics here is no different than it is anywhere else. If people hear a message enough, they forget where they heard it. It gets repeated so often and it becomes fact. That's what the cable news networks have done."

"When did you get so smart?"

I loved the way her freckles seemed like glitter across her nose. "I learned it in a sociology class."

I shifted the topic from Dahlia's vendetta against me to Carly's future. "I'm really glad you're going to school. I've got no problem with you coming back to the ranch eventually. But I think it would be a good idea for you to try something else first. Use that degree while you can. After a few years, if you still want to ranch, then you'll at least be able to make an informed decision."

She drew in a long-suffering breath and leaned her head back to stare at the roof of the cruiser. "Right. Like you did. Like Mom did. You both knew what you wanted when you were my age, but somehow, I'm too young and immature to know my own mind. Despite the last four years I've had."

I jumped on that, not wanting to talk about how my life had turned out. I'd always thought coming back to Hodgekiss after college was right for me. Now I wasn't so sure. "Tell me about those years."

She laughed again, holding no grudge for my unsolicited advice. "Nice try, Kate. That's classified."

"But Diane knows." I hated this part.

Carly sobered up and looked out her window. "Yeah, well, it's a need-to-know situation, and she needs to know."

Dang, I wanted to ask more questions, but Carly was locked up tighter than nun's knickers.

There was more I wanted to say on the subject, but my phone rang, and I answered on speaker. "Sheriff."

It was Cindy Doak. "Myrna said you called, and she told you who all was at the branding. So, have you figured out who took my spoons?"

Carly gave me a questioning look, a sparkle of humor in her eyes. She mouthed, "Spoons?"

Sheesh. "I intended to start investigating this morning, but something's come up. I won't be able to do much more today."

She paused. "I suppose you're working cattle for your family or something."

Carly opened her mouth in silent offense. She flashed her middle finger, showing what she thought of Cindy Doak.

No denying I felt exactly the same. But an elected official needed to act with dignity, and more than that, Dad had drilled into us the importance of politeness. "Sheriff business is my top priority. I understand your frustration. I promise to investigate your case."

Carly's eyes twinkled and she mouthed, "Case?"

I glared at her. "But there's a matter of citizen safety I'm attending to right now."

Cindy sounded excited. "What's going on?"

Carly rolled her eyes.

"I can't talk about it. I'm sure you understand."

Cindy didn't answer immediately. Did that mean she suspected me of lying? "Sure. Guess that makes sense."

"I'll be in touch." We said our goodbyes and hung up.

Carly couldn't wait to get the skinny. "What was that all about?"

I told her about the theft. I couldn't call it a break-in because nothing was locked.

"Damn." Carly clicked her tongue in exaggeration. "Got any hot leads?"

"It may not seem like spoons and a novelty sword are much, but they're important to the Doaks, and someone is being deliberately malicious."

"Sure. Someone named Dahlia."

All indicators pointed in that direction.

We approached the Johnsons' place. The Monte Carlos were parked on either side of Ramona's Mustang. I could understand the attachment they had for their cars. My first love, and the most enduring, was my 1973 Ranchero, Elvis. "Good, they're home."

Carly rubbed her hands together. "I can't wait to meet this woman who's captured Newt's and Earl's hearts, with a stomach strong enough to handle the way they smell. Also, I need to know the badass who owns that sweet car."

I pulled the keys from the ignition. "She's got them and the house all cleaned up."

Carly hopped out of the Charger. "It's a freakin' miracle." She opened the rear door and invited Poupon out. For her, he jumped down to the ground and even wagged his stubbed tail.

Before we made it up the porch steps, Newt squeaked open the screen door and poked his head out. His eye had passed the swollen red stage and moved on to overripe plum. "Well, Katie. And Carly, too." He pulled his head back when he saw Poupon. "You brung that beast."

Carly snapped her head down to look at the dog. "Him? He's deputy. Sworn to uphold the law."

Newt's eyes went from Carly to Poupon, showing doubt, but he didn't argue.

He opened the door and stepped out, looking nervous in his clean Western shirt, baggy Levi's, and stocking feet. "We ain't been fighting. I swear."

Carly made a show of looking him up and down. "Well, Newt, I don't think I've ever seen you looking so handsome."

He beamed, and even his teeth looked scrubbed. "I know you're teasing." But he looked pleased.

From behind him, Ramona approached. She wore another prairie dress, this one in a mint green. "Don't stand there, Newty. Invite them in."

Newt looked alarmed at his neglect. He held open the door. "You can take your shoes off there. Ramona put a rug out so we don't drag dirt all over the house." He held his palm up.

"Newt!" Ramona scolded him. "That's for us. Not company." She waved us in. "You can leave your shoes on."

Newt gave me a stern look. "That deputy's got to stay outside. Mom never let animals in the house. Said they weren't clean."

Funny she allowed her sons in, though. "Stay," I said to Poupon, who didn't show any interest in staying or going.

I introduced Ramona to Carly, and she showered Carly with the same welcome she'd given me.

"Come in." She waved us toward the living room. "I want to show you the good work the boys are doing with the drapes."

Carly waggled her eyebrows at me when Ramona and Newt led the way to the living room.

Earl stood on a kitchen chair holding up a curtain rod while the other end rested on the top of the window trim. An empty chair was pushed up to the window edge. He tilted his head back and spit his words at Newt. "Would you git your rear into that chair and hook that in before my arm breaks off?"

Ramona demanded an addition. "Please?"

Earl tightened his lips for a second, then shot Newt a stink eye. "Please."

Carly stood back and assessed the drapes. They were a hideous plaid with various shades of green. Maybe Ramona was keeping with the color scheme of the kitchen and would pick out turquoise and gold furniture. "Where did you get those? They're so retro," Carly said.

Ramona threaded an arm through Carly's. She seemed as hazardous to the Johnsons as a kitten was to a bunny. "Aren't they? I'd prefer ultramodern, but this is for the boys, and I thought they'd be more comfortable with something more familiar."

Carly nodded and caught my eye. "That's thoughtful."

Earl and Newt still held the rod. Earl spoke in a sweet voice I'd never have thought possible for him. "How does this look, Mona?"

Ramona snapped her arm from around Carly and frowned. "We've talked about this," she said with a sharp bite. "Please don't call me that."

Earl couldn't have looked more wounded if she'd shot him with a poisoned arrow. "I apologize."

She rearranged her face into soft lines. "You know I'd forgive you anything." She gazed at the drapes. "Up a little more on your side," she said to Newt. "Perfect."

Ramona picked up an electric screwdriver and the hardware to secure the rod to the wall. Carly took them from her. "Let me do that." She pushed another chair up and climbed on.

I hated to pull the plug on such sweet domesticity, but this was all based on lies. Speaking gently, I said to Ramona, "I spoke to Verde Mesa this morning."

She cocked her head and gave me a quizzical look, her round face open and curious. "Mesa Verde? The cliff-dwelling place?"

Her confusion seemed sincere. "No. Verde Mesa. The health-care facility." I watched her closely.

She studied my face as if trying to glean the mystery of the universe there. She didn't seem convinced when she said, "Oh. Yes. How silly of me to forget."

"They said you were scheduled to return a few days ago, and they're worried about you."

Her forehead wrinkled, and her eyes took on a worried gleam. "They did? I'm sure I wasn't supposed to be there." She clucked her tongue and brightened. "But if they said so, they're probably right. Thank you for coming out here to tell me. I'll call them and apologize for the bother."

This wasn't going as I'd expected. "They'd really like you to return as soon as possible."

Ramona stared at me as if she didn't quite understand. "But I'm here now." She seemed confused.

Maybe she was being treated for dementia. "Are you taking your meds?"

She brightened. "Oh, yes. Newt and Earl remind me every day."

"Don't you think you should return to Verde Mesa?"

"This is a good place for me. Safe."

What did she need to be safe from? "Do they treat you well at Verde Mesa?"

Her eyes opened wide, and she nodded. "Oh, they're lovely. But this is where I belong. Newt and Earl need me." She giggled and leaned in close. "And I need them."

It seemed like a good fit, I admitted. "But I still need to take you to North Platte to wait until tomorrow. Verde Mesa is sending someone to drive you back to Tucson. Maybe after they see you and you can explain your position, you can come back here."

The three others scrambled off their chairs and gathered around.

Newt beamed. "What do you think, Ramona? It's pretty good, huh?"

Earl took a slight step so he was now in front of Newt. "Them's the nicest curtains we've ever had. You got good taste."

Ramona smiled at the brothers, and it was as if the sun burst into the small room. "They really add some color. I think they're just right."

Only a brute would break up this comfortable scene. Some parts of my job felt like biting down on foil with a mouthful of fillings. "I really think it would be good for a doctor—"

My phone erupted into the room, and I stopped. A reprieve.

The others continued to admire the drapes and discuss what else they might need to complete the décor of the room.

Carly watched me walk out to take the call.

"Sheriff."

A timid voice answered. "I hate to bother you, Kate."

It took me a second to recognize Mel Patrick, from a ranch on the southwest edge of Grand County. I stepped onto the porch. "That's fine, what's up?"

Her voice cracked. "I don't know what's happened, but Mist is gone."

"Mist?" I looked around for Poupon and located him in the shade of a straggly lilac bush on the edge of the yellowed lawn, more crabgrass than anything. His head rested on his paws, but his eyes followed me with what I took for resentment at his exile.

She cleared her throat. "My cuttin' horse. We turned her out to a pasture a ways from the homeplace. You know, along with the other horses. But today I went back, and she's not there."

The horse had probably wandered away. Maybe been spooked by a coyote or snake. But what if this was another crime? "Are any of the other horses missing?"

Mel sounded choked up again. "That's the thing that has me so worried. All the others are still there. They're all ranch horses. Some of them are pretty good roping horses but not like professional quality. But Mist was a champion. She's won ribbons and probably worth a few thousand dollars." Her voice sounded jagged. "But I'd never sell her. She's more than good cuttin' stock to me."

I'd seen Mel working Mist on a few occasions at the Grand County fairgrounds. They had an obvious connection. In every horse person's life there is one, maybe two horses that are a part of your soul. I liked horses, but I wasn't what you'd call a horse person. There's a difference, and I was aware Mel was the other kind. Losing Mist would be like losing a child. "Is there any evidence of someone being there? Like a cut fence or tire tracks around the gate?"

She started to cry, raw, heaving sobs. I waited while she recovered enough to speak. "I didn't see anything. Rusty is in Cheyenne checking out a new tractor, and I'm here by myself. Can you come check it out? Maybe I missed something." Rusty was Mel's husband, and I was sure being alone had added to her anxiety.

I considered Ramona. She didn't seem like any kind of threat to Newt and Earl. I could leave Carly here; as she said, she knew how to take care of business. "Yeah. I'll head out your way and be there in about a half hour."

I returned to the house and found the four of them in the kitchen, where Ramona was pouring water in the coffeemaker and Newt and Earl were at the refrigerator.

Newt hip-checked Earl. "The ginger cookies is what goes best with coffee."

Earl threw an elbow into Newt's side. "Everybody knows chocolate is what's best."

Carly stood back, humor beaming in her eyes.

Ramona pushed the on button and spun around to the brothers, crossing her arms on her chest. "This is the kind of childish behavior that led to Newt's black eye, and I won't have it in my kitchen."

My kitchen?

"If you two don't behave, we won't have any treats with the coffee."

They stood ramrod straight, guilt covering their faces in place of the old grime. I had a hard time reconciling them in their clean Western shirts and jeans and shaved cheeks with the men I'd often encountered slinking around in their cruddy camo with grizzly faces.

Ramona waited as if checking to make sure they understood, then she said, "Put out some of each and let Kate and Carly decide what they'd like."

To me she said, "We had a talk about fighting. When we were young, the boys nearly killed themselves over a lovers' rivalry."

I hoped my face didn't show how my innards cringed over thinking of Ramona, Newt, and Earl in the same breath as the word *lovers*.

"But we're too old for all that foolishness. Now we're a family. More than friends, and all together in one unit."

Newt and Earl nodded, both glowing in their adoration.

And I was going to tear that union apart. I tapped Carly on her sleeve and motioned her outside.

We stood on the front porch as a meadowlark trilled across the sundrenched yard. "I hate to ask you this, but can I leave you here to babysit while I run out to Mel Patrick's place?"

She grew serious. "What's up?"

"Mel's cuttin' horse is missing, and I need to look into it. But I can't leave Ramona alone with Newt and Earl."

Carly puckered her lips and blew out a breath. "Dang. Mel loves that horse. How did Dahlia work that crap?"

Things were getting out of hand, and I had to put a stop to these malicious antics. All I needed was a break to find proof of Dahlia's interference. But that wasn't going to happen until I resolved the Ramona issue.

In the two and a half years I'd been sheriff, I'd dealt with missing persons, theft, kidnapping, and murder. But mostly, the job entailed title inspections, serving divorce papers, keeping the lid on teen partying, and an occasional domestic violence call. "I don't know."

Carly watched me. "You need to do something about her."

"She'll get tired of her games soon, and if not, she'll slip up."

Carly tilted her head in thought. "Let me take care of this."

I held my hand up. "Oh, no. I'll handle it. But for now, I need you to hang out here and keep an eye on Ramona."

She flashed me her typical Carly brightness. She glanced toward the screen door. "I don't mind staying, but why do you want me to?"

It felt silly saying it. "Ramona has a history of violence."

Carly let out a guffaw. "You want me to be Newt and Earl's bodyguard against that sweet little old lady?"

That was exactly how I felt. "I know it seems ridiculous, but stranger things have happened."

She laughed even harder. "Like father, like daughter. You're starting to sound like him."

Busted. I often resorted to Dad's folksy sayings when I ran out of reasons.

We tromped back into the kitchen. Ramona was pouring coffee, and Newt and Earl were carrying the cups to the table.

Ramona looked over her shoulder at us. "Do you take cream and sugar? My father made me drink it black, and I got used to it. He said coffee was good enough on its own. And the boys never doctor their coffee. So, I'm afraid we don't have any cream. But we've got milk and sugar, of course."

Carly was full of her usual charm. "Black is fine. And I'm going to have a cupcake and a cookie. They both look delicious."

Newt already sat at the table, his focus on the plate of ginger cookies. I'd bet he'd reached for one before we came in and had his hand gently slapped by Ramona.

"Thanks for the offer, but I've got to take a call. I'll be back as soon as I can, and then I'll need to take you to North Platte." I tried to get it out there all at once, the old Band-Aid-ripping method.

Ramona blinked at me.

Newt and Earl whipped their heads toward me in unison. Earl spoke first, a wrinkle of concern across his forehead. "You're what, now?"

Newt jumped up, banging the table and sloshing coffee. "You want to take Ramona away?"

Ramona recovered and smiled serenely at the brothers. "Of course I'm not going away. We're a family, and family belongs together."

Frog farts. I tried for my most soothing voice. "I explained earlier. Ramona needs to go back, at least for a little while. She has to take care of a few things before she can come to Nebraska full-time. It's been a good visit, I'm sure, but now she needs to go home."

Newt and Earl echoed each other. "This is her home."

She wasn't going to go easily. I said, "We can work on the situation for sure. But the first thing is to get Ramona back to Arizona. At least temporarily."

The two brothers stared at me with all the skepticism of soldiers who'd fought in a questionable war. "You're taking her to Arizona?" Newt asked.

"I'm taking her to North Platte, where a person from where she lives will pick her up and drive her back home."

"What about her car?" Earl asked.

Good point, and one I could use. "Why don't you keep it here until she can come back?"

They nodded and stared at me with hard expressions. This gig was bound to lose me some lifelong friends.

Carly gave cheery input. "I'll hang out here and help Ramona get her things together. It'll be okay. You know Kate's going to do everything she can to make this right."

The three didn't say anything. Ramona continued to look confused, and Newt and Earl seemed to have lost all interest in the coffee and treats.

My heart cracked to see this circle, so newly formed, broken apart. Maybe the staff person and I could work out something so Ramona could stay close and eventually come back to the house. But twenty thousand other things needed my attention. "I've got to go."

Carly walked me out to my cruiser and watched while I encouraged, then demanded, Poupon to jump in back. "I'll help Ramona pack up." She gazed out on the green pasture. "But I'm telling you, Kate, if you don't corral Dahlia, you're going to be in real trouble."

20

I sped away, taking the turns on the gravel road too fast but not caring. When my phone rang, I nearly tossed it across the cab. I didn't need one more problem. Before I launched it, I checked the ID, and one band of crushing tension eased. I heard the welcome in my voice. "Aunt Deb, how are you?"

Deb was Mom's sister I hadn't met until the trouble almost two years ago. She lived in a Chicago suburb. Diane, Louise, and I had taken a long weekend to visit last fall. If I had to lose a mother, I'd gained an aunt I loved getting to know better.

She sounded perky, her harsh Chicago accent now so familiar. "I've been thinking about you. Louise mentioned you met a handsome young man at a branding, and I wanted to hear how that went."

That was a whole suitcase full of stuff that stopped me short. I unpacked one shirt at a time. "Louise?"

Deb's laugh always made me smile, even now. "I was giving her tips on making latkes."

"Why is Louise making latkes?"

I pictured Deb relaxing in her single-story ranch home on her quiet street, the tiny yard shaded by an elm. "She wants to embrace her Jewish heritage. She said she feels she missed out."

It would be like Louise to begin her cultural exploration with food. "And the handsome man?" This part would be a doozy.

Eager for details, she said, "I'm sketchy on all of this because I didn't want to gossip about you with Louise. I thought I'd come to the source. So?"

"You're going to have to give me more than that. I can't think of any single men around here I've had contact with." Nor did I want to think of any single man I'd care to see.

"I can't remember his name. Something a little different. Not like Bill or Tom. She said he's tall and is a successful lawyer and has a son the same age as her twins."

Oh, Louise. I thought she'd given up trying to hook me up.

Mention of the twins sidetracked Deb, a good thing for me. "I'm dying to meet those two boys. And your brothers, too. I was telling Jimmy I think we should plan a road trip for later this summer. Mother would be okay for a week, I think. The staff and her neighbors could watch her and keep her company."

My grandmother Ruby. We'd all hoped to kindle a relationship with the older woman, Louise especially. Dad's mother, Grandma Ardith, was such a force in all our lives, even after moving to the old folks' home in Broken Butte. We assumed with another grandmother we'd double the love. Sadly, Ruby hadn't welcomed a passel of grown grandchildren she'd never met from a daughter she'd written off.

Still, I felt lucky to have gained Deb. Who, it turned out, wasn't all that distracted by the new subject. "We can talk about that later. Right now, I want to know about this lawyer. Louise said there was definite chemistry."

Louise needed a hobby. "Garrett Haney. He's Sarah's brother." I paused, giving Deb time to wind through the complicated and many Sandhills relationships. I'd had a lifetime to follow the threads of family and friends, parents, grandparents, siblings, cousins, and it was as familiar to me as the freckles on my arms. "He's visiting here for their branding. But there's nothing between us. No chemistry. Barely a conversation. And he's married."

"Huh." She filled that syllable with suspicion. "Is there anyone else you might be interested in?"

I rubbed the bridge of my nose. I'd paddled down this river before and wasn't a fan of the scenery. "I'm doing fine. My garden is started. The job is going well."

In the second before she spoke, I could see her tilt her head and frown, as if unsure how to continue without hurting my feelings. "That might be okay for now. But your divorce was four years ago. You don't want to stay alone too long, or you'll forget how to live with someone."

I hadn't told anyone about Baxter. I thought Diane and Carly might have some inkling. That particular heartbreak didn't feel like something I'd get over, and if there was a risk of that kind of pain again, I'd rather forget how to care about someone. "I'll keep that in mind." I gave that an end-of-conversation tone.

With a falsely casual tone, she said, "One more thing, dear."

I didn't say anything, hoping she'd take the hint that I didn't need one more thing.

She didn't. "Louise said your father is acting out."

I kept massaging my forehead and didn't respond.

"She thinks maybe you could talk to him. That he'll listen to you. I know he's hurting after Miriam left. But he's nearly seventy, and running around, burning the candle at both ends, probably isn't good for him."

I'd almost rather they meddle in my life instead of his. So, here we go. "I'm having a situation I could use some advice about."

Delight tinged her voice, though I knew it wasn't because I had a problem, only that she could help. "What is it?"

"When I took this job as sheriff, I thought it would be for one term only, kind of a way to tread water until I found another ranching position. But I've come to like it. I feel as though I'm doing good work and helping people. But there are parts of the job I hate. And it might be causing some hurt feelings with the family. Carly offered me the ranch foreman job at her place."

She spoke in a steady tone, as if encouraging me to talk. "Now that you bring it up, Louise might have mentioned something about you being sheriff."

"What did Louise say?"

Deb hesitated, as if trying to figure out how to dig out of a hole. "Your mother's past and then her leaving so abruptly has devastated Louise. I'm afraid it's kind of a shoot-the-messenger situation. She's convinced that if you weren't sheriff, Miriam would never have left."

I grumbled. "Miriam, Marguerite, Mom. Whatever you call her, she wasn't who we thought."

Deb stayed supportive in the way I'd want a mother to be. "You're right, of course. Don't worry. It'll take Louise some time to process it, but she'll come around. But I think working with Carly on her ranch would be ideal."

"Yeah, but." I inhaled. "I would be in charge for a year or two until she came home to stay. Then I'd be working for her. Not my own boss."

"And you are in charge as sheriff?"

"Yes and no. I mean, there are elections, and it seems someone is always unhappy about what I'm doing. But I love my house on the lake." The more I talked, the more confused I got.

"Well, you know what your mother would say."

I squeezed my eyes shut for a second as I drove on the one-lane black-top, wincing at the stab of pain at the mention of Mom.

"She'd tell you to search your heart. And I agree. The answers you need are in there. Take the time to listen."

I mumbled some kind of agreement to let her know I appreciated her concern but couldn't hang up quickly enough. "Thanks for calling. It's always good to hear from you. Let me know when would work for you to come visit, and we'll figure out where you can stay. Bye now." I punched off and stomped on the brakes, stopping in the middle of the road.

Deb's words should have been Mom's. My *mother*. She was the one I wanted to hear from. She'd dropped her damned cluster bombs and left us to clean up the carnage. The molten rage bubbling inside me was because I loved her and hated her the way only a child could feel for a mother. A woman who might not ever have loved her.

Or loved her enough.

21

The half hour drive to Mel and Rusty's place would have been a nice outing since the sun was bright and I could almost hear the flowers blooming and the calves getting stronger. The hills were filled with leaping calves enjoying their freedom. Black cows buried their heads in the grass, doing what cows love to do, eating the prairie's juicy sweetness. All of God's creation seemed to be enjoying the heart-expanding perfect day.

Except me, and soon Ramona, Earl, and Newt. I was breaking up their fresh-formed family. I felt lower than an egg-sucking dog. After my experience with Mom, I understood mental illness was nothing to mess around with. Ramona might seem sweet and harmless, but what would happen if she didn't take her meds? She already acted forgetful and muddled.

I forced my thoughts from the woebegone trio to the crime spree plaguing Grand County. "How am I going to get to the bottom of it?" I asked a dozing Poupon. "And does it really matter?"

Since he was likely to keep eating, pooping, and napping in any event, he didn't bother to answer.

If I took the job with Carly, Ted could take over and Dahlia would stop. That would leave Chester County scrambling for a sheriff. "Who am I kidding? I'm not walking away midterm."

The Six Circle Ranch, Mel and Rusty's place, had been in his family since the 1880s. Towering cottonwoods rimmed a path to the headquarters with the hallmark massive wooden barn that always seemed to have a fresh coat of striking red paint, with the brand— the number six within a circle—prominent on the haymow door. Twice a year Mel and Rusty hosted ropings with dozens of people attending.

Mel met me in the dusty ranch yard in front of the barn. She was a tough woman, tall, with the solid look of someone used to hard work, but her tanned face was puffy and her eyes swollen from crying. "Jump in with me, and I'll take you to the pasture."

I parked the cruiser, unrolled all the windows, opened the back door, and told Poupon to be good. He responded with a yawn and closed his eyes. I climbed into her four-wheel-drive dually pickup that could pull an eight-horse trailer without strain. We barreled away from the house and barn and through the hills on a trail road, with me getting out to open and close the wire gates twice.

"Had the roping last weekend, but I'd turned Mist out earlier that week because she had a little bit of a limp, and I didn't want to work her. I checked on her this morning and she's gone."

My heart twisted to see the obvious pain pinch her face. "Can I get a list of names of who was at the roping?"

She flicked her eyes to me in shock. "You don't think anyone here would take Mist? They're our friends. They wouldn't do that."

I did think it was someone from the Sandhills, a specific someone. We all wanted to believe our friends and neighbors wouldn't hurt us, but after living with Ted when he was sheriff and then my own term, I'd learned that people you trust the most can be the most dangerous.

Unbidden, Baxter flashed into my head. Again. Turds on toast. Every time I thought about betrayal and loss, there he was. Sure, Ted had cheated on me and ripped out the rug from under my life. But that rug had been moth-eaten and full of holes. He'd probably done me a favor by revealing his true nature.

But Baxter was something different, deep and honest. And I'd wrecked it. I carried the entire blame for losing something so precious. At that moment, I related to Mel's shredded heart.

Mel recounted a list of names. Sid and Dahlia weren't on the list, but Violet, Dahlia's sister, had attended. Minions.

I didn't want to disillusion Mel unless I had to. "I'll start the investigation by interviewing them to see if they noticed anything suspicious."

She seemed relieved. "Oh, sure."

We pulled up to a clanking windmill. The pump spilled icy, clear water into the full tank. The overflow pipe drained the runoff to create a tiny creek with thick, vibrant grass and dandelions growing several feet down a hill until the water soaked into the sand. Purple and yellow coneflowers danced in the breeze. "This is the pasture they were in. I already moved the rest of the horses closer to the house."

I asked a question even though I knew the answer. "You checked the whole pasture? The fence line?"

Her eyes filled, and she nodded and swallowed. "She's not here."

"Let's take a drive around the fence and see if we can find anything." I honestly didn't know what else to do. But I wanted to make sure she hadn't missed tire tracks or a severed wire, like Dick Fleenor's Brenner pasture.

A click in her throat let me know she was struggling not to break down. We rumbled from the windmill and around a few low hills until the fence appeared. Strung taut, the cedar posts planted firmly. I couldn't see any point of exit or where a horse might wander through.

Mel's voice was tight and high, as if filtering through a sieve. "I got Mist when she was a yearling. I broke her and trained her. She's a natural. So smart. She knows what I want at the moment it comes into my head."

I didn't doubt that connection. I'd seen it with others, a rare kind of telepathy. I had just enough of Mom in me to sometimes believe in things I couldn't touch. "I've seen you work with Mist. She's special."

She sniffed, and we continued to run the fence line without speaking. The pickup chugged up a tall hill, and I focused on the wires. A brown curlew dipped, and I lifted my gaze to watch. "Oh."

Mel whipped her head around at my exclamation. She let out a squeal and slammed on the brakes. She was out of the pickup before I had a chance to say another word.

Mist, with a bright blaze down her muzzle, trotted across the prairie toward us. Her tail raised, four white socks flashing. She seemed as anxious to get back to Mel as Mel was to get to her. The large woman slipped between the wires of the fence so fast it looked like a magic trick.

My throat closed, and I blinked back tears watching the reunion. All I could think was the phrase *love is love is love*.

Mel asked me to drive her pickup back to the ranch, and she pulled herself on Mist.

At least one thing had gone right today. But something told me this wasn't going to be the trend.

22

By the time I found myself on the gravel road passing the tractor's dead hulk on the way to the Johnsons' house, it was past late afternoon and still no sign of that rain the forecast had teased about.

I resisted the urge to drive slower. Ramona needed help. I wasn't a mental health professional and had no way of knowing the depth of her illness. Her confusion was an indication not all the pots were boiling.

I came down the hill to see the Monte Carlos and Mustang parked where they usually were. I eased the cruiser into line beside them and pushed myself out. Dragging my feet, I climbed the porch steps. This wasn't going to be easy. A quick knock and I walked in. "Hello."

No sounds filtered from the kitchen, and when I entered, the only things greeting me were the coffee cups drying in the strainer. I retraced my steps to the porch and listened. Carly's laughter floated on the clear air, and I started for a barn that looked like a fart would bring it down in a heap of sawdust. It had once been painted white, as evidenced by the few flakes left on the gray wood.

I found Newt and Carly by a pile of hitches. All manner of hitches. They would fit any ball, any vehicle. Rusted metal, shiny chrome.

Newt held up one with two hands. "We got this one at the Gordon sale pert near five years ago. A bargain because it's heavy."

Carly tilted her head. "But it's broken."

Newt puffed up with how clever he and Earl were. "That don't matter. We can sell it for the steel."

Carly nodded. "But you've had it for five years and you haven't sold it."

"It was a bargain, and they didn't even know it." Newt seemed to miss the point.

They didn't see me approach, and both jumped when I started to speak. "Where's Earl and Ramona?"

Carly turned her attention from the hitch to me. "At the house, planting gladiolas bulbs."

Newt dropped his head to the pile of hitches and didn't say anything.

A shot of acid dropped into my gut. I spun in the dirt and tore off for the house.

Carly started behind me. "What?"

I hit the porch steps and burst through the door. "Ramona? Earl?" I shouted, not expecting an answer. I took the stairs two at a time. The wood needed sanding, and you wouldn't want to make the trip barefoot.

Carly thudded right behind me. She sounded as breathless as I felt. "Where are they?"

I turned on her. "You were supposed to keep an eye on them."

"They're two old people. How far could they get?"

I responded with an evil eye and rushed back down the stairs to find Newt. Even though Carly and I hollered for him, it took several minutes to locate him behind the chicken house, sitting in the shade from a pile of old washing machines.

I grabbed him by the sleeve of his shirt, which now sported a few grease stains to match the smeared grass stains on the knees of his jeans, and pulled him to his feet.

His sorry face pointed toward the ground.

"Where are they?"

So much like one of my nephews when I'd caught him trying to light a campfire in the basement, Newt shrugged in misery.

I jammed my face close to his. "Tell me."

He shook his head and still didn't make eye contact. "If I tell you, then you'll take Ramona away. She would be scared and alone."

I dropped my hand. "You don't understand. Ramona needs help. She might be dangerous."

He straightened. "Ramona ain't gonna hurt Earl. We're a team. That's what she says."

I stared up at the sky. Where would they go?

Carly joined us. "I think I figured out how they left, anyway."

Newt's head snapped up, and he focused on her.

Carly gave him a reproving glare. "Newt wanted to show me how his lawn mower worked."

He butted in with enthusiasm, either because he loved the mower, or he wanted to distract us. "It's a real doozy. Got it from Rasmussen's dump. They thought it wouldn't work. But I gave it the good Newt treatment, and it fired right up. I can't tell you what I did because it's my trade secret. But now it works."

Carly wasn't having it. "While he fired it up so I could see how well it ran, I'll bet Earl and Ramona took off on that old Honda."

The edges of Newt's mouth turned up, as if proud of their cleverness.

"Is that true?" I stepped toward him.

The tiny smile dropped. He turned down the corners of his mouth before saying, "I can't tell you."

"This is important." I wanted to grab him and shake him until I rattled the information loose.

He folded his arms across his chest and clamped his lips together.

There were millions of places Earl could take Ramona. Newt and Earl roamed across four counties that covered a fourth of the state of Nebraska. They knew all the old buildings, line shacks, sheds, and abandoned homesteads. Two elderly people on a small motorcycle could come to so much harm. That's if Ramona remembered to take her pills.

If she forgot, who knows what could happen?

I clasped Newt by his arm. Thin as it was, the muscles bunched under my hand. "Come on."

His eyes held an element of panic. "Where are we goin'?"

"I'm hauling you in until you tell me where Earl took Ramona."

Carly stepped back to allow me to drag Newt toward the cruiser. She took Newt's side. "Come on, Kate. You don't need to do that. Ramona is harmless."

I whipped toward her, letting out my frustration. "You don't know that."

Newt refused to walk to the cruiser on his own, and when I gave her a meaningful look to give me a hand, Carly held both arms up and stepped backward. "Don't look at me. This whole idea of locking up Newt is ridiculous."

"You should listen to that girl," Newt said. "She's got some sense."

With one hand clamped around Newt's bony wrist, I started yanking him across the dirt ranch yard toward my car. "Someone from the Verde Mesa facility is on their way to get Ramona. They wouldn't send a staffer all this way if they didn't think Ramona needed to be in their care."

Carly followed behind me, her lanky legs having no trouble keeping up. "Sure they would."

Newt strained backward. "She's right. Them places get gov-a-mint money for how many people are there. They prolly want to lock Mona up for the profit."

With gritted teeth, I tugged him along. "I don't think that's true."

He fought, but I was sure if he needed to, he could get away. He made it unpleasant and a chore to drag him in, but he was going with me. "You saw her, Katie. Mona wouldn't hurt a fly."

Carly spoke over my shoulder. "I was here all afternoon, and I can vouch for that. She was as sweet as can be."

I opened the back door of the cruiser.

Newt jumped back, and I nearly lost my hold. "You got that...that... deputy back there."

Poupon sat up and shook, getting his bearings after an epic nap. Hair flew in the sunlight. He seemed amenable to jumping out and took off for the nearest bush.

I stuffed Newt inside. "Until I speak to the person from Verde Mesa, my plan is to send Ramona home. At least temporarily."

Newt pushed his head toward the open door and spoke to Carly. "I'm 'onna need my ride when I get sprung from jail. Will you bring my car?" He didn't need to tell her the keys were in it. Hardly anyone in the Sandhills removed their keys when they were at home.

She nodded. "Which one is yours?"

Newt's mouth dropped opened as if she'd hurled a supreme insult. "The good one."

Carly shifted her eyes to me, and I said, "Turquoise."

Newt sat back with my gentle nudge. "I never. That rig of Earl's is a mess. He don't take care of it like I do mine. Carly had to be messin' with me."

"I'm sure she was." I closed his door, loaded a disgruntled Poupon in the front seat, and piled in.

I tuned out Newt on the drive as he whined and complained and told me over and over how it was a crime to put him behind bars.

"Then tell me where Earl and Ramona are. Save us both from a night in jail."

He threw himself against the back seat and folded his arms over his chest. With his chin jutted out and his mouth clamped shut, he glared at me through the rearview mirror.

When we made it to the turnoff to Stryker Lake, I said, "We're going to stop at my place for a minute. I'm going to fix a sandwich. Want anything?" I could order something from the Long Branch, but I wanted to avoid anyone finding out I had Newt in the holding cell. There's no accounting for the magical transfer of gossip in the Sandhills.

Newt unfolded his arms and looked out the window with a sulky set of his mouth. "I could eat."

We rumbled along the dirt road toward my bungalow. The sun had finished its main work for the day and was making its own dinner plans. Not much was left of the afternoon. With the windows down, early summer couldn't help but invade the cruiser. I wanted nothing more than to finish planting my garden and mow my grass.

What if I was on the Bar J with Carly? We'd be working for a few more hours yet. Fencing or repairing haying equipment for summer. There was always something to be done, and time off was even harder to come by than it was with being sheriff. But there wouldn't be an old bachelor junk guy in my back seat, even if he didn't carry his signature garbage reek, and I wouldn't be ripping a quirky family apart.

Dad's pickup was gone, and I figured he'd been called to work. If I could get Newt to cough up Earl and Ramona's whereabouts, I could look forward to a two-hour drive to North Platte, however long it took to have Ramona admitted to the hospital, and maybe an overnight at a hotel. I wanted to be on hand when the staffer from Verde Mesa picked her up. I felt like I needed to report to Newt and Earl. And no doubt, Carly would grill me about Ramona's well-being, too.

I pulled up in front of my yard. "If I let you out, you're not going to take off, right?"

Newt pursed his lips like an old lady. "I ain't got nowhere to run to."

I let Newt and Poupon out, and they both followed me up the cracked sidewalk to the house.

"When we was little, we used to fish in that lake," Newt said. "Me and Earl'd catch a mess of perch, and Mom would clean 'em and fry 'em up for us. They was good."

I didn't own the lake. About half was on Jim Strong's and the other on Troy Stryker's. But neither of them did much with it except turn horses out to graze the surrounding pasture once in a while. "You're welcome to fish here anytime."

We plodded up the steps. "I'm not one for cleanin' fish. They stink."

Newt being put off by a fishy smell was about as logical as May Keller being allergic to oxygen. I tugged the screen to the front porch, and Poupon preceded me inside. The front door was open; guess Dad had left it that way. Poupon walked in and headed for the couch.

I took one step into the living room and caught my breath. One of my dining room chairs was knocked on its side. Fishing poles looked like they'd been tossed on the floor, and a tackle box spilled lures and bobbers outside the kitchen door.

I rushed through the living and dining room to find even worse mayhem in the kitchen. What sent my heart into overdrive was the amount of blood.

23

Newt stood behind me in the kitchen doorway. "What d'ya suppose happened in here?"

Bloody handprints marred the white paint of my cabinets. Smears of crimson covered the counter and sink. An empty paper towel roll littered the floor along with wads of soaked, pink-tinged kitchen towels.

Since the handprints looked small and didn't reach the upper cupboards, it didn't take a Congressional hearing to assume they were from my nephews and Tony. Something had gone terribly wrong on the fishing expedition.

"Dang." Newt sounded awed. "That's a lot a blood."

Phone in hand, I dialed Sarah. She sounded worried when she answered. "How bad is it?"

If I hadn't been concerned before, that spiked my blood pressure. "I just came home, and there's blood everywhere."

"You must have just missed them."

Newt stood in the doorway, mouth open, looking terrified.

"What happened?" I asked.

Brie gurgled in the background, probably perched on Sarah's hip. "Garrett wasn't clear. All I understood was something about balancing on an old fence post and Tony fell and knocked his head and blood."

"There's a lot a blood," Newt echoed, even if he couldn't hear the conversation.

"Where are they now?"

Sarah must have heard Newt's comment. "Yeah. You know how head wounds bleed. Garrett and Sheila treat that kid like he's made of glass, so I'm sure even a little blood would freak them out. I don't know how bad it is. I sent him to Louise's place. He can drop off the twins, and Louise should be able to tell if it's a big deal."

I started for the front door, motioning for Newt to follow me as I squeezed past him. Poupon needed a jerk on his collar before he agreed to jump off the couch and join us.

Sarah inhaled. "Garrett is such a drama queen. Tony was crying. The twins were making so much racket I could barely hear. If it's not too much trouble, would you mind checking up on them?"

I let Newt ride up front and gave Poupon the back seat, making everyone happier than the earlier ride, I was sure. "On my way."

She sounded relieved. "I know Louise will know what to do with the kids, but who knows how traumatized she'll make Garrett before it's all done. Not that he couldn't use some traumatizing, the prick." Whether it was her general disdain for her brother or he'd done something specific, I didn't know.

"I'll rescue Garrett and Tony and call you back with an update."

I slipped my phone into my shirt pocket.

Newt shook his head. "That was an awful lot a blood."

I thought about turning on the lightbar and even adding a siren. Not because it was necessary—it wasn't, since there were no cars on the highway to town—but because it might excite Newt. We took the corner before crossing the railroad tracks and sped along the road until I slid into the alley between Beverly's (the aging widow who'd lived there since before my oldest sister was born) house and the one I'd grown up in.

A newer Ford F-150 Supercab was parked next to Louise's aging Suburban. That must be what Garrett had borrowed from Alden for the fishing trip. I hopped out and opened the back door for Poupon. "Come on inside," I said to Newt. "You're still in custody."

Newt didn't protest and followed along, keeping a good distance between him and Poupon. I didn't knock but burst into the kitchen when I heard a ruckus inside.

Everyone gave us a quick glance, then went back to business.

Tony, his face a smear of blood, snot, and tears, sat on a kitchen chair bawling. His thick chestnut-colored hair was clumped with blood near his forehead. A fresh rip in the right knee of his jeans and whole layer of kid-grime made him look pretty rough.

Louise stood above him, holding a dishtowel on his head, her brow wrinkled with worry. Two of her chins wobbled when she turned to me, but she didn't pause lecturing Garrett. "What were you thinking? You can't just take them out and turn them loose. They're children, not dogs you let go at a dog park. We're lucky you didn't kill them all."

Mose and Zeke squatted in front of Tony. They'd developed an ability to tune out their mother. I couldn't make out their words, but they sounded quiet and comforting.

Garrett stood three feet away, his face pale and his eyes frantic. He held up his phone. "I'm going to call 911. Get the ambulance here and take him to Broken Butte."

Louise lifted the towel, soaked bright red. She peered at the wound. "I think it needs stitches. What do you think, Kate?"

I lifted a finger to Garrett in a wait-a-minute gesture and hurried around to Louise.

Poupon plopped in his favorite place in the corner of the kitchen behind the picnic table Louise had kept when her family had moved in after Dad left.

Newt wandered in and closed the door. He didn't venture far into the room and spoke in a soft voice. "That's a lot a blood."

Garrett swallowed hard. "It is. That's not good."

Louise dabbed at the wound and pressed down for a second.

Zeke patted Tony's knee. "I had stitches." He twisted his forearm to show the neat centipede scar. "It don't hurt at all. But it itches like crazy."

Mose nodded and in a sad voice added, "But yours are gonna be on your head where no one can see."

Zeke's eyes widened. "Unless they shave your hair, and it doesn't grow back. That would be awesome."

Tony sniffed and hitched his breath in an effort to stop crying. Maybe the prospect of being a bald badass with a snaking scar on his scalp bolstered his courage.

Louise pulled back the cloth, and I leaned in to see the gaping half-inch slit fill with blood in an instant. She clamped the rag back down.

"Yep." I caught Garrett's eye. "Stitches."

He started to punch his phone.

"Hold up. It'll take the EMTs fifteen minutes to a half hour to gather up because most of them live in the country."

Garrett blinked, probably remembering he wasn't in Scottsdale with ready medical care. In a breathy voice bordering on panic, he said, "Then you can get us to Broken Butte. Siren and lights."

I nodded. "I can. But I might have a better solution. Let's get you guys in the car."

Garrett started to protest, but Louise and I exchanged a look, and she gave her agreement with a dip of her chin.

She turned on Garrett. "Go with Kate."

Louise held out her hand to Garrett, and he took a tentative step toward her. She clamped onto his wrist and thrust the bloody towel into his palm and placed it back on Tony's head before Garrett could squawk.

I noticed Newt still watching the scene, and I turned to Louise. "Can you keep an eye on Poupon and Newt until I get back?"

Newt's eyes flicked to Poupon, then back to me. "I can go with you. I'll be good."

Louise reached into a cookie jar, and an unexpected arrow jabbed into my heart.

The ceramic urn, big enough to hold a double batch of Louise's monster chocolate chip cookies, had been made especially for her by Mom. In a swirl of green and blue, it was a true work of art.

I pushed away the thought of missing Mom. She'd deserted us. Not the other way around.

Louise pulled out a cookie and grabbed a paper napkin from a dispenser on the table. Sounding like she scolded Newt, she set the cookie on the picnic table and said, "Sit there and wait."

The twins immediately clamored for a cookie and left Tony's side.

I leaned down and placed a palm gently on Tony's elbow. "Let's get that head of yours examined."

Leading him, with Garrett holding the towel to his head, I ushered them out to the cruiser and into the back seat. From there, it was a matter of a quarter mile straight to the end of the block and into a gravel lot.

Garrett sounded alarmed. "Oh, no. Not the vet."

I popped out of the car and held the back door open. "You can trust him. He's good. Stitched up my head over two years ago and I haven't had a problem."

Garrett stared at me with his brown lawyer eyes. "Show me the scar."

I leaned toward him and pulled my hair back to reveal the top of my forehead. The scar wasn't anything a plastic surgeon would brag about. But for a veterinarian, I thought it scored a solid seven, maybe even an eight.

Garrett wasn't so generous. He leaned back, one arm around Tony, the other holding the bloody rag. "Looks like he closed it with a crochet hook."

I grinned at Tony, whose sobs were reduced to periodic hiccups. "I think it looks like I'm a pirate. What do you think?"

With big, watery eyes, he leaned away from Garrett and studied it. A microscopic twitch at the corner of his mouth hinted at a grin. "It looks like a velociraptor took a swipe at you."

Garrett's reprimand was quick. "Tony!"

I laughed as loud as I thought would sound authentic. "I'm going to use that. Thank you, Tony."

He squirmed away from Garrett, who still kept the towel on his son's head. "Zeke says stitches don't hurt."

Garrett locked eyes with me, clearly conflicted about what he should do.

I took Tony's hand and said to Garrett. "Quick and easy. They're on the top of his head where no one will ever see."

He inhaled deeply in surrender, and we trooped into the clinic that smelled like disinfectant mixed with the stinging scent of medicine and the corrals out back.

"Heath," I called out.

A second later, the trot of boots on concrete alerted us to the handsome blond man who rounded the corner from the exam room. In a second, his eyes greeted me, swept over Garrett, and settled on Tony. His glance came back to me. "Oh, no."

It took a fair amount of reasoning to convince Heath, but he caved, as I'd felt certain he would.

Heath considered Tony a second. "Do you like bunnies?"

With his eyes full of trepidation, Tony answered with a serious nod.

Heath disappeared through a door behind the counter. The crates for small animals were in a room there and the barn with stalls for the large animals beyond that. In a few seconds, Heath stepped back in holding a tortoise-shell lop-eared rabbit.

Tony gasped as Heath placed the bunny in his arms. "Lester's family is away for a few days, and he could use some company."

With Tony occupied making friends with Lester, and Heath threading his needle, I turned to Garrett. "I promised to call Sarah."

After explaining the situation and listening to Sarah's disdain for her gentrified and entitled brother, I signed off and waited.

The clinic door opened, and Garrett stepped out. "Everything okay?"

He looked pale but calm. "Yeah. Heath's letting Tony put Lester in his cage and feed him. Tony seems fine, but Heath says he'll probably hurt when the numbing agent wears off."

He turned his deep brown eyes to me. "Thank you for taking charge at your sister's place. I think we were coming to blows before you showed up."

His appreciation surprised me. "Louise takes some getting used to, but she means well."

Something seemed to snap in him, as if the polite conversation was too much. He turned away. It only took him a second to get control. "Sorry. I'm not very good at this whole father thing."

In a knee-jerk way, probably learned from being married to Ted, I rushed to reassure him. "It's obvious you love him. So that's a start."

That smooth lawyer exterior crumbled, leaving a vulnerable man, eyes blinking back tears he refused to shed. "It's pretty late to jump into this. Tony is ten, and I've spent most of that time in an air-conditioned office on the tenth floor piling up billable hours." He swallowed, and his Adam's apple bobbed down his throat. "I've missed too much."

What could I say to that? I treasured the times I'd spent with all my nieces and nephews, especially Carly. If Garrett had forfeited his moments with Tony, he'd never get them back, and I had little comfort to offer. "Then you shouldn't miss what's coming next."

He stared at the door to the clinic, his face etched with despair. "I can negotiate settlements, stride into court with confidence, manage the business side of a successful partnership. But I can't keep my son safe on a stupid fishing trip."

I chuckled, and his scowl showed me he didn't appreciate it, so I sobered up. "Kids are on a suicide mission half the time. Unless you hover over them, pad them and helmet them twenty-four-seven, they're going to find a way to get hurt." The Fox clan, with nine kids, had accumulated countless bloody wounds and broken bones, not to mention the scythe-bearing specter of cancer that had stolen Glenda from us. "And Louise's kids have all managed to get injured under her watch, no matter what she admits to."

Garrett's shoulders slumped. He didn't say it, but his posture shouted that he felt like a failure.

The clinic door eased open, and Tony walked out. I added, "Some of my best memories are when I spent time with my niece while she was sick. You don't have to do anything else but keep them as comfortable as possible and pay attention to them." An image of six-year-old Carly flushed with fever hit me. I'd taken a shift babysitting to give Glenda a break. Carly cuddled close on my lap while I read *Charlotte's Web*. I still felt the warm weight of her, the trust and love.

Garrett looked at me like I'd given him an idea, and his face brightened a little. He dropped a hand softly on Tony's shoulders. "Dude. Ready to go home?"

We drove back to Louise's, and I retrieved Newt and Poupon, said goodbye to the Haneys, and started for the courthouse.

Newt looked out the back window at Garrett's pickup. "That Haney guy. He done all right for hisself. Kind of a surprise after how he was raised."

That made me curious. "What do you mean?"

Newt swiveled back to me and mumbled something.

"What?"

He looked up at me with sad eyes. "Earl'd be mad for me talkin' out of school. We don't like to tell tales on folks 'cause if it got out we gossip, folks wouldn't want us on their place."

People generally didn't want the Johnsons digging through their private dumps, but that hadn't stopped them from sneaking onto ranches and finding their discarded treasures.

"'Cept bein' your CIs, naturally."

"Naturally." Newt and Earl fashioned themselves my confidential informants, and surprisingly, they'd been helpful.

Newt squinted in the side mirror, probably looking at Garrett. "Alden Haney, he didn't do right by that boy."

This was news to me. Sarah believed Garrett had been treated like a prince. "What do you mean?"

Newt fidgeted and got that mournful droop to his face. "That boy learned how to take a beating. That's all I got to say about that."

I settled Newt into the holding cell and didn't balk when Poupon jumped into my desk chair and wrapped into a ball. "I'm going to slip home for a shower and change of clothes. Then I'll get us some burgers and be right back."

Newt gripped the bars, his skin-and-bones build and buzz cut making him look especially prisoner-like. He puckered up his face in indignation. "You're not going to leave me alone, are you?"

I almost told him I was leaving my deputy in charge, but I figured Poupon's presence wasn't much comfort. "I'm starving, and I'm sure you're hungry, too. And since Twyla banned you, I'll bet you're craving Bud's special sauce."

Newt pulled out his pout again and eyed Poupon. "Can you get some of the sauce in one of them little cups so I can have it on my fries?"

"While I'm gone, maybe think about how we don't need to stay if you tell me where Earl and Ramona are."

Again, his gaze popped over to Poupon. He seemed to consider his options, then folded his arms again and pursed his lips.

This was going to be a very long night.

24

Home after dark, again. And I wouldn't even get to sleep in my own bed. If I was going to have to spend the night in my office, I at least wanted an air mattress and sleeping bag. The luxury of a good night's sleep, something I needed, would have to wait. But I didn't have to live like an animal.

I pulled next to Dad's pickup. The lights weren't on in the house, so I assumed Dad had made it home from a trip and was sleeping.

I let myself in quietly and showered. A clean uniform left me feeling much better—about my hygiene if not my life. With my hair hanging loose down my back making my shirt damp, I found Dad sitting on the porch step, gazing out at the lake and the silvery ripples reflecting the half-moon.

I plopped down beside him, deciding supper could wait a few more minutes. "How's it going?"

He didn't answer for a few seconds and then let out a breath as if he'd been holding it. "I ought to say it's good."

My heart sank. "But it's not so good?"

He leaned forward with his forearms on his knees. "I'm running as fast as I can, but I'm not getting anywhere."

We were quiet for a while before I spoke. "And I've planted my feet in one place and making the same progress."

His chuckle had no humor. "What a pair." He stared into the darkness, the lake and the frog chorus out there. "She broke my heart, Katie. And I don't know how to fix it."

It hurt to hear him say it. Mom told me she needed her kids and grandkids around to chase the ghosts away. She'd escaped, but I wondered if she hadn't left the ghosts behind to haunt us. "It's a blow. You can't expect to get over it right away." That might be true, but it wasn't helpful.

"All I know is that for forty years, I counted on love. And now that's gone, I'm empty."

Around the lump in my throat, I managed to croak, "I'm sorry."

He didn't look at me. "But I'm not hopeless. Life isn't over, and I believe I'll find love again. But not the way I've been chasing it. And you," he twisted his neck to face me, "you need to stop doubting that you are lovable. It'll happen for you, too."

Even if I hadn't wanted to have the talk with him as others had urged, it looked like I was in it up to my earlobes. "Obviously, my retreating from involvement isn't working. But I can't see as your overactivity is any better."

"Your mother would advise meditation and yoga."

"Yeah? Well, she can skinny-dip in a piranha pool."

He tilted his head back and let loose a laugh like I hadn't heard from him in a long time. "Fair enough."

The frogs croaked, and a soft breeze ruffled the leaves on the elms.

Dad planted a hand on my knee. "What are you going to do about Dahlia's mischief?"

It shouldn't have surprised me he'd figured it out, but I hadn't known he was paying attention. "It'll play itself out. No one is going to listen to her, anyway."

"I don't know about that. If she talks loud and long enough and creates the right kind of doubt, she might get what she wants."

I let that sit.

His words floated into the darkness. "The question is, what is it you want?"

Since that seemed to be the query of the day, with no ready answer, I phoned in an order to the Long Branch and wished Dad a good night.

Nothing much had changed at the courthouse since I'd been gone.

Newt sat on his bunk watching Poupon snooze in my chair. "That burger smells good. I wondered if you forgot about me."

I held the bag just outside his reach. "Are you ready to tell me where Earl and Ramona are?"

He stared at the bag, then at me, his mouth dropping open at my betrayal. "You can't not feed me. There's prisoner laws about that. But no, I ain't sayin' nothing even if you starve me."

I slipped his bag between the bars. "Of course I'm going to feed you. But you could make it easier on both of us if you'd come clean. You can't think this is good for Ramona."

He took the bag and sat on the bunk. I gave Poupon his two patties, and he wolfed them down without a thank-you. We didn't speak again until we'd finished eating and I'd let Newt use the bathroom to clean up before bed.

Leaving Newt in his cell, I took Poupon out for his evening business. I stood on the front lawn of the courthouse while Poupon sniffed and wandered, his main form of daily exercise, and thought about Ramona. It was an hour earlier in Arizona, but still well after business hours. At a residential facility, though, maybe someone was around to answer questions.

I found the number in my phone for the front desk and gave it a shot. After enough rings, I thought I was out of luck, but then someone answered with a soft, "Verde Mesa. Can I help you?"

I snapped myself back to attention. "Yvonne Cartwright doesn't happen to still be there, does she?"

The woman gave a deep-throated chuckle. "Not by a long shot."

I figured, but I thought if I left a message, maybe I'd be priority number one tomorrow. "Could you leave her a message that Sheriff Fox called?"

She sounded as if this wasn't her normal job. "Sure. Let me find something to write with, and I'll get your number."

She fumbled around a moment and said, "Sheriff Fox. Your message?"

"I'd like a little more information about Ramona Hinze. What I might expect from her."

"Did you say Ramona? Mona? Do you know where she is?"

I didn't know how much I ought to say to an unidentified person on the other end. "Do you know Ramona?"

Her voice sounded tight. "Of course I do. I'm Alba Torres. Director of Food Services. Mona works for me."

Now it was my turn to be confused. While I tried to decide what to ask first, Alba must have recognized my confusion.

"I don't normally answer the phone. I'm in my office planning menus, and who knows how all the calls got routed to my number. I've called IT, but they probably won't be here until tomorrow. This call, at least, I can handle."

"You said Ramona works for you?" Ms. Cartwright said Ramona was a recent transfer. Something was off here. Was it possible the director was out of touch with her patients? Maybe she'd confused them.

"Oh, yes." She had the slightest Hispanic accent. "For many years. Part-time, of course. And she's always been reliable. So, I was worried when she didn't show up for her shift two days ago and I haven't been able to reach her."

Maybe Ramona was having a breakdown of some kind. "She seems really confused."

Alba gave a little moan. "Oh no. I've noticed she's getting more forgetful lately. I was going to urge her to see one of the doctors here and get tested for dementia, but that's such a hard conversation, and I kept putting it off."

Way more than a hard conversation, it would be awful to have to confront someone with that kind of decline. "I think testing would be a good idea."

Alba sounded concerned. "But she's okay? She's with you? Where are you?"

"I've spoken with Yvonne Cartwright. We have plans to get Ramona back to Tucson. But I'm a little concerned about her medication. Do you know anything about her prescriptions and instructions?" I hoped Alba wouldn't cite HIPAA and clam up.

Alba inhaled. "Yvonne knows where Ramona is? She never told me about it. But I'll tell you, I'm happy to hear she's on her way home. I've been worried about that old girl. She is getting more and more forgetful all the time."

"Would not taking her medication make the problem worse?"

Alba hmmed. "We're a tight group in the kitchen, but I'm her boss, so I don't know everything. But I wasn't under the impression she took anything more than blood pressure medication. Maybe vitamins."

"Then there's no worry she'd get violent if she missed a dose or so?"

Alba laughed that throaty, carefree sound. "Mona? Oh, she's a sweetheart. Wouldn't hurt a fly. She's kind of lonely, though."

"Oh?"

"Well, her husband died a while back, and she's been alone. Some kind of car accident, and I think Mona was driving. She misses him and maybe feels guilty."

That jibed with what Newt and Earl had said. "Anything else you can tell me about Mona?"

"Just that she'd do anything for you. She's such a sweetheart."

That was what I thought. "Thank you. I appreciate you talking to me."

"What's your number, and I'll have Yvonne call you back." She hesitated. "I'll tell her you called, anyway, but whether she calls you back is anyone's guess."

Didn't sound like Alba had much respect for Ms. Cartwright. I left my number and thanked her again.

When we returned to my office, Newt was perched on the edge of his bunk, looking miserable. I left the desk light on and stretched out my mattress and sleeping bag and removed my boots, then wandered to Newt's cell and leaned against the bars. "I'm worried about Ramona. The care facility says she can get upset easily."

Newt studied his hands, maybe surprised to look down and see clean fingernails. I know it shocked me. He spoke cautiously, as if not sure he ought to tell me. "Most of the time Ramona is good. She talks a lot about when we was young. Back then, me and Earl, we both wanted to have her for our sweetheart."

"May said you were split over her." That wasn't exactly what she said, but that was the gist.

A swell of red heated the back of Newt's neck. Before Ramona came into their lives, the skin would have been so caked with dirt I wouldn't have been able to see color. "We been through a lot together since then, me and Earl. We got to the war, and that took the fight out of us."

I couldn't help laughing at his odd choice of words.

He jerked his head up, with a puzzled look wrinkling his forehead. Then he nodded. "Oh. 'Cause we get to bickering from time to time."

Their bickering had them rolling in the snow at the side of the road, shoving each other into their open trunks, elbowing in the ribs that knocked the wind from their lungs. Not to mention the constant insults and offended snits.

"But that's not like real fighting. We made a pact in the war that if we got home, we'd be friends forever. Nobody to come between us. Like the band-of-brothers stuff."

"Then you drew guns on each other in the Long Branch."

He shrugged. "We're over that now."

"After you got back from Vietnam, what were you going to do about Ramona?"

A hint of a smile tugged at his mouth. "We figured to let Ramona have her pick. The other one would have to man up and step aside. But when we come home from the war, she'd already picked another."

"That must have hurt."

He dipped his head lower, and his neck flamed darker. "She got the right to do what worked for her. Me and Earl understood. She had to get away from her dad. And Bob Blakey was a important guy with college learning. We only wanted her to be happy."

"Do you think she had a happy life?"

He raised his head and looked at me, his eyes probably blue once but faded to a gray. I saw longing and a touch of sadness, but mostly, they had that look of devotion some dogs have for their owners. Not that it applied to me, of course, because my dog was Poupon. "I think mostly she's confused."

"There's talk that Ramona came back to get Earl's and your money. That maybe you have a fortune amassed somewhere."

His mouth dropped open in the over-the-top way my ten-year-old niece's might. "Me and Earl got some money. Mom always said we need to save for a rainy day. But when she was with us, we never had no money. And after she was gone, Earl and me were careful. I want to know who said we got a lot of money, 'cause they ain't supposed to say nothing at the bank, and that's all who knows what we got."

Maybe they did have a stash. "I don't know it's anything but gossip.

People know you and Earl work hard and don't spend much. So, they're probably guessing."

He folded his arms across his chest and looked smug. "We done all right. But it ain't nobody's business." He lifted his chin in defiance. "And if me and Earl want to give it all to Ramona, that's our business, too."

"Of course it is. But your friends are concerned. They want what's best for you."

He sniffed and raised his chin a bit higher and sat like that for a minute. Then he unfolded his arms and focused on me with a serious face. "Ramona was pretty shook up the night she got to our place."

I hoped he was opening up, and I didn't want to spook him. "Oh?"

"It was that night last week that we had that storm." He waited for me to nod. "And it rained, and the wind blew something terrible. Me and Earl already hit the rack. We was planning on going out to Bill Lister's place—you know the old homestead where his great-grandfolks lived—'cause we thought maybe with the wind blowing from the south like it was, it might uncover something in a dump we had our eye on."

I fixed him with my most encouraging stare.

"So, we don't hear nothing, but Earl, he's got the room up front there, he sees headlights pull in. And so we get the guns and go out to look, and there she is."

"Ramona?"

"Yep. She's sittin' in that Mustang, and the lid's down and she's getting wet. She's all shivery. And she's staring straight ahead with eyes like they ain't seeing nothing."

"What did you do?"

"It took a minute to figure out who she was. We ain't seen her in pert near fifty years. But then Earl, he's got the flashlight, he says, 'Mona?' And she shakes herself and tells him her name's Ramona. And we both say howdy, and then she kind of snaps out of it and looks at us and gets all excited. She says, 'Hello, boys,' and then we get her inside and warmed up with some of that hot chocolate mix. And we even made it with milk instead of water, 'cause it was a celebration."

"How did she end up here?"

He turned away from me, and I thought he might not answer, so I said, "Come on, Newt. We need to help her."

His gaze returned to his hands in his lap. "She don't remember."

I exhaled. "This isn't good."

He spoke to his fists. "She said she was at that truck stop by Big Springs. You know the giant one that has the showers and the store and restaurant and all them pumps for the big rigs in back and the car ones in front?"

"Sure." I answered because I was afraid he'd keep describing it to me if I didn't.

"She said all she remembers is coming out after going to the bathroom. The car lid was down, and it was raining and windy and she didn't know why she was there or how she got there. She had the car keys in her hand, but she didn't know how to put the lid up. Then she remembered she wanted to go home, and this is where she thought of home. So, she drove here. But that was pert near two hours in the rain, so it makes sense she was played out. Like a homing pigeon or something. She said she wanted to be safe, and this was the safest place she could think of."

25

Between Newt farting and snoring and Poupon's claws clicking along the floor as he paced the small office, I didn't get much rest. At one point, I considered if Poupon wasn't going to use that comfy dog bed I'd provided, maybe I'd try it out. It had to be more comfortable than the deflated air mattress. I might have dropped off to sleep somewhere around six a.m.

At least, I felt like I'd only slept fifteen minutes all night when my office door burst open at 6:15 and a livid May Keller stormed in, slapping on the light and slamming the door.

"What the ever-living hell is going on here?"

Dang. Why hadn't I bothered to lock the back door when I'd returned from the Long Branch last night?

Poupon stood from his plush bed on the floor and wagged his tail before bowing to stretch his front legs.

Newt was standing, clutching the bars before I pushed myself to standing. His eye had faded to the color of a mashed banana. "Did you come to break me out?"

May stood with her hands on her hips. "I've seen a lot of foolishness in my time, but this takes the cake. Twyla told me you'd locked up Newt, but I had to see for myself."

How Twyla knew this information was a mystery, but she had her ways.

I reached for my boots, my back and hips stiff from my night on the floor. "Earl took off with Ramona, and I'm keeping Newt until he tells me where they went."

May glanced around the office and snatched the cell key from my desk. "Why the hell didn't you tell me that chippy absconded with Earl? I know where they went. And you wasted a whole night on this nonsense."

May was more the two-bits-word type as opposed to the ten-dollar kind, so I took it that she was fired up. She headed for Newt's cell with the key ready.

I jumped up and stopped her. "Hold on. You can't let him out without my consent."

Her slick-soled boots slid to a stop. "What's your plan, sister? We need to save Earl, and that tramp is sly. I'm tough, but maybe we could use some backup. So, if you're going with me, you can't leave Newt locked up here alone."

I plucked the key from her hand. "Where do you think they are?"

Newt's fingers clutched the bars, and he looked hopeful. He didn't want to stay in jail any more than I wanted him here.

"I don't *think*. I know. Lover's Leap."

Newt gasped, and I knew May was right. "I've never heard of Lover's Leap."

May gestured for me to unlock the cell. "Nobody calls it Lover's Leap except these fools. And the only reason I know it is because they let it slip last time they got tangled up in this twaddle."

Newt's face flared red, and he looked to the floor. "I didn't know you knew about that."

May shoved my elbow toward the lock. "I know lots of things. But that night before you went to the deployment place in Denver, I was afraid you were gonna do something stupid. And sure enough, you tried to."

Newt couldn't look at her.

May explained it to me. "They swore they were in love with Mona Hinze. Mona's dad had that place at the bottom of Tree Horn Ridge."

The butte had a gradual rise on the eastern slope and ended in a cliff that dropped about fifty feet to a dry creek bed. The house, now nothing more than a sanctuary for mice and 'coons, stood several yards from the ridge. Another bit of property owned by Troy Stryker but not cared for. The house used to get rented to teachers or others who stopped in Grand County for a while and moved on. At one time, it was a sweet little cabin, with towering trees and a view of the valley. Now the trees were mostly dead and the yard overgrown.

Troy Stryker lived in Denver and sold off most of his family's land, for some reason clinging to a few parcels close to Hodgekiss. Maybe he speculated the town would have a boom and his land value would skyrocket. For now, without livestock or renters, it didn't do more than cost him property tax.

May kept on with her story. "So that night, these yahoos dare each other to drive off the cliff to declare their love for Mona."

Newt snapped his head up and spoke with uncharacteristic force. "But we didn't do it."

May looked surprised.

"Because Mona come up and told us not to. She said she loved us both equal and she'd never forgive herself if we come to harm. Mona said we were a family and we belonged together."

May snorted. "And then what? You go off to war and she marries some dandy and moves away."

Newt thrust his chin at May. "Mona, she needed somebody to take care of her. Earl and me, we ain't never held a grudge about that."

I stuck the key in the lock, and the mechanism clicked. "Okay, let's go to Tree Horn Ridge and see about collecting Earl and Ramona."

May stepped back to let Newt out. "Better take your gun."

We used the courthouse bathrooms and dropped Poupon at Louise's.

"I'm going to grab breakfast sandwiches to go," I said to May, who rode shotgun while Newt took his place locked in back. "Do you want anything?"

May Keller growled at me. "I had eggs and biscuits hours ago, at breakfast time. But you can get me one of Twyla's sweet rolls."

How could a weathered rope of a woman hold so many carbs?

Newt caught my eye in the rearview mirror. "What the devil is a breakfast sandwich?"

I rubbed my hands together in anticipation. "You're in for a treat." I'd have described it to him, but Bud's sandwiches were a daily grab bag. You ordered the breakfast sandwich and left it up to Bud if it was on an English muffin, sourdough, Texas toast, or, once, raisin toast. It could have ham, or bacon, sometimes a small hamburger patty, most of the time cheese, always an egg, but it might be fried or scrambled. I'd seen them come with hash-browns, or not. But I'd never had a bad one.

I slipped into the kitchen and gave Twyla my order, then waited by the front counter, knowing Bud would give me priority.

My shirt vibrated. This damned phone felt like a stick of dynamite in my pocket. Every time it rang, something exploded in my life. Maybe that was an exaggeration, but wouldn't it be nice to be out on the range, moving cattle from one remote pasture to another, or in a tractor putting up hay, and no one to bother me? I could safely leave the phone in the pickup or put it on mute. It wouldn't be my job to answer the cursed thing. Maybe I'd once again call it a phone instead of a damned phone.

This time, the ID told me it was Kim Matthews. After a short hello, she said, "I had a second, so I did a little follow-up on Ramona Hinze."

"What made you do that?" With as busy as she seemed, and no real reason to follow up, since Ramona was a resident of Verde Mesa and not a wanted criminal, taking the time to look up a name might be a lot.

Kim was calling from the same chaotic background as usual. An eruption of voices like blackbirds in my elm trees and general activity filtered beyond her voice. "The name sounded familiar. I mentioned it to some older detectives, and someone remembered something. It didn't take much time."

"Thanks for that. What did you find?"

"In 2013 she stood trial for killing her husband." Kim let that drop, and I couldn't pick it up for a second.

"How did it happen?" I couldn't picture docile and cheerful Ramona killing someone.

"According to the prosecution, she pushed him off a trail on Mount Lemmon." When I didn't answer right away, she said, "It's a mountain just north of Tucson. Tall. Even has a ski area."

I wasn't interested in the geography; I was trying to grasp the situation. Ramona would have been in her sixties then. She'd hiked a mountain with her husband and shoved him off to his death. Plump and domestic in her prairie dress. Not like some other women that age in yoga pants and sports bras, cycling, running, working out. This was Ramona. She must have mellowed a lot in the last few years to go from athletic hiker, full of enough venom to kill someone, to the woman baking cookies and cupcakes for Newt and Earl.

"She must not have been convicted if she's not in prison." There had to be an explanation. No proof, circumstantial evidence? Just because she was on trial didn't mean she actually did it.

"According to the detective I talked to who remembered the case, she was batshit crazy. And nobody doubted her. He said it was nuts watching her slip into different personalities in court."

"Still, if she is mentally ill, they wouldn't let her out." Right?

Kim gave out a high-pitched skeptical *hmmm*. "Turns out she didn't get convicted. She was released as incompetent and remanded to a forensic hospital. From there, who knows what happened. Maybe she got better. Or they thought she got better. If they thought she was functioning, they could have released her to a regular mental health facility with fewer restrictions. Who then might have given her a weekend pass."

I finished for her. "And when she didn't return, asked for help finding her."

"Probably something like that. If you're interested, I sent over the online article. I scanned it, and it didn't say anything more than I told you."

Ramona told Newt and Earl she'd killed her husband. But I'd assumed she was confused. Killed him, as in not recognizing he had a heart condition before the heart attack killed him. Or baking treats for him until his diabetes downed him. Not as in actually killing him by shoving him off a ledge.

"One more thing." Kim broke through my thoughts. "The detective said her first husband died, too. Suspicious circumstances, but they couldn't find evidence she'd done anything. That's speculation. But, you know, where there's smoke."

Yeah. Just how much smoke was Ramona blowing up our skirts?

26

It only took a few minutes before Twyla handed me the bag. "When May complains about how gooey the roll is, tell her I packed extry napkins."

Grease already pocked the bag, and the smell of spicy breakfast sausage nearly made me faint. Before she could slip away, I asked, "How did you know I had Newt locked up?"

Her bloodshot eyes told me she had no patience for stupidity, and my question clearly qualified. "I don't reveal my sources."

But the answer popped into my head, and I mentally slapped my forehead that I hadn't thought of it earlier. Carly. "What else did she tell you?"

Twyla knew who I referred to. "We think Dahlia's out to sabotage you. Going around committing crimes to make you look bad."

Was that all? The warmth of the sandwiches felt good on my palm, and I couldn't wait to get back to the cruiser and dig in. "You two better not be hatching any plans of your own. I'll deal with this." I had no idea how, exactly. Without solid proof, which meant more than a few loose tie-ins to each incident, I couldn't accuse her of anything. Yet, nearly a dozen people had been to the golf course, had access to Doaks' house, and had attended the roping at Six Circle. The fence in Fleenors' pasture, the one they shared with Sid and Dahlia, certainly narrowed it down.

Twyla leaned on the counter next to the cash register and rubbed at her temples, the hangover still graying her face. "Unless you do something to stop her, she's going to get the job done. And so far, I ain't seen you doing squat."

With an obviously fake hearty wish for her to have a good day, I hurried back to the cruiser.

The ride to Troy Stryker's place didn't take more than twenty minutes, and we all munched our food as the countryside passed by. The wind picked up, scuttling heavy, low-hanging clouds.

Newt only spoke once. "I never knew Bud could do this. Did you get one for Earl and Ramona?"

May swiveled to him. "If they haven't ate by now, they might as well wait till dinner. Half the day's over." It was 7:30. In the morning.

Newt sat back with a peevish scrunch on his face, clearly not happy to be chastised.

We drove across an Autogate with a crumbling anchor post on one side and the wires broken on the other. The pit under the metal rungs was completely filled with sand so that cows could comfortably cross, if there were any cows in the pasture.

May grumbled, "That numbskull."

"Who?"

She glared at me as if I ought to know. "Troy Stryker. I tried to buy this place three or four times, and he won't let go of it."

We bumped closer to the house that looked like a whispering ghost would topple it. "Why do you want it?" It didn't butt up next to her land, unless she'd acquired a few thousand acres I didn't know about.

She stared out the window so I couldn't see her face. "I don't, necessarily. But from time to time, it might come in handy."

Why, May Keller. Like buying up the house and land so Blanche Johnson could remain in her home and raise her boys. Apparently, she was a one-woman charitable organization. Maybe she had someone in mind who could use a house. And maybe it was for a future need.

The house looked slightly bigger than my place, probably built around the same time. Unlike my little bungalow, this place had no front porch, just two concrete steps to the front door.

A small Honda motorcycle leaned against the side of the house. The wood siding of the one-story house showed no signs it had ever been painted. Windows were broken out and frames and eaves splintered. A bent aluminum screen frame hung drunkenly from one hinge at the front door. We parked in front of a mangled ornamental metal fence that separated the sandy road from the tangle of weeds and thatch of prairie grass that was once a lawn.

The westerly wind sent waves rippling through the front grass. Cottonwoods and ash trees gave a hint to what had been a sweet and pleasant yard. Now dead branches and suckers gave witness to neglect. One dead cottonwood looked like maybe a lightning strike had torn off the top, leaving it jagged and now white-trunked, like a standing skeleton. Gusts tugged the branches of the old trees. A definite chill in the humid air and a crystal-wet scent promised rain.

May sprang from the front seat, and before I let Newt out, she was already banging on the door. "Listen up, you vixen. You open this door this instant and let Earl free from your claws."

Newt hung back, and I was sure May couldn't hear him say, "Aw, don't be like that. They're my family."

As I came up behind May, Earl opened the door and stood barring the entrance. "How'd you find us? Newt, I swear if you ratted us out—"

Newt shouted behind me, "I never!"

Before I could clear Newt, May beat me to it. "I don't need Newt to tell me you'd come back here to the scene of the crime."

Earl and Newt both answered in sync. "What crime?"

May landed a hand on Earl's upper arm, attempting to shove him aside. "It's a manner of speaking." Stringy Earl held strong against May, and when he didn't budge, she demanded, "Where is she?"

Earl tried for an innocent face, which looked silly with his wrinkles, grizzled cheeks, and graying buzz cut. "Who?"

May tugged at his arm. "Don't toy with me, son. I'm gonna tear her limb from limb if she so much as skinned your knee."

It's probably a good thing May Keller never had kids of her own. I hated to imagine if someone pushed her little Johnny down on the playground. Nobody likes to think about murdered children.

"Okay, May." I used my best sheriff voice and lowered it an octave for added authority. "Step back."

To my surprise, the voice worked. Or else May didn't want to admit she couldn't get past Earl's blockade. She aimed and fired a murderous glare at Earl before slipping to the side of the door to let me get closer.

Newt hovered just behind me, ducking and weaving around me, probably trying to catch sight of his beloved inside.

I tried to laser reason and logic into Earl. "We've found you, so there's no point in hiding Ramona. I know you don't want her to leave, but she has to. At least for now."

Earl stuck out his lower lip. "Who says she has to leave? It's a free country."

In a perfect world, the three of them would totter around that old house, Ramona making sure they brushed their teeth and washed behind their ears, and Newt and Earl providing a peaceful home in the country. That is, when they weren't bickering.

A figure moved in the shadows behind Earl. As it approached, I made out the prairie dress and then Ramona's tired face. Her bright eyes and pink cheeks had turned dull and pale since yesterday afternoon. The light from the open door revealed dust and grime on her dress and a tear down the left side seam. Her hair looked matted on one side and tangled on the other. Maybe not by May Keller's standards, but Ramona was an old woman and obviously didn't have the stamina for all this foolishness.

I lowered my voice and made it soft. "You aren't teenagers. All this running around and sleeping on the floor, and probably eating pretty bad food, isn't good for any of you."

Newt pushed beside me. "How are you feeling, honey? I can get you a breakfast sandwich from the Long Branch if you come out. I had one this morning, and I know you'd like it."

Earl whipped his head toward Newt. "You Aaron Burr. All you had to do was not tell. And they dangled food in front of you and you caved."

I was schooled enough in Newt and Earl lingo to figure out Earl meant Benedict Arnold.

Newt's mouth dropped open. "I never. They locked me up and kept that beast outside my cell to make sure I didn't escape. It was torture. But I never cracked."

Earl spun toward me. "You put Newt in jail? That's lowdown."

Ramona came closer toward us and placed a plump hand on Earl's shoulder. Her voice sounded sweet, if exhausted. "Hey, Newty. Did you bring your friends out for coffee? Come in, and I'll get it started."

Newt stared at her a moment, then turned a questioning expression on Earl.

Whatever Earl communicated to Newt, he backed Ramona up. "I brung a camp stove we had, and Ramona packed us plenty to eat. We got coffee, but I'm not inviting you in."

I watched Ramona to gauge her reaction. "I spoke with Alba Torres at Verde Mesa. She seems very nice. Don't you think going back there would be a good idea?"

She stepped past Earl's barrier, a look of curiosity on her face. Her little girl's voice spilled out. "Ms. Torres? She's so kind to me. But I don't live there anymore."

May Keller *hmphed*, and from her expression, I thanked heaven she hadn't brought a gun.

The brothers fell all over themselves with their duet of reassurances. If devotion was all she needed, Newt and Earl would be better than any doctor.

Apparently, May could only take so much, and they'd exceeded the limit. "You dimwits shut up. This bit of fluff has never brought you anything but heartache. I say good riddance."

I couldn't agree with May. Eliminating Newt's and Earl's body stench alone improved the living standard of everyone in Grand County and beyond. Ramona had given their lives a boost, made them interested in living and striving to step into the world, instead of scurrying around the edges as they'd been doing. But Ramona's greatest value was the obvious affection Newt and Earl felt for her. She brought love and order to their home. I couldn't see the harm in that.

But she clearly needed help. "Ramona."

She smiled at Newt, then beamed at Earl, but didn't seem to hear me.

I tried again, sterner this time. "Ramona." When she dragged her gaze to me, I said, "Have you taken your pills today?"

She tilted her head and wrinkled her brow, her eyes looking pensive. "I think so." Her face cleared. "Yes. I definitely did. I remember looking in the mirror over the sink and thinking that we should replace that old wood medicine cabinet with a new one, maybe with those mirrored wings that fold in on either side so you can see the back of your head." She raised her eyebrows as if asking the brothers for their approval.

Earl took her hand. Not to be left out, Newt took her other one. Earl spoke softly. "That was yesterday at the house, honey. I helped you take both of them pills this morning. Before you made us oatmeal."

She stared at him a moment while she thought. Then she let out a giggle. "Oh, that's right. Where is my head?" She sounded completely back to herself. And she turned to me. "I'm a little worn out. All this excitement being at the old place."

I didn't know how to respond.

She stepped outside. "I was tickled when Earl suggested we camp out here. So many memories." She poked Newt and Earl on their chests one after the other. "The best ones were of you two." Then she turned to me. Although she seemed perkier than a moment ago, there were dark circles under her eyes, and her skin had a slight gray tinge. Even if she'd been keeping to her blood pressure meds, or whatever she took, being dragged around was wearing on her, and she needed to stop. "Of course, there's no electricity or water, but Earl made us a campfire and we brought a water jug. I managed that oatmeal without letting it stick to the pan."

I'd seen Newt and Earl's water jugs. Gallon milk containers covered in layers of burlap. When you wet the burlap, the evaporation cools the water, in theory. I hoped Ramona had insisted they go a more modern and hygienic route.

I gave her a friendly smile. Then said in a conversational tone, "Earl. I want you to ride that motorcycle back to town with Newt. May and I are going to drive Ramona to Hodgekiss, where I'm going to drop May off. Then I'm taking Ramona down to North Platte to meet the person Yvonne Cartwright sent from Verde Mesa."

Earl stepped in front of Ramona, bolstering for battle. "'Cause she didn't remember when she took her pills?"

Newt also took up her defense. "That don't mean nothing. I'll bet you forget things all the time. Like where you put your keys or somebody's phone number."

May added her two cents. "She's nuts, plain as snot runs from your nose in January. And if you think elsewise, I'd say you're a few slices short of a loaf yourself."

Newt drew himself up, and his face looked as stormy as the sky. He panted twice as if building up his steam. "You can quit that hateful talk now, May Keller. We're none of us crazy. We can take care of each other."

I couldn't imagine the courage it took for Newt to speak out like that to May. It showed his deep feelings for Ramona.

Earl raised his chin and stood shoulder to shoulder with Newt. "We're a family."

May *hmphed* again and stomped away, throwing up her hands. I figured it was only a display of irritation to give her an opportunity to light up. Which she did.

Like smacking a puppy, stealing a lollipop from a toddler, or kicking a cat, I was about to do something despicable. Carly's offer wavered before my eyes. Peaceful ranch life. My choices never involving hurting another person. Looking after cows and horses who depended on me for food and care but not for emotional support. I wouldn't be called upon to break anyone's heart.

I placed a hand on Ramona's spongy elbow, her aging skin soft and yielding, and nudged her toward the cruiser. "Go on, boys. This is how it's got to be."

Newt and Earl gave me their stony faces again. I couldn't tell what hare-brained tactic they'd come up with next.

Ramona pulled away from me. She turned to the brothers and placed one palm on each of their grizzled faces and studied them, her face etched with deep kindness. "You boys keep the house neat and do your laundry every week." She patted their cheeks. "And don't forget to change your beds and put on clean sheets."

May tossed her cigarette butt to the dirt and ground it under her boot, her expression skeptical.

Earl's face melted. "We can steal you away."

Tears filled Newt's eyes. "You don't have to go."

Even May Keller had nothing to say as we trudged to the car.

While sprinkles dotted the windshield and an occasional gust cascaded grit against the cruiser, Ramona chatted from the back seat on our way to town. "My family moved here when I was in high school. Back then, me and Newt and Earl used to have the most fun. We'd have picnics on Lover's Leap and have the wildest card games. They were always so much fun and the perfect gentlemen."

May watched her. "Oh yeah? Then why'd you up and marry Bob Blakey the minute them boys shipped out?"

From the rearview mirror, I saw Ramona's face scrunch in confusion. "Bob Blakey?"

I'd never heard of Bob Blakey before Newt had mentioned him, and I cast May a questioning glance.

She gave me an impatient aside. "An accountant from Broken Butte. Was doing the school audit. I was on the board then, and I can tell you that man was a wizard. Saved us a bunch. Smart." All the wrinkles in her face seemed to glow with disapproval when she focused on Ramona. "Until it came to her. I don't know as she even graduated before she ran off with him."

Ramona watched us with what appeared to be idle curiosity, not as if May was talking about her.

May addressed her. "Where'd you haul him off to after you got your claws in him?"

It took her a moment to think about the question. Then Ramona's eyebrows drew together as if in anger. From the rearview mirror, I watched her whole bearing change, making her appear more sturdy and solid, and almost aggressive. Her face set in grim lines. "My husband."

When Ramona didn't go on, May twisted around and prompted her. "That's right. What happened to him? Did you throw him over for something better like you did to them boys?"

Ramona zeroed in on May with almost a sneer. It didn't look like the

Ramona I'd seen before. Gone was the little-girl voice. "My husband is dead. He wasn't a good man. He treated me bad." The way she said it sounded mechanical, almost like reciting lines in a play. Was this behavior what Kim Matthews's coworker had described as different personalities?

May spit her words at me. "Bob Blakey was salt of the earth. There's a real ugly story here, mark my words."

Was this what Yvonne Cartwright warned me about? Even if Ramona had taken her meds, the stress of the last day might be too much for her. It would be good to get her to an expert who could help her.

By this time, we were pulling into Hodgekiss. Cars and pickups lined the corner of Main Street and the highway in front of the Long Branch. Twyla and Bud served senior lunch three days a week, and today was hot roast beef sandwich day. Always a favorite.

We continued up the hill and around the front of the courthouse, where I stopped next to May's pickup to let her out. While the sun climbed toward noon, clouds hid its progress. We'd had a string of beautiful days like pearls. That kind of perfection never lasted long, and we'd probably have some cold, rainy days right around the bend. They were necessary for the grass, but I took a moment to appreciate the periwinkle sky and sweet-smelling lilacs drifting on the breezes of the last few days.

"I could drive on down to North Platte with you," May said. "I don't like the idea of you being alone with her. She's sly."

I started to assure her I was fine when my phone rang. "Sheriff."

Twyla croaked into the line. "You better get your butt in here."

27

My stomach lurched with the sense I was smack in the middle of Dorothy's tornado with problems swirling around me like witches on bicycles. "Why?"

Dishes clinked and silverware clacked and voices rose in conversation. Twyla gave me a terse reply, probably busy with the hungry seniors. "There's some ol' gal asking about Mona Hinze. Says she's from Arizona and supposed to pick her up. I'm guessing Mona went back to her maiden name, which seems disrespectful if you ask me."

Why hadn't I questioned that before? Did Ramona change her name back because she'd murdered her husband?

Twyla broke into my thoughts. "I'm not liking the looks of her."

This all seemed jumbled, and a caution light flashed yellow. "I'll be right there."

May Keller had stopped to listen. "If you've got something to take care of, I'll keep an eye on Mona."

From the back seat, we heard a soft plea. "Please don't call me that. I'm a whole person. My name is Ramona Blakey."

Let's address this. "But sometimes you go by Hinze."

She furrowed her brow. "That was before I married Bob." Her face fell. "I do miss him so."

This was a flip from seconds ago when she'd said he was a bad man. "But you're Hinze now."

With a polite smile, she said, "No."

Except Alba had referred to her as Mona Hinze. Ramona Blakey. This was starting to be something like the Shakespearean rose, except, by any other name, it was starting to stink.

Whatever demon Ramona had released earlier seemed to be under control again, and she looked timid and more than a little afraid of May. I considered a moment, then shut off the cruiser and pulled the keys. "I'm going to put you in the holding cell while I take care of this." Since it was Saturday, there was no one at the courthouse to babysit. "May, you can stay with her, can't you?"

May speared me with one of her impatient scowls. "I told you I was on duty. And I'm a hell of a lot more reliable than that Betty Paxton. You get her locked up, and I'll take a puff and be right in."

Which was what I resorted to. With May settled into my chair and her feet on the desk, and Ramona sitting on the cot in the cell looking pensive, I left them, promising to return as soon as possible. This cell was getting too much use lately. At this point, I didn't know if Ramona needed to be locked up, but I was having serious doubts.

It would be faster to walk than drive, so I slipped out the back and hoofed it down the alley and across Main. A glob of seniors shuffled from the Long Branch, and I took a moment to agree with them that we'd had some fine weather and the coming rain was welcomed. As Ted used to say, it's always campaign season.

I slipped into the restaurant side to see mostly empty tables with the cream-colored diner dishes littering them, discarded napkins wadded up, the smell of beef gravy heavy in the air. Lunchtime started at noon and ended by one. The leavings were like a battlefield with the casualties awaiting burial.

Twyla shot from the kitchen carrying a large gray bin for the dirty dishes. "Look at this mess."

The detritus rivaled any other post–senior dinner. Restaurant service always set Twyla off. Sheriffing may or may not be the right business for me, but the service industry was definitely wrong for Twyla. Though getting her Jack Daniel's at wholesale probably made up for waiting tables. "Doesn't Donnell work at noon?"

Twyla blew air out her nose. "She up and quit. Got a job at the old folks' home in Broken Butte. As if driving all that way and putting up with those cranky old-timers is better than waiting tables here."

Yeah. As if. "Is that her?" I tilted my head to a dark-haired woman sitting at the far booth.

Twyla glanced at her and lowered her voice. "Asked for a glass of water. That's all."

No wonder Twyla suspected her of no good. If she'd have ordered a shot of Jack Daniel's, all would have been right.

I smiled as I approached, and she watched me. "I'm Sheriff Fox."

Eyes so dark brown they seemed black in the artificial light of the Long Branch, skin a rich bronze, she studied me without a hint of friendliness. Her voice sounded rough, like it pushed through a tumbleweed. "I'm Brenda King. From Verde Mesa. I came to get Mona Hinze and take her back to Tucson. She is staying with an Earl Johnson, I believe, and his brother. Do you know where they live?"

She shoved a few pages at me, and I scanned them. They were a release form authorizing me to remand Ramona Hinze to Brenda King's custody.

It surprised me she knew Newt's and Earl's names, since I didn't remember mentioning them to Ms. Cartwright. I eased into the booth across from her. "I thought we were going to meet at the hospital in North Platte."

Her mouth turned up in an unconvincing smile, revealing uneven teeth. "Sure." She nodded. "That's right. I decided to drive up here instead of waiting. So, where is she?"

Maybe Twyla had more reasons not to trust her. "Sorry about not getting Ramona to North Platte yesterday. She seemed upset about going back to Tucson, and she ran away. But she's ready to go now."

Heavy brows furrowed. "You lost her?" She had a bulky appearance, not fat but sturdy, as if alligator wrestling might be a hobby.

I hated having to admit that and tried to run over the top of it. "I hope the extra day wasn't a problem. Where did you spend the night?"

She watched me closely and seemed to consider before she answered.

That husky voice snaked out. "I stopped in Big Springs for the night. That place on the interstate with the gas station."

Popular place. "Ramona's had some rough days. I'm wondering if you ought to stay a day or two in North Platte before you tackle that long drive again. Make sure she's up to it."

A hardness entered Brenda's eyes. "Thank you for your concern. I'd planned on doing just that. So, if you can tell me where to find her, the sooner we get on our way, the better."

It didn't feel right to me. "Before I take you to her, I'd like to make a call to Veronica Cartwright. I'm sure you understand my caution." I waited to see her reaction.

She inhaled and squinted as if challenging. "That would be Yvonne Cartwright." She sat back in the booth and waved her hand. "Go ahead. I'm glad you're being thorough." She didn't seem glad.

I stood and walked down the aisle and squeezed by Twyla, who bussed the tables close to the kitchen. Leaning against the restaurant door, I dialed Yvonne's number and slipped outside.

In the deepening gloom from the approaching storm, an eighteen-wheeler roared past on the highway, and I barely heard her answer. After identifying myself, I started in. "I just met Brenda King. She's here in Hodgekiss to pick up Ramona Hinze."

Yvonne paused. "Oh? I thought you were meeting her in...what town?"

"North Platte. At the hospital."

Yvonne sounded distracted again. Obviously, you had to be able to multitask to run a nursing home, and I questioned Yvonne's aptitude. "Yes. That's right. But you say she's there in your town? How far away is that?"

It seemed like a loose operation if they sent someone up here and she never checked in. "Over a hundred miles. Did she know Ramona was up here? Where was she staying?"

Yvonne hesitated, and I assumed she was thinking. "I don't remember telling Brenda about Hodgekiss, but I must have. I tried to call Brenda after I spoke to you yesterday, but she didn't answer. I assumed she either had no signal up there or maybe she was gassing up and left her phone in the car. At any rate, I left a message. I meant to call her back, but things got wild around here and…" She stopped and sighed. "Things got wild around here. With Brenda gone, we're short-staffed."

I might look into Verde Mesa. More than ever, I considered trying to move Ramona up to a facility nearby where Newt and Earl could keep an eye on her. "Brenda's here now and wants to take Ramona."

A door banged shut on Yvonne's end, and voices spoke in the background. "That's fine. Brenda is more than capable. She's been with us for several years and knows Rami well."

That nickname again. Kim Matthews said the neighbor had called her Rami, too. I didn't think it suited Ramona, but it wasn't up to me. "I might recommend Ramona stay a bit in North Platte to rest up. She's been through a lot of excitement."

Yvonne sounded distracted, as if she tossed off the sentence without thought. "Thank you for your care and concern."

That didn't satisfy me. "Would you like to talk to Brenda?"

The voices in the background grew louder. "Would you do me a favor? Have Brenda check in with me after she's seen Ramona, and she can give me an assessment. If Brenda thinks they should stay a night or two along the way, then we'll make that call."

I tried again to get some sense that Yvonne Cartwright gave a damn about Ramona. "She's driving a convertible Mustang. Seems amused it reminds her of *Thelma and Louise*."

Yvonne cleared her throat. "Yes. Well. We had a new activities director. A young woman just out of college. She took over movie night, of course, as her job. She asked the residents for suggestions and then, I guess she's young enough she'd never seen it and didn't know how it ended. Or the subject matter. So, she screened *Thelma and Louise* for the residents."

I'd think a romantic comedy or an animated film would be a better choice than a movie dealing with rape and ending in two women sailing into an isolated canyon.

Yvonne sounded annoyed. "It triggered some residents. I wasn't aware that Ramona was one of them. She seems pretty tough." She let out an unamused *ha*. "Needless to say, that activities director is no longer with us."

I didn't like the way they seemed so casual with Ramona's well-being.

But they knew her better than I did. Maybe it would be best to get her home quickly.

I returned to Brenda's table. She'd finished her water and seemed impatient to be on our way. "All good?"

"I need to check your ID. Then we'll get Ramona."

Her dark eyes drilled into me. "I left my bag in the car. My license is there."

I eased out of the booth. "Let's go get it."

She leaned forward, placing a well-muscled arm on the table and reaching behind her. With a flick of her hand, she whipped a lanyard with a laminated card dangling from the end. "Will this do?'"

I took the badge. An official ID from Verde Mesa with *Brenda King* printed on it. Yvonne Cartwright trusted her. She checked out. Just because Twyla and I felt a little uneasy, that didn't mean anything. Kim Matthews's term "icky hairs" flitted through my head.

My phone rang. This Pavlovian stomach clench couldn't be good for my health. After taking a moment to close my eyes—what Mom used to call a one-second meditation—I answered. "Sheriff."

"Sherwood Temple here. I've had no status report from you today, and since I haven't seen your delightful self here, I wondered if you've got the case wrapped up and will be returning the statue to us forthwith." *Forthwith? Seriously?* Snooty, arrogant, poke-my-fist-in-his-eye tone and all.

I felt like a boxer who'd been punched into the ropes and bounces back for more. "I'll be back at it this afternoon."

He paused. "So that would mean no, you haven't made any headway."

"I'll get back to you later." I punched him off, sad it was a button on my phone and not a finger to his eye.

"Okay. She's at the courthouse. I can ride with you." It wouldn't hurt to check out her vehicle.

Brenda wore black jeans stretched across muscular thighs. A sleeveless black T-shirt and black hiking boots completed the outfit that looked more biker thug than health-care professional. Although she had no visible tattoos, her dress and demeanor made that seem like an oversight on her part. Tough, wary, and street-smart oozed from her. Nothing about her made me want to kick back and share a few laughs.

We made our way to an older gray Taurus parked along the highway. I directed Brenda around the block and to the courthouse. While she pulled up, I popped open the glove box.

"Hey." She sounded as if she'd like to deck me. "What are you doing?"

I held my arm up just in case she threw a fist. "Looking at the registration."

She leaned back. "What is it with you? I've showed you ID. You checked with Yvonne. I'm legit. Just give me Mona and I'll be on my way."

Mona. Not Rami. No wonder Ramona seemed so confused if even her name changed constantly. Now I understood her insistence on using her whole name. The registration sat on top of the car manual. The 2008 Ford listed Verde Mesa Care Facility, Tucson, Arizona, as the owner. "Okay, it seems in order. You ought to be glad I'm being careful to not turn over a patient without verification."

She blew out an exasperated breath. "Right. Let's go."

With Brenda on my heels, I headed for my office, surprised to see the door closed. May might have become claustrophobic in that tiny space. I reached for the knob, and it didn't turn. Alarm pounded into my gut with the force of a sucker punch. I reached into my pocket for keys and in seconds opened the door.

A garbled growl focused my attention on the cell. The door was wide open. Ramona was gone. But May Keller, trussed up like a roped calf, coiled on the cot, a bandana in her mouth and knotted behind her head.

Anchovies and toe jam. I should have felt lucky May Keller was sturdier than Ramona and wasn't likely to suffer a stroke or heart attack. But the fury on her face was enough to mask the many wrinkles, and forget about shooting daggers with her eyes. May looked ready to launch torpedoes.

I was right there with May in declaring war on the Johnsons. Stinging acid shot through my blood, and when I found Newt and Earl, I sure as shootin' wanted to hog-tie them, too. There weren't enough curses for my rage. In a flash I had the bandana off, May drawing in breaths as I started on the frayed bit of rope at her wrists.

She wriggled as if I tried to hurt and not help her. "Them boys. I'm gonna beat bumps all over their hides. Then I'm gonna string 'em up by their ankles so they can watch me slap that girlie upside the head."

Brenda loomed over us in the cell's doorway. "What the hell? Where's Mona?"

May Keller spared a glare for Brenda. "Who're you?"

I succeeded in loosening the knots. Newt and Earl hadn't tied May with any intention of keeping her there permanently. "She's from Tucson. Going to take Ramona home."

May sat up and rubbed her wrists. "Well, you're too late." She shot up and immediately fell back to the cot. "Damn pins and needles in my feet. I'm gonna kill those yahoos."

Brenda spun around and slapped the wall with a resounding smack. Thank goodness it wasn't someone's head. I'd have thought someone working with psychiatric patients would have a more serene vibe. "You let someone kidnap Mona? We have to find them."

They wouldn't go far. I addressed May. "Suppose they're back at Tree Horn?"

May's hands shook, and I figured she was overdue for a smoke. "I wouldn't put it past the knuckleheads. But I'm tellin' you, that girl didn't look all that good. I don't think even them dimwits would drag her around much."

Brenda's fists clenched, and her jaw looked like iron. "If anything happens to Mona, there will be consequences."

Her threat sounded sincere, but that wasn't what worried me the most. What if Ramona lost control and became violent? "When you say she didn't look good, are you talking about physical or mental?"

May reached for her shirt pocket and pulled out her pack of cigarettes, already pushing herself to stand. "She's not made of sturdy stock. Like a silk pansy. She looked all played out."

Brenda towered over us. A good swipe from that powerful arm might smash us like mosquitos, which seemed like a possibility since she didn't have patience to spare. "Where are they?"

If the current of frustration running under Brenda's skin set me on edge, it didn't seem to affect May at all. With the tingling in her feet under control, May stomped toward the cell door and elbowed Brenda. "I got a few ideas, and I ain't gonna stand around here discussin' it." May stuck a cigarette in her mouth.

Brenda's heavy boot pounds followed May's cowboy boots clacking toward the front door.

Running around the hills checking out the Johnson brothers' hidey holes didn't seem like the most efficient way to unite Brenda King and Ramona Hinze.

Before I dropped into my chair to plan a course of action, my phone rang.

I closed my eyes for a long blink, saying a quick and silent prayer it wasn't another of Dahlia's nuisance calls, or one of my brothers or sisters insisting I interfere in Dad's life, or even Sarah with her excuse for siccing her married brother on me. "Sheriff."

"We're really sorry we done what we did to May Keller."

It had to be one of the Johnsons. I made a guess. "Newt?" A sledge-hammer of emotions smashed into me. Mad, relieved, worried, mad again. "Where are you?"

His voice had an edge of panic. "We thought we was doin' the right thing. Ramona ain't a criminal to lock up."

"You're right. But she needs help, and I want to get it for her." I kept speaking slowly and calmly.

He sounded on the verge of tears. "You gotta come out here, Katie. Ramona is having trouble, and we don't know what to do."

"Where are you? Is she agitated? Can you get away from her?"

His voice shook. "We brought her home 'cause she looked like she needed to rest. But I guess she's agitated, if you mean is she carrying on. We don't know how to help her."

I was already out of my office and racing for the door. "Hold on, I'm on my way."

"Hurry. She ain't acting right."

28

I hadn't alerted May or Brenda I was leaving and hoped May would be more engrossed in her nicotine break, and in the best case, both would be talking and not hear me leave.

No such luck as I caught sight of May's blue pickup in my rearview mirror when I crossed the railroad tracks heading north. The tall figure next to her had to be Brenda. Guess we were all heading to the Johnson house.

The wind kept pushing more clouds to pile overhead, but they seemed reluctant to let go of their moisture. A steady rain would relieve man, beast, and grass alike. But a raging storm always meant trouble.

May stayed on my tail as I raced down the highway and turned onto the gravel road, only hanging back when I hit the trail road and the dust got too thick. As it was, they braked next to the Mustang only seconds after me and trotted to catch up as I climbed the porch steps.

At the front door, I spun and held my hand up, and May pushed her chest into it. I pointed to the small rifle in her hands. "Nope. Put that back where you got it."

She had it pointed down to the deck but at the ready. It looked like a pellet or BB gun, not lethal, but not something we needed. "That's a bad idea. Everyone thinks this girl is harmless, but I know better."

Before May could say another word, I shot my hand out and wrenched the gun from her grasp. "Not messing around with you."

May's mouth dropped open. "I didn't know you had that in you. But you might be sorry you disarmed me."

Brenda King seemed mighty interested in the gun. I propped it by the front door. "You two stay out here. I'll let you know when you can come in."

They didn't respond, and the belligerent expression they both gave me looked remarkably similar coming from two such different faces.

The screen door screeched when I pulled it open. "Newt? Earl?" The entryway and living room seemed dark after the cheery scene yesterday.

Thudding came from above and descended the stairs two at a time. Then stocking feet—only slightly dingy—then jeans, shirt, and finally Newt appeared. He spoke in a quiet voice, but his eyes had a wild sheen. "She's up here."

He loped up, and I dashed after him. I followed a flutter of subdued but urgent voices into the nearest bedroom. It didn't surprise me to see an old mid-century pressed-wood bedroom set with a shiny, varnished veneer. The double bed had a plain headboard and matching footboard. A mirror was attached to the dresser along one wall, a long, ruffled doily on top.

Ramona was propped on the bed, her prairie dress blending with the mint-colored chenille bedspread. Earl and Newt perched on either side of her. Earl leaned close to her and spoke in a soothing voice. "See, the sheriff is here now. Remember Katie Fox? She's a good one."

Ramona's face was streaked with tears. Fear sparked in her hazel eyes, and she shook her head at me. "I don't remember." Her voice shook. "I'm sorry. I don't remember."

Earl patted her hand, and Newt took over. "It's okay. We all forget things. Don't you worry."

She inhaled a sharp breath and stared at Newt. "I don't know you." Then she whipped her head around to stare at Earl. "I don't know you, either. What am I doing here? I want to go home."

A sudden explosion that sounded like a buffalo stampede rushed up the stairs. None of us moved as we focused on the bedroom door.

Brenda King stormed in. She looked like a bear in the doorway, all black clothes, dark skin, and hair wild. A fierce hurricane of determination lit her face, and she looked ready to rip Ramona from the two men and haul her out.

Ramona let out a scream. "It's you!"

29

Brenda rushed to the bed and bumped Earl out of the way. She leaned close to Ramona. "That's right. I'm Brenda. I've come for you. Like I always said I would."

From the doorway, we heard May banging up the stairs. "I'm gonna knock some heads together when I get up there. You two nitwits better not think you're getting away with hog-tying me and leaving me for dead." Not exaggerating or anything.

Ramona stirred on the bed and whimpered.

May clumped into the bedroom, wheezing. She might be able to outwork us all, but not if she had to do it on a run. "What in the blue blazes is going on in here?"

Ramona blinked at Brenda with something like wonder. "I know you. I remember. The night and the wind." She glanced at the window as a gust shook the glass. Her face cinched with worry and fear, pulling at her round cheeks. "It was cold. The rain. I got lost." She stared at Brenda, and a spark of recognition in her eyes made her face relax. "Rami."

Brenda's hard face didn't crack, and in her raspy voice she said, "That's right, you're Ramona. I'm Brenda. We're friends. From Verde Mesa."

Newt stroked Ramona's hand. "We're here for you, honey. We won't let nothing bad happen. Family."

Brenda's glance at him was murderous, then she spoke directly to Ramona, giving her a mesmerizing stare that made me think of a hypnotist. "I've come to take you home. You want to go home, don't you? Remember, we talked about home?"

May pushed past the bed where Earl and Brenda crowded next to Ramona. "If you're gonna have a party in here, you gotta let some air in. Too much humanity stinking up the place." She wrenched the old wood window frame up, letting in welcomed summer perfume with a damp promise.

Ramona stared intently at Brenda. "Yes. I remember. I told you all about home. You told me about your home." Her face brightened, improving her pallor. "Look. You're here." She pulled her hand from Newt's and took hold of Brenda. "We're friends. The same. We had bad husbands, and now they're dead."

Newt and Earl both sucked in a breath. "We know that's not your fault," Earl said.

"It's okay, honey," Newt said.

Brenda's smile looked hard. "That's right. You know me. I've always helped you."

Earl leaned between Brenda and Ramona. He let a worried glance linger on Brenda before he spoke gently to Ramona. "I think it would be a good idea for you to stay here and rest a little bit. You can get your strength back before you leave."

Newt's attention flicked from Earl to Brenda, to Ramona, and finally landed on me. In a high-pitched voice, he pleaded with me. "You ain't gonna let this stranger take our Ramona away. Not until she feels better."

Brenda's rough voice slapped Newt. "I'm the best thing for her right now. Your half-assed redneck care has nearly destroyed her. You need to back off."

Ramona pulled her hands back and covered her ears. She squeezed her eyes closed. "No fighting. I can't take fighting."

Earl tried, but his slender body couldn't block Brenda from Ramona. "Okay. We won't fight. No fighting. See?"

Ramona peeked from slitted eyes and slowly let her hands drop. "I want to go home. Please. Take me home."

Brenda gave us a victorious nod. "Okay. Let's get going." Brenda straightened and held her hand to Ramona.

Ramona smiled sweetly at Brenda and took hold, letting Brenda pull her to her feet. She arranged her dress. "Road trip." She seemed to shed a heavy load. "Isn't that what you said? And now we're going. Home. In the car, like Thelma and Louise."

Brenda's tough exterior cracked into what looked like the first genuine smile I'd seen lately. "That's right. The two of us on an adventure, like Thelma and Louise."

Thelma and Louise had an epic friendship, sure. But Bill and Ted were buddies, too, and they had more excellent adventures if you asked me. In fact, as far as buddy movies went, Thelma and Louise felt bleak.

They walked hand in hand out the door and down the stairs. Newt and Earl looked stunned, then started to follow.

May stood at the top of the stairs and hollered, "Don't you think I've forgotten what you boys did. There will be a reckoning. Count on it."

The boys were halfway down the stairs when Brenda opened the screen door.

Earl hollered, "Wait."

Ramona, who had been staring up at Brenda, turned slowly and gave Earl a curious glance.

Earl jumped the last step and landed in front of her in his stocking feet. "Don't you want to get your things?"

Brenda waved an impatient hand in the air. "She doesn't need any of that. Keep it or toss it. We're on our way."

May and I exchanged looks. "That don't make no sense," May said.

I went after Brenda and Ramona as we all emptied onto the front porch. The sun had declared defeat, and the dark clouds dominated. The wind carried a chill. I reached them and spoke up. "Before you take off, I want to call Yvonne Cartwright."

Brenda held onto Ramona's hand and scowled at me. "Why? I've shown you the documents. You've already talked to her and made sure I'm authorized to take her."

Icky hairs. I needed to trust them. "I have doubts about Ramona's condition to travel."

It felt like Brenda wanted to chomp me down and poop me out. "Yvonne isn't here to assess her. In my professional opinion, the sooner I get Mona to Tucson, the better."

Ramona's eyes gained a certain clarity, and she yanked her hand from Brenda's grip. "Ramona. My name is Ramona. I'm a full person. Not a half."

Brenda's response was quick and firm, not a lot of warmth. "I know your name, girl. Look at me. Remember? We're a team, right? You and me."

My undergrad degree in psychology didn't make me an expert in therapy or dealing with someone who had a fragile grip on reality. Even growing up with Mom, who some might argue lived in a haze of mental illness, didn't make me qualified to know the correct methods to use with a confused person. Maybe the doctors and staff at Verde Mesa had been treating Ramona long enough to know how to soothe her and gain cooperation. And maybe that called for a firm hand, not soft and sweet.

Earl, Newt, and May crowded behind me on the porch.

Ramona tilted her chin at them and scowled in mock anger. "You aren't coming outside in your stocking feet, are you? That'll take a gallon of bleach to soak out the dirt."

Brenda tugged at Ramona and mumbled something I didn't hear.

Ramona peered into Brenda's face. She relaxed again. "A team. I remember. Thelma and Louise."

Brenda urged Ramona down the porch stairs. "That's right. We look out for each other."

Ramona's giggle sounded girlish and carefree. "I've got your back, and you've got mine. Because we're meant to be together."

May pushed around me. "That sounds like a bunch of bull hockey. There's something sour about this whole thing."

Newt tugged on my wrist. "You can't let her take our Ramona away."

Earl nudged my shoulder. "Ramona don't seem right, and that woman doesn't treat her good."

Brenda herded Ramona toward the Mustang with long strides, never hesitating about what vehicle to take. She seemed in a hurry to get Ramona inside.

Ramona looked back at us standing on the porch. Her face clouded, and she turned to Brenda, tilting her head up and studying her as if trying to read a book in a new language.

This was about as right as a snowman in Tucson. I started down the porch steps. "Brenda."

In a flurry of black hair, Brenda opened the passenger door and shoved Ramona inside.

30

I lurched forward and stepped into the space between the Mustang's door and passenger seat as Brenda swung it toward me. The edge caught me on my hip. Even though I'd braced for it, all that heavy steel hitting flesh and bone sent a wave of pain ricocheting through my hips, up my arms and down my legs.

I grew up with a herd of brothers and sisters who had unbreakable loyalty with non-family but were more like hyenas among ourselves. They'd attack if they detected weakness, and I'd learned to keep a straight face even when I wanted to holler. I glared at Brenda.

Her dark eyes showed surprise and cunning I didn't think appropriate for someone who cared for people with mental health problems. "You want to call Yvonne? Fine. But we've got a long drive, so we're going to start."

Earl and Newt protested behind me, but I wasn't concentrating on them.

Ramona whined from inside the car, sounding like a weak kitten. "I'm hungry. I didn't eat lunch."

This seemed like a good opportunity to delay their trip. "Good idea. Let's go to the Long Branch, and while you grab a sandwich, I'll touch base with Yvonne."

With dead eyes and a bit of a cocky smirk, Brenda said, "Sure," and started for the driver's side.

"Why don't you and Mona ride with me." I made sure it sounded like more than a suggestion. "One of the boys will drive the Mustang, and the other one can bring his car to drive home."

May stomped to her pickup. "I'll meet you there. I ain't missing out on this hoo-ha."

Everyone took their assigned rides, and we left in a caravan down the dusty road.

Brenda refused to engage in the small talk I kept throwing out. She grunted one-syllable answers to my inane questions such as, "Do you like Tucson?" "How long have you been there?" "What made you go into health care?"

I gave up and we drove in silence, only broken when I unintentionally let out an irritated grunt of my own.

Dahlia's shiny new Ford F-250 was parked on the highway across from the Long Branch, with Ted's two-year-older and a little less shiny Ford F-250 snugged up behind it. Dahlia bought a new pickup every two years and handed down her old one to Ted. It was a tradition they'd carried on since before I'd married Ted.

Brenda gave me a side-eye at my outburst but, when it wasn't directed at her, showed no more curiosity.

I angle parked on Main Street, and Earl took the spot next to me in the Mustang. Like a parade, May pulled in next, with Newt in his turquoise Monte Carlo finishing the line. We made our way down the cracked sidewalk with the wind spitting dust and gravel into our faces, the cold biting as much as the dirt. Though it would be temporary with the sun brightening as soon as the storm passed, right now it felt more like winter than June. The clouds had marched closer, threatening heavy rain within the next hour or so.

I entered first and held the door open to the bar side for everyone else. The restaurant only had tables for four, but in the bar we could pull up tables to sit together. Before I followed the group, I glanced into the restaurant at Ted, Roxy, and little Beau sitting with Dahlia and her two sisters, Rose and Violet. Beau's face was smeared with chocolate syrup and ice cream, and he wrangled a spoon in a melted sundae. He sat across from the great-aunts, who had their backs to me. Dahlia sat in a chair at the end of the booth, and Roxy and Ted squeezed together facing me. Beau caught sight of me and squealed. "Kay-Kay-Kay!"

Dahlia whirled around, a horrified look crossing her immaculately—if a bit garishly—made-up face. She replaced it with a smile so fake it could be sold on a New York City sidewalk.

Dahlia hated me for several reasons, the main one for beating Ted in the election. But this repulsed expression seemed excessive.

Roxy jostled Ted and squiggled against him, trying to make him move so she could get out. When he finally stood, she popped out of the booth and bounced toward me, all bubbly boobs in her pink, low-cut, and remarkably tight T-shirt with rhinestones spelling, "Cowgirls don't cry. They reload."

She saw me reading her shirt, and we shared a split-second connection on the appropriateness of her wearing that. I'd seen Roxy deliver a shot center mass and take out a man threatening her son. She might not be a typically nurturing mother, but I knew Beau would be protected. Which was a damn sight more than I could say about Mom.

The silent acknowledgment lasted a fraction too long and ruined any chance for my escape.

Roxy shoved open the glass door and threw her arms around me in the cramped foyer.

It didn't matter what sins I'd committed in this life or any before, Roxy's unbridled affection was a hell I didn't deserve.

"Oh my God! I haven't seen you since the whole Garrett thing. You have to tell me everything."

Darn the swift and deadly advance of gossip in the Sandhills. Nobody was supposed to know about Tony getting stitches. I needed to shut this down before it got Heath into trouble. I started with playing stupid. "What Garrett thing?"

She tugged me into the restaurant. "He's so handsome. And I think you make a perfect couple. I mean, he's smart and you're smart."

Couple? Nothing to do with illegal stitches. This town made me crazy. "I don't know what you're talking about."

She stopped dragging and, thankfully, removed her hands from me. Giving me a conspiratorial elbow nudge, she clamped her mouth shut, pantomiming locking it and throwing away the key.

For the love of mustard on a fudgesicle. I shouldn't even try to explain, but I couldn't help myself. "There's nothing between me and Garrett Haney. He's married. He lives in Scottsdale." Saying that made it sound as if I'd been considering such a thing. "He's a dick."

She giggled. "Oh, I think the lady does protest too much." Shakespeare scholar she wasn't.

I stepped back and thumbed over my shoulder in the direction of the bar. "I've got to get over there." The less I said about who was there and why, the better. I tossed a casual wave to Ted, said hello to Violet and Rose.

Draining as much friendly from my voice as possible, I finished with, "Dahlia."

She only half turned her head, enough to give me a side view of her aquiline nose, and put the least effort into an almost smile.

I started to leave when my phone rang, giving me a premonition of what hot flashes were going to be like. "Sheriff."

"You gotta get here now." The woman's voice on the other end sounded urgent.

Another twist to an already bendy day. "Who's this? Are you in danger?"

"Jesus, Kate, no one's got a gun to my head. It's Kasey Weber. Someone's driving out in our north pasture, and I think they're trying to herd the bulls."

Kasey and Dwayne Weber had been building a reputation for the last few years with their rodeo stock and had some success. Good rough stock could run into a lot of money, and competition could be fierce. It wasn't unheard of for "accidents" to befall a particularly fine bloodline.

I glanced at the doors into the bar. "If you can keep track of them without being seen, do that. Don't engage."

"Aren't you coming out?"

I scrutinized Dahlia and wondered if this was another of her tricks. If not, I needed to check it out. "As soon as I can."

Dahlia couldn't hide a smirk before she gave an alarmed, "Oh my gosh. What is it?"

Roxy slapped a hand on her chest as if waiting for a shocking revelation. Ted was trying to get Beau to stop flinging melted sundae. Violet and Rose hadn't turned around.

Dahlia exaggerated her distress. "Do you suppose it's another crime? Grand County is becoming like the lawless Wild West."

For the love of cheese.

Ted wasn't paying attention to us. He grabbed a wriggly Beau and a handful of those worthless napkins Twyla squeezed into the metal dispensers. Beau arched his back and whipped his head from side to side. Ted's crisp white shirt was doomed, which tickled me because it would annoy Ted a great deal.

For all Dahlia's manipulations over the years, she couldn't act any better than my niece Kaylen when she played a pilgrim in her first-grade production of the first Thanksgiving and insisted on wearing a tutu.

There were only a few other tables occupied with people having afternoon coffee. But they watched, and I felt their judgment.

Dahlia had the stage, her voice booming and dramatic. "Ted should go."

Okay. Game over. "I'll take care of what's going on in my county."

Shifty eyes landed on me, and Dahlia sneered. "Don't you have a situation you're dealing with already? Your people in the bar are waiting for you."

I couldn't let Ted save the day. "He's here with his family. Day off."

Roxy's focus skipped from me to Dahlia. "Oh, that's okay. I know from being married to the sheriff that sometimes the job has to come first. And it's really important for all of the sheriffs to work together. So, it's totally fine for Ted to go, like, figure out the crime scene and stuff. Whatever you need to do here, Kate, you should do that and feel confident Ted's got your back."

The scary thing was that Roxy probably believed everything she said and that Ted would be doing me a favor. Maybe she didn't remember Dahlia's scheming before the last election. A child was caught in those crosshairs. Thank goodness everyone came out safe and sound, and I won the election on top of it. But Dahlia's meddling had consequences.

Ted could generally be trusted to come through in the end, but he always had to take it as far as possible in hopes of the most advantageous outcome for him.

It wouldn't take long to drive the few miles to the Weber place, look around the scene—which I was sure was another of Dahlia's schemes—and get back to town. I could leave May to keep an eye on Ramona and Brenda while they ate. But if Newt and Earl could get the better of her, as they had in the jail, she didn't have a prayer if Brenda became aggressive. I could call Carly, but even if she was at the Bar J headquarters and not in a far-off pasture, it would take too much time to get to town.

I considered Dahlia and nodded my head. "Roxy's right. I need to call on backup, and Ted's the obvious choice."

Dahlia lifted her nose in smug satisfaction.

Ted hadn't succeeded in cleaning up Beau. All he'd achieved was a screaming toddler who'd swiped sticky chocolate not only across Ted's shirt but on his chin and nose.

Roxy got to Ted before I did. She pulled her hands back in a clear indication she had no intention of getting messy with her child. I reached to the counter where dishes, silverware, and other supplies were stacked and grabbed the bar rag Twyla kept in a used tomato can of cleaning water for wiping tables.

"Incoming," I said. While Ted grappled with his squirming son, I made an airplane noise and when Beau giggled, I wiped away the chocolate, ending with a swipe at Ted's chin.

He pulled back with a look that told me how much he wanted to swat me. I pointed to my nose to show him he had more chocolate. He rubbed at it.

Roxy beamed at me. "That's what I love about you. Nothing grosses you out. That's why you're such a good rancher."

Dahlia moved in behind me. "Kate needs your help with a string of thefts she hasn't been able to solve."

Ted's scowl cleared, and he gave me a serious nod. "What do you need?"

"It won't be too tough. I need you to babysit for me."

He sent a questioning look to Dahlia. I doubted he was in on her plans, but he probably picked up the sizzle of her frustration.

I motioned for him to follow me toward the bar. We moved through the foyer and into the darker room. Nothing smells quite like a daytime bar. Stale beer, the lingering grease and savory scent of noon's beef gravy. A week ago, with Newt and Earl in this closed-in space, we'd have smelled a whole raft of unpleasantness. Thank you, Ramona.

The five of them sat with laminated sheets in front of them, a sign Twyla had been there to toss the menus out but hadn't been back for their orders. They all lifted their heads when we approached the table.

Brenda assessed Ted with interest. For what, I didn't know.

Ramona gave a welcoming, if distant, smile.

May regarded us with a challenge. She probably wanted us to hang Brenda and Ramona from the windmill on Main Street. It wasn't a working windmill, just one anchored in the pavement as a kind of tourist attraction.

Newt and Earl looked worried, but I didn't think it had much to do with me and Ted.

"I've got to check something out, and I'll be gone for a little bit." I addressed Brenda. "This is Sheriff Conner from Chester County. He's going to hang out with you until I get back."

Brenda dropped a palm onto the table. "This is ridiculous. We need to get on the road, and I'm not waiting around for your little games."

I slapped Ted on the shoulder and spoke to Brenda. "I'll probably be back before you finish your lunch."

Without waiting, I spun around and headed for the door.

As luck would have it, I spotted Dahlia reaching for the door handle of her fancy ride. I changed directions and trotted toward her. "Hold up," I shouted.

She languidly turned and leaned against her pickup, folding her arms across her chest. "Yes?"

Temper popped and bubbled like a sulfur pit in Yellowstone. Before I reached her, I started in. "I know you're behind all these stolen things. The sculpture, the Doaks' spoons and sword. You cut Dick Fleenor's fence, and you let Mel's horse out of her pasture. No doubt you've got Kasey calling."

She gave her eyebrows an arrogant raise. "Or is it you can't deal with small crimes around here and you want to blame someone?"

It took all my restraint not to pull out my finger and drill it into her chest with every point. "Malicious mischief is a real crime. You're pulling me away from protecting citizens to satisfy your petty grievance."

"Oh? Is that what you call it?"

"I won the election fair and square. Ted lost. Grand County is better off for it." Normally not one to make sweeping claims, I was hopping mad and couldn't help myself.

She remained unruffled, which made me want to throttle her. "The voters will decide who's better for the county. I don't think it'll be much of a contest since you don't seem able to keep any kind of law."

"I'm going to prove you're behind this so-called crime spree, and it will ruin any credibility Ted might have left." How I was going to find the proof to back this threat eluded me enough my stomach churned.

She laughed. "You'll never find the stolen goods. They're history. Enjoy your last year as sheriff, if you last that long. You won't be reelected."

I fumed while she opened the pickup door and pulled herself up. The engine roared, and she pulled away, that self-satisfied smirk leering at me from the rearview mirror.

She'd said, "They're history." An interesting choice of words. And one that pricked a memory.

31

Once in the car, I dialed Yvonne Cartwright's number. The phone rang four times and turned to voicemail. I left a message, then pulled to the shoulder. I searched for the main number for Verde Mesa and dialed that.

A voice that sounded like a young man answered, probably a front desk person. I asked for Yvonne.

He sounded rattled. "Uh, um. You know. Now is not a good time."

With a firm tone, I said, "This is official business. I need to speak to her."

"Well, um. She's not available right now. I can take your number and have her call you back."

"Please let her know it's urgent and to call back as soon as possible."

"I will. Yes. Of course."

He said of course, but I had doubts. Still, there didn't seem to be much I could do about it, so I gave him my number and hung up.

The Webers lived only a few miles from town. Their modular home, new pole barn, and collection of pens could be seen from the highway just east of Hodgekiss. Kasey waited for me on the dirt road in front of her house, a few yards from the barn. I sped toward her, rolled down my window, and braked, sending a cloud of dust over us. The clouds had swallowed what was left of the afternoon sun. We could only hope they held moisture and not simply more of this hostile blustering.

Everything about Kasey was long, from her legs to her thick blond braid. She earned her nickname of High Pockets. She leaned down and shouted above the rumble of my motor. "I think I might have scared 'em. I drove up the hill, and they must have seen me because they left off from behind the bulls and headed toward the north."

"Is there a gate up there?"

She shielded her eyes against the sun even though it wasn't out, and looked in that direction. "Yeah, but it's in a weird spot. You have to know where."

"Climb in. We'll go check it out."

It took her a moment, as if she didn't want to come with me. Then Kasey dashed around the car and into the passenger side. "Go around back of the barn. I'll get the gate."

After she closed the gate and got back in, we rumbled down a sandy trail around a stunted hill to a pasture with the wire gate undone and lying on the ground. Kasey said, "The bastards must have come through here while I was in town getting the mail. They left the gate open. It's a wonder the bulls didn't get out."

"I don't suppose they planned on there being any bulls left in the pasture," I said.

Kasey watched out the side window without turning to me. "I didn't expect you'd respond as fast as you did."

"I was in town. Why wouldn't you think I'd get here quickly?"

She still didn't look at me. "I mean, Roxy says you're usually out at one of your brothers' or sisters' places doing day labor. And I heard they're branding at the Magnuson today."

"County business comes first."

With her wide eyes and fawning tone, Kasey oversold her sincerity. "We're lucky you're our sheriff. Roxy says Ted stays at the courthouse or patrolling in Bryant most of the time. But she's not, like, putting you down or anything." Kasey and Roxy were the definition of frenemies, a term as ridiculous as Roxy herself. Kasey's tone took on a sly edge, and she watched me. "She was more like complaining like maybe she thought Ted was a little lazy."

Did that make Roxy my champion? That was the kind of support I didn't need. "I'm not seeing any fresh tracks after the morning sprinkles. You sure they came this way?"

She turned back to the window, and her braid swayed down her back. "I don't know. Maybe they came through the gate."

My phone blared, and I glanced at a 480 area code. Since it wasn't one of my brothers or sisters, I couldn't ignore it. With one eye on the trail and the other searching the hills for the intruder, I barked into the phone. "Sheriff."

A second of silence, then a man said, "I'm sorry. This must be a bad time. Sarah gave me your number."

Garrett Haney. What would he want, and why had Sarah coughed up my number? Whatever it was, I didn't have time for it. "I'll call you back."

"Sure. But I only wanted to thank you for yesterday. Helping with Tony."

Kasey no doubt heard a man's voice, even if she didn't know what he said. A smirk spread across her face.

What about me being busy didn't he understand? "No problem. Thanks for calling."

Apparently, my abrupt manner didn't clue him in that I didn't want to talk. "I thought maybe I could buy you a steak at the Long Branch."

Kasey might've been hearing more than I'd thought, because her eyebrows shot up and she watched me intently.

Maybe the bull hole I hit in the sandy trail wasn't purely by accident.

Kasey flew from the seat and smacked her head on the doorframe on the way down. "Ow!"

Garrett heard that. "I'm sorry. I'll let you go. But call me. At least let me take you for a drink."

The last thing I wanted was to plan a get-together with Garrett. "That's not necessary. I've got a lot going on right now. I don't know if I'll have any time before you head back to Scottsdale."

"I'm—"

I didn't let him get going again. "Say hi to Tony for me." I hit off and dropped the phone in the console.

"Who was that?" Kasey asked. "He sounded yummy."

Yummy? That was a word that should only be used for food and only when talking to someone younger than three. "No one."

"Maybe. But he was interested. Why wouldn't you go out with him? I mean, what else have you got going on? Are you a lesbian or something?"

I scanned the hills. "Where did you say that gate is?"

"Because Roxy said the reason Ted started the affair was because he wasn't getting any at home."

Ted was getting plenty at home. "You saw the vehicle out here? What color? Make? Any details?"

But Kasey wanted to gnaw on this bloody bone. "Of course, after they started in again, she said they both realized they were soul mates."

I slammed on the brakes, and Kasey slapped her hands on the dash to keep from bashing her forehead. "We're trying to find someone messing with your livestock."

She sat back, and her glare told me how unreasonable she considered me. "Okay. Only trying to be friendly."

She directed me to where the gate was located in a taut fence line. Along the way, we passed individual bulls grazing without care.

"How many bulls are in this pasture?" I asked.

She sounded pensive. "Eight."

We came to the gate, which was closed, and I idled in front of it. No tracks in the rain-pocked sand. "I counted eight."

"Huh," she said. "I guess maybe I was mistaken."

I stared at her for a moment. "Right." *Or Dahlia put you up to this. Maybe she bribed you with hanging out at the Creekside Golf Club, where you could drum up investors in your rough stock. And you'd call and I wouldn't respond, and then you'd talk it up in the Long Branch.*

I didn't know what was in it for Kasey. But she and Dwayne generally had no love for the law, and she might just enjoy a little mischief at someone else's expense. We didn't talk as I roared back over the pasture and waited for her to open the gate at the back of the barn. I drove through and waved at her, not bothering to give her a lift back to her house.

This whole operation didn't take more than an hour, and I felt reasonably sure Ramona would be safe for that amount of time. But with May, Newt, and Earl involved, anything could happen, so I raced back to town just the same.

By now a few errant spits of rain smacked into the windshield. My phone rang, showing a 520 area code that must be Yvonne Cartwright. "Sheriff."

"Is this Kate Fox?"

She'd called my number and I'd answered; not sure who she thought it'd be. "Yes."

There was a flurry of noise on the other end before she said, "This is Yvonne Cartwright. I've been trying to reach you."

I'd called her own phone and left a message with Verde Mesa, so her questioning the sheriff being Kate Fox seemed stupid. She didn't bolster any more confidence in me about her competence. I'd look into her board of directors or some oversight entity on Monday. "I'm glad you called. I—"

"It's so awful." She blurted it out and started to cry.

Dang. Bad news. I knew it. But what brand of bad? My breath caught, and I narrowed my vision as if I could see through the phone. "What's happened?"

The drops on the windshield hit like cluster bombs, leaving smatterings that might be used for a natural Rorschach test. Black clouds swirled with a shimmer of greenish gray. That could indicate hail. Seemed early in the season for that, but the weather had quit being predicable some years ago.

"Oh, dear." She sniffed and blubbered until I wanted to scream. Another few seconds and she haltingly said, "I'm sorry. It's just, I can't seem to process it."

As director of a psychiatric hospital, I'd think she'd have more control of her emotions. But most of the Foxes had learned the fine art of stuffing our emotions, so I was no judge. "Ms. Cartwright. Yvonne. Tell me what's going on."

A gust rocked the cruiser.

She caught a sob and sniffed again. "Right. Yes. It's Brenda King. You said she was there today."

A chill laced up my spine. I hated the way this was starting out. Something was off about Brenda King, and I'd sniffed it on her when I met her. "Yes. She's here now. With Ramona Hinze. They're waiting until I speak to you before they start on the way back to Tucson."

She bawled a bit more and then blew her nose.

Enough rain smacked my windshield to start my wipers; no need to use drops as ink spots to analyze my mental state. Plenty frenzied, I'd say.

All the while I wanted to crawl through the fiber optics and shout into her face. "What is it?"

She hiccupped her way through the next bit. "I-I don't know what's h-happening. But it's impossible that Brenda King is-is-is...wherever you are."

That made my stomach twist. "Grand County."

"Yes. She can't be there because..." She lost it again.

Because, because, because.... *Why couldn't Brenda King be here?*
"She's dead."

32

I nearly keeled over with that news. Brenda King was anything but dead. She was tough and mean and sitting in the Long Branch with my friends.

It took me another round of sending calm questions to Yvonne before she could pull herself together to explain it to me.

"They found her b-b-body," a long, shuddering breath, "behind the Dumpster this morning. They think it happened not long before that."

"But she's..." I started again.

Yvonne kept going. "She was strangled. Her car stolen. They don't have any more information and wouldn't have had that if she hadn't had a credit card in her pocket."

I wasn't wrapping my head around this. Brenda King was here. "Could someone have stolen her card?"

"They—" She broke down again. "They sent a picture of her b-b-body by the Dumpster. It's so awful."

My mind dipped and spun. "What Dumpster, where?"

After another shuddering breath, she began. "At a gas station in, wait." It sounded like she shuffled papers. "Big Springs, Nebraska."

Big Springs is where you'd exit I-80 to head up to Hodgekiss. It was a natural place to stop before the two hours of no services that it would take to get here.

Wind buffeted the cruiser as I held onto the wheel, steering into the growing storm and trying to think this through. "If Brenda King is dead, who is here picking up Ramona Hinze?"

"Whoever it is, you can't let her take Ramona. You need to get Ramona to a hospital where they can monitor her meds and make sure she stays in a calm environment. Any kind of stress can set her off. And you'll have noticed, she's not easy to control if she gets agitated. It's taken several of our strongest aides to subdue her."

Ramona? "She's pretty weak right now. I don't think she'll be much of a problem. I spoke with Alba Torres last night. She said that in all the years she's worked with Ramona Hinze, she's never seen her show a temper. And as far as she knows, Mona doesn't take any medication except high blood pressure pills."

Yvonne sniffed and sounded put out. "Alba Torres is not a doctor. She doesn't deal with patients."

"She seemed to know Mona pretty well."

"Mona? Who's Mona?"

"Ramona Hinze. She must have work therapy or something because she has a shift in the kitchen. Alba Torres said she's worked there for years."

"Ramona Hinze has only been at Verde Mesa for a few months. And we don't do work—" She gasped. "Mona? Mona in the kitchen?"

Rain sluiced down the windshield, making the world distorted. "Yes, I—"

"But her last name isn't Hinze. It's Blakey."

The line died. I hit redial, but it rang to voicemail. Yvonne's reaction knifed into me with stinging force. Why would she panic about Blakey versus Hinze? The puzzle wasn't coming into focus.

With Yvonne gone, along with any chance of clarification, I turned back to Brenda King. Something nagged at me. I pulled over and thumbed through my email. It took a second to find the attached article from Kim Matthews, and I clicked to it. The photo below the headline was far bigger than my phone screen, and I manipulated it, moving back and forth. When I finally scrolled across the first sign of brown skin, my breath locked in my chest. My fingers pushed across the screen until I found an eye. A very dark eye. One that had scowled at me not an hour ago.

I clutched my phone to call Yvonne, but it rang. It was her. I answered with, "Brenda King is Ramona Rodriguez Hinze."

33

The sweet woman in Newt's and Earl's life was Ramona Hinze Blakey. She'd lost her husband in a car wreck. Ramona Rodriguez Hinze might have murdered two men. After meeting her, I thought that was a real possibility.

And she sat with my friends at the Long Branch. The air around me sizzled with my fear for them. I lurched onto the wet highway.

Yvonne panted into the phone, barely able to control her panic. "Rami Hinze is our patient. Mona Blakey is an employee. Alba Torres says Mona hasn't been in all week."

Clouds dropped lower, as if carrying too much weight. I put the phone on speaker. "What does this mean?"

"Rami is delusional. According to Alba, Mona might have some dementia, though she hasn't been diagnosed. She wears out easily, not in robust health. Alba says she's easily confused and influenced."

"What are they doing together?"

Yvonne sounded as if she'd run a marathon, huffing and barely getting the words out. "Rami was checked out of the unit to attend her mother's funeral. But she had to have a sponsor. When I reviewed the log, I see she was released to Mona Blakey."

I blurted it without thinking. "You release patients to a food service employee?"

"She described herself as a friend of the family, and Rami is highly functioning when she's on her meds."

When she's on her meds…. Toe cheese and jam. "Mona's maiden name is Hinze. You've got two Ramona Hinzes at Verde Mesa."

Yvonne sounded like a freight train, and I wondered if I ought to suggest a paper bag over her head. "I'm forming a theory. I have no way of knowing if it's correct."

The rain tumbled from the clouds like it couldn't hit the ground fast enough. It battered the road so loud it sounded like a Husker touchdown in Memorial Stadium. The barrow pit began to fill. My tires skidded as I accelerated, driving not nearly as fast as my racing heart. "Give it to me."

Like an asthmatic before using an inhaler, she wheezed her words. "Perhaps Rami and Mona found each other in the dining room and discovered they shared the same name. I don't know, but with one being called Rami and the other Mona, maybe they made some bizarre conclusion about being united. Alba says Mona asked to use Hinze instead of Blakey a few weeks ago."

Oh my God. "Ramona insists she's a whole person. The only time I've seen her show any anger is when she's called Mona. Alba called her Mona, so maybe this is a recent development, like maybe she's trying to fight Rami's hold on her?"

Yvonne's voice sounded shrill. "I don't know. I don't know."

I raced toward town, my wipers doing double time and not making much progress against the deluge. "I'm going to detain both of them. When you've got some answers, call me back." That was all the nice I could put on that.

Even given the tragedy and shock of the real Brenda King's death, Yvonne Cartwright didn't have the capability to run a facility where people depended on a clear head.

I barely braked when I hit the town limit and sped toward the Long Branch. One swipe of my blades caused my heart to contract and my blood to fire. "Damn it!"

The orange Mustang wasn't parked on Main Street.

34

I hit the glass doors of the Long Branch and jetted into bar. I shouted, not only because I couldn't help it but because the rain roared against the windows. "Where are they?"

Newt and Earl sat facing me, all four eyes wide, their faces flushed and their hands flat on the table.

Ted's back was to me, and he twisted around, maybe worried I'd attack, which I was tempted to do.

Newt and Earl jumped to their feet like pinballs loaded in front of the same plunger. They were around the table and on their way to the door before Ted could shout.

"You two stop there." Ted shoved his chair back.

The women's bathroom door opened, and May Keller walked out, unlit cigarette poked in the corner of her mouth. "Well, maybe we can get this dog-and-pony show wrapped up. I want to drag the meadow up north while the ground's wet."

May's work schedule wasn't my concern. I didn't think I sounded as breathless as Yvonne Cartwright had, but it might be close. "Where's Ramona?"

Newt and Earl fell-to with a jumble of words that didn't make sense.

I held my hand up and cut them off, my attention on Ted. "What did you do?"

His dark eyes smoldered with defensiveness. "You can't keep them here. They didn't break the law."

Froth didn't actually fly from my mouth, but I was sure he understood my fury. "You let them go?" My mind spun through what to do about it.

He doubled down on his decision, sounding authoritative and, in perfect imitation of his mother, lifting his eyebrows to show his superiority. "Brenda seemed capable. And she showed me the paperwork. It looked all in order."

Newt or Earl—I didn't turn to locate the black eye to see which one spoke—said, "He shouldn't have let that woman take our Ramona. She was scared."

The other brother filled in. "That woman kept callin' her Louise. How can you let Ramona go with a lady who don't even know her name?"

I swung my full attention on the brothers and now saw it was Newt talking. Part of me noted Newt in a red plaid shirt while Earl wore blue, easier ID than a fading shiner. "And that lady put down the top on the car."

Earl said, "Any fool could tell the rain was gonna start."

Newt pointed an accusing finger at Ted. "And he wouldn't let us follow her. And she needs us."

As if tattling on a bad babysitter, Earl added, "He pulled his gun and told us if we didn't sit down, he'd toss our butts in jail."

Ted raised his hands up to show innocence. "They kept saying they needed to rescue Ramona, and I didn't want Newt and Earl to harass Ms. King and Ramona Hinze."

I zeroed in on Ted. "That woman isn't Brenda King. She's a violent mental patient who suffers who knows what kind of delusions. They call her Rami. She took our Ramona Blakey, who she calls Mona. Rami and Mona. One Ramona in her eyes."

Newt and Earl both gasped.

Even May Keller stared in surprise before forming all her wrinkles into an epic frown. "Well, that'll frost your tomatoes."

Ted tried to pass that off with a puff of air but seemed to understand how seriously I took it. "The release looked official. How was I supposed to know?"

"It was official." I didn't call him an idiot, yay me. "Because it was official for Brenda King. Brenda King is dead. Murdered. Her body was just discovered in Big Springs. The likely culprit is Ramona Hinze."

One of the brothers said, "Another Ramona Hinze? Like our Ramona before she was married?"

Ted's frown showed he thought I was making this up.

Using their nicknames to try to explain, I started, "Rami somehow got Mona to believe their destinies are intertwined. And they watched *Thelma and Louise* and now are on a road trip that they plan to end by sailing that Mustang off into a canyon."

May Keller wasn't so convinced. "I've seen crazy, but that tall drink of water didn't look crazy to me. Maybe like she could be a lumberjack with all that muscle. And why would this other Ramona come all the way to the Sandhills? If I don't misremember, them women in that movie was headed to Mexico, not Nebraska."

Newt jabbed my arm. "Ramona wanted to come home. She was always goin' on about home."

Earl jabbed Newt, not because he disagreed but out of nervous energy. "And sometimes she got all crazy, saying she killed her husband."

"And one time she said they were going out on their own terms, but she didn't tell us who the *they* was," Newt said.

Earl: "But that was only sometimes. Then she'd be our good ol' Ramona again."

Newt turned his mournful eyes to me. "Our Ramona ain't feeling good. She's tired out."

Earl looked on the verge of tears. "We thought that woman was taking her to a hospital to get her heart checked out. But now we don't know what's happening."

No one moved or spoke for a few seconds. I was trying to push aside my feelings of worry over Ramona's condition and feeling helpless in the face of Newt's and Earl's distress. Rami must be the other part of *they* Ramona talked about. Where would Rami Hinze take Mona Blakey?

Maybe that was what the Johnson brothers were considering too, and they reached a conclusion before I did. Their discussion took place in their no-words way, because without a sound, they bolted for the front door.

No one made a move to stop them.

I turned to May. "What do you remember about why Thelma and Louise go to the canyon?"

She worried the cigarette in her mouth. "Welp." She raised her gaze to the ceiling and let some seconds tick by. "They was gonna get caught for killing that shitheel back at the bar when he was after Louise. And they didn't want to mess with that or go to prison or go back to their lives."

While she spoke, I suddenly knew where they'd go.

Newt's turquoise Monte Carlo sped by the window, heading east on the highway.

35

The race to Tree Horn Ridge was punctuated with back tires skidding on the wet pavement and the slap of my wipers trying desperately to keep up with the downpour. Thunder growled at quick intervals, like elk signaling their readiness to fight. The first crack of lightning hit as I dropped from the highway to the rough gravel of the ranch road.

Newt's tire tracks were disappearing fast as the rain kept its steady pace. Puddles formed in the lower, more packed parts of the narrow road. The clouds marched closer and lower, making me hunch my shoulders to keep from brushing the sky.

If I drove to the decrepit house, I'd be below Lover's Leap. That would leave me there to pick up the pieces, not where I could prevent their flight. I kept an eye on the road to track Newt's car. He'd know how to make it to the top.

Even though the Johnsons had never watched *Thelma and Louise*, they'd heard me talk about driving a car off a cliff. They must have figured Tree Horn Ridge fit the bill. The whole scenario seemed so outlandish that if Newt's tire tracks didn't show the way, I wouldn't be sure I had it right.

Another bolt of lightning sizzled across the sky. To the far west, a band of blue sky chased the clouds, but it looked like a slow-motion race. We were in for more rain, and from the way the gray-green swirled in the black, we'd be lucky not to get pelted with hail.

The tracks left the sandy road, and I had to lean forward and concentrate to follow their trail. A crushed soapweed, a tire tread in a bare spot, and an occasional smashed bunch of grass led me to the east end of the pasture where a gentle slope grew increasingly steeper. Bless my trusty Dodge Charger that could traverse the most rugged Sandhills terrain.

While I climbed the slope, occasional flashes of lightning lit up the ranch yard below. The dead cottonwood gleamed white, reaching the jagged and charred top as if daring another strike.

Rain kept its endless drumming accompanied by a nearly constant rumble of thunder. But every few minutes, a cymbal crashed almost instantaneous with the flash of lightning, making me clench from my teeth to my toes.

I topped out on the butte and lost the trail, but I accelerated on the rough prairie, bouncing along with such violence I feared I'd either break the axle, destroy the shocks, or scramble my liver, kidneys, and intestines like eggs in a skillet.

Through the wet windshield and the murky light, I finally spotted headlights. In a few more yards I saw they shone on Newt's Monte Carlo, like a target painted on the prey's belly. The turquoise beauty sat parallel to the edge of the cliff. Newt was willing to sacrifice the love of his life, his car, to block Rami from sailing the Mustang off the drop.

The Mustang's top was down, rain having its way with the women seated inside. A pop of lightning hit so close it raised the hairs on the back of my neck and felt like it stopped my heart. The clouds swirled in a rage. Gusts sent waves spreading across the grasses and drawing the air itself into the battle.

Newt and Earl ran from the Monte Carlo, closing the twenty yards toward the Mustang. They split up at the hood of the Mustang, with one brother flying to each side of the car.

I gunned my cruiser to nose up to the Monte Carlo, forming a wider barrier to block the Mustang. I slammed on the brakes and shot out of my car. Despite my adrenaline and focus, the icy curtain that doused me made me gasp. As weak as Ramona was, this exposure would be dangerous. If she had a fragile heart, this might do her in.

The weather gods upped the stakes as the first sting of hail hit the back of my neck. Tiny at first, like mini razors slicing my skin. Frail Ramona had no protection from this storm, which threatened to get much worse before it passed. To prove my point, the hail increased in size and came down harder, roaring like a barreling train.

I shouted but probably couldn't be heard above the storm and the Mustang's engine revving. "Stop!"

Earl was braced in the wet grass outside the driver's side. One hand grasped the top of the door, and the other tugged the handle. Neither he nor Newt seemed to notice the ice pelting them.

Rami flinched and drew up her shoulders as the hail battered. Her wild, black hair was plastered to her head. She managed to keep hitting at Earl. With a mighty thrust, she shoved the heel of her hand upward on Earl's chin.

He squirmed free and threw himself at her, reaching inside the open vehicle.

I pumped my legs as I ran from the cruiser, slipping on the wet weeds and crashing to one knee before I jumped up again, reaching for my gun and pulling it from the holster.

On the passenger side, Ramona remained slumped in the seat. I hadn't seen her move or even open her eyes. Despite the rain and hail hitting me and making me squint and blink, I thought her pallor looked pasty and maybe her lips were blue.

I raised my gun, thinking to shoot out the tires. But shooting tires wasn't as easy as they made it look on TV, and I doubted it would stop Rami from gunning the Mustang over the cliff. With Newt, Earl, and Ramona all gathered close to Rami, shooting into the car wasn't an option. I shoved my gun back into the holster.

"Rami." I yelled at the same time another lightning strike detonated, and it sounded like the earth split open. A blinding flash erupted close to the house down below. The dead tree in the front became a whole lot deader as it smoldered, frustrated it couldn't burst into flames because of the rain.

With my slick cowboy boot soles, it felt like I ran through soap suds. I slipped and skidded, not getting close enough to the Mustang to make a difference. The boys fought valiantly, but they were no match for four thousand pounds of steel and an engine with more horsepower than the Bar J.

With her beefy arms, Rami swung at Earl. Her fist connected with his jaw, and his head snapped back on his neck. He lost his grip on the car.

Rami pulled her arms in and focused inside the Mustang. It looked as though she manipulated the gear shift between the seats, probably ramming it into reverse, because the wheels started to spin.

Newt reacted with astonishing speed and swung a leg over the car door behind Ramona. He hurled himself into the miniscule back seat, still leaning into Ramona's lap.

Momentarily shed of Earl, Rami hefted herself up, leaving one hand on the steering wheel and rotating her upper body to flail at Newt.

In the clamor of the storm, shouts were like mumbles. Despite racing toward Earl, I made frustratingly slow progress on the slick prairie.

Earl was already on his feet, lunging after the Mustang.

Hail accumulated on the ground like spilled salt. One stone winged the tip of my nose, smarting more than it seemed possible. The assault continued across my head and shoulders, like a torrent of icy arrows.

Newt dodged and ducked, standing in the back seat and leaning over Ramona, keeping his body between her and Rami. The blows Rami managed to land on his kidneys and back didn't seem to faze him.

Back in the fight, Earl sped toward the Mustang from where he'd fallen behind it, and I was closing in on them from the front. Trying to understand Newt's position and what he was struggling with, I realized Ramona's hands were bound together and knotted to something inside the cab.

Rami's animal scream cut through the roar of the wind and rain. "Together."

"No, Rami!" I kept running, hardly believing that scrawny, almost-seventy-year-old Earl could outrace me. His desperation must be fueling him. With my eyes on Earl hurtling toward the car and Newt's struggle over Ramona, my foot landed in a gopher hole and electric jolts of pain shot from my ankle to my knee. I went down while yelling. "Rami. Don't."

At a slight side angle, I saw her glance up, but I was sure she wasn't seeing me, only gauging her route to the cliff edge. Her lips moved, but whatever she hollered was lost in another eruption of thunder and lightning. This strike popped on a fence post several yards away, and a fireball zinged along the barbed wire.

Earl made it to the rear of the Mustang and used the car to stabilize himself until he reached the driver's door again and leaned inside, maybe to grab the keys.

Again, Rami let loose a scream that sounded straight out of a horror movie. She wrenched Earl's hand from inside and twisted his arm.

He screeched in pain but stretched his good hand back into the car. Rami punched the gas, and the Mustang jolted ahead, enough that it threw Earl off his feet. He slipped, and his legs slid under the car.

By now I was back on my feet in a limping run but too far away to pull Earl out of the way. "*No!*"

Rami didn't brake as she ran over Earl's legs. He shrieked, the sound slicing through my skin.

Newt jerked his head as if slapped. As the Mustang steered at an angle to skirt the barrier of cars, Newt threw an arm around Rami's neck, catching her in the crook of his elbow.

He must have wrenched her foot off the pedal, because the wheels slowed, nearly stopping.

Rami swiveled her head to Ramona. My ankle protested and buckled, but I pushed myself.

It wouldn't be enough to intervene.

The Mustang's wheels spun on the hail, but with a jerk, they found traction. Rami spun the wheel to get around the cars blocking her way to the rim. Inside, Newt seemed to hover over Ramona, protecting her from the worst of the rain. He dipped his head in front of her, as if resting it on her chest.

Rami grimaced and writhed under the onslaught of the hail, but she kept her focus riveted to the edge. When she'd angled far enough to make it without hitting the Monte Carlo, the engine roared even louder than the storm.

There was no way I could close the few yards left between us and stop her.

The tires rolled faster.

Newt's head poked up and whipped from side to side. I suppose he took in Earl lying on the wet prairie, propped on his palms, mouth open in a primal wail at witnessing his brother flying over the edge of Lover's Leap to his death.

No longer feeling my ankle or the stinging bullets of ice, I raced to throw myself at the car, hoping that maybe it would make enough difference to derail the plan. Knowing it wouldn't and I'd end up under the wheels.

As the Mustang gained momentum toward the edge, Newt stood upright in the back seat. A length of rope flew from his hands, whipped by the wind and sailing across the prairie. He lunged for Rami.

But she had the car on a straight course now, and there wasn't anything he could do. Rami took her eyes off her path for a split second to look down in Ramona's lap. She reached over and clasped Mona's hand, raising it up. That stupid iconic moment when Thelma and Louise seal their friendship before ending their lives in a fiery crash.

"Newt!" I know I screamed it. So futile. My friend, the cranky, sweet, loving, innocent Newt was going over the edge. I couldn't stop it. Loyal to the end.

He never hurt anyone. He didn't deserve this.

I howled again. Lightning struck a soapweed between me and the car, and the plant exploded, sounding like a munitions factory under attack.

I must have instinctively closed my eyes, because when I opened them, I saw the taillights of the Mustang in a blink before they disappeared below the rim.

Earl's wails hit me, and I noticed the hail had let up, though rain still smacked.

I dropped to the prairie, my head stripped of everything but a black heaviness.

Newt.

Ramona.

36

I buried my head in my arms and stayed there for a moment. The hail stopped as suddenly as it had begun, taking the rain and the roaring wind with it. Thunder rumbled far away, and the blue band of sky to the west surged closer.

Then I heard it. I didn't believe it at first, but I whipped my head to the sound.

"Gonna need a little help here." Newt's voice carried from the ridge.

Earl yelled, and now that the wind had dropped to a mild gust, I heard him plain. "Katie's comin'."

I pushed myself to stand and fell over, my ankle like a live electrical wire. I tried again, treating it a little more gently but still rushing toward Newt's voice.

Slight though it was, the breeze across my wet clothes sent a cascade of shivers over me and made me clench my teeth to keep them from chattering. Newt would be at least that cold, so I hurried even more.

Behind a small hillock, in a slight depression not visible from where we'd been on the top of the butte, Newt lay curled around Ramona. She quivered and whimpered. Probably shocky and freezing, but alive.

I spared a glance over the cliff.

My stomach flipped and dropped with a queasy splash, and I swallowed to right it. The Mustang had nosed into the creek bed and bounced backward. Crunched and dead in the wet ranch yard.

Rami Hinze hadn't stayed inside, of course. She'd gone airborne, and her final resting place was atop the smoldering tree. Facing the heavens, she draped along the sharp teeth of the trunk.

In the movie, they never show you what Thelma and Louise look like after the crash. This was a vision that would haunt me.

I turned back to Newt, working my throat until I could form words. "That was very brave."

He gathered Ramona in his arms. She was twice his size, but he managed to hold her close. "We love her. You gotta do for people you love."

37

At six o'clock in the evening, the sun still smiled from a sky so blue and vast I felt swallowed whole. The town smelled of lilacs and hope, mingled with the spice of a fresh-mowed lawn. Someone's Rainbird sprinkler chuck-chucked. If happiness had a season, it'd be summer. And June was the garden gate into three months of bliss.

Well, maybe that was on the poetic side, especially for a Fox. But darned if I didn't love summer and wearing a simple T-shirt dress with canvas loafers. With my hair loose and falling casually down my back, I looked and felt nothing like the Grand County Sheriff. I was unofficially taking a night off. Of course, if an incident happened, I'd have to respond, dress and loafers notwithstanding.

I'd parked Elvis, my Ranchero, in my spot behind the courthouse to leave room for all the vehicles crowding up and down Main Street. Listening to the chorus of blackbirds who seemed as pleased with the day as I was, I joined others making their way up the hill to Zoe's baby shower.

The drama that played out at Tree Horn Ridge two weeks ago had been the talk of the town and had garnered me a touch of hero status. Enough that gossip about the other crimes had died down somewhat. It hadn't cooled Sherwood Temple's jets any. In the last weeks, I'd spent time at the golf course and had interviewed, either in person or by phone, most of the

people who had been on the premises during the time the sculpture might
have been stolen.

It wouldn't make any difference now, but it showed Sherwood I was
putting in an effort, and I was growing fond of the green fairways and
multitudinous marigolds.

Diane pushed a ribbon-festooned stroller up the middle of the street.
"This is making a hole in my entire week. Who has a baby shower on a
Tuesday night?"

"Someone who spends every weekend at rodeos," I said.

Panting and struggling to keep up, Louise lugged her heft alongside us.
Diane had arrived at Louise's last night after eight o'clock, and I'd been
summoned into town to help build the stroller that Diane had picked up
after work. Susan and Carly had shown up about the time we'd finally
figured out how to attach the wheels. We'd ended up hanging out until
after midnight, laughing and gossiping, something that was all too rare.

Between gasps for air, Louise said, "Last night was fun. It was how we
used to be. A loyal and tight family."

Diane gave her a side-eye and my stomach clenched, wondering where
she was going, because Louise wasn't one to wander around.

She swung her arms to give her momentum. "Like it used to be before
you took the job as sheriff and investigated our mother."

Diane growled at her. "Knock it off."

Dahlia, with her daddy longlegs stride, caught up to us. Her arm
threaded through Sid's, the clacking of her high-heeled cowboy boots
quickening as she passed.

Sid twisted his head around. "Nice work helping out Mona Hinze."

Dahlia jerked his arm and uttered, loud enough for several folks on
their way to the Legion Hall to hear, "But she didn't save that poor crazy
woman. She's dead now, no thanks to Kate."

Sheriffing wasn't easy in any county, but I was getting tired of taking the
blame for the actions of others.

Diane let the stroller loose, and it rolled downhill a few inches before I
grabbed the handle. In her fuchsia pumps and cheerful tea dress, Diane
made impressive progress to Dahlia's side. Using a voice that must
command attention in boisterous board meetings, Diane said, "I'll bet Ted

feels terrible letting Rami Hinze kidnap Ramona right out from under his nose. If Kate hadn't acted quickly, more lives would have been lost."

Dahlia quit walking, making Sid stumble. Her mouth flew open enough I thought it might crack the top layer of her makeup. "Ted wouldn't have been there if Kate had been handling her job."

In her understated natural look that only money could buy, Diane raised one eyebrow. Speaking in a voice as arching as that expressive eyebrow, she said, "And Kate wouldn't have had to take off if someone hadn't been faking crimes."

Wearing tight jeans and a ruffled shirt, Dahlia didn't have the same flair as Diane, but that didn't stop her from smirking. "There's been a rash of crime in this county because they know with Kate as sheriff, they'll get away with it."

Diane's mouth tweaked into a smile that would stampede the Wall Street bull. She used a casual tone. "Oh, I don't think they'll get away with it."

Dahlia couldn't hide the stab of worry that momentarily creased her forehead before she returned Diane's deadly gaze and sweet inflection. "Good luck to her. But I'm afraid the damage has already been done." With a jerk, she prodded Sid to continue with her to the Legion.

We crowded into the cavernous room with floor tiles probably as full of asbestos as the ceiling tiles, since the whole place was constructed in the sixties. An industrial kitchen stretched behind a metal roller window that was opened to display servings of white cake, homemade pink mints, mixed nuts, and a punchbowl of Hawaiian Punch with 7 UP.

The rest of the world might have progressed to savory canapes and fancy tarts, but Grand County was destined to stick with tradition.

Family, friends, neighbors—many folks qualifying in all those categories at once—milled around, exchanging information about the amount of rain and size of hail from that big storm. I figured a few of them talked about the way Newt, Earl, and I had saved Ramona from a killer.

Most of the kids were turned loose to play tag, or the ever-favorite Pass-Run-Tackle-Smear-Kill, a kind of Red Rover-football mix unique to Grand County.

The Fox clan took up one whole corner of the hall. Even Douglas made a rare trip to town, and he and Michael had their heads bent together. Both tossed a nod in my direction, and I assumed Michael had gotten over his snit. They went back to mumbling in their twin language. It reminded me of the way Newt and Earl communicated.

As if I'd conjured them with my thoughts, the door opened, and the Johnsons wandered in. Earl creaked past on crutches, one leg in a cast. The other leg had survived with bruises. Newt's black eye had faded. A few scrapes on their hands and faces—which didn't look that much out of the ordinary for them—was all that remained of our episode at Tree Horn Ridge. I'd even abandoned the ortho boot they'd given me and no longer felt as though I walked on a splintered glass ankle.

Newt and Earl hadn't reverted to their old camo outfits, but maybe that was because they hadn't discovered where Ramona hid them. Their plaid shirts showed signs of wear and a lack of recent laundering, and grass and grease smeared their Levi's. I didn't smell them until they passed right by me on their way to the refreshment table. They'd promised Ramona a weekly bath, and that probably wouldn't happen for a few more days.

I tailed them and waited until Newt had filled two plates with cake, mints, and mixed nuts—which were mostly peanuts and Brazil nuts. He took Earl's to the end of the counter by the kitchen, within easy reach for refills.

"What have you heard from Ramona?" I asked.

Mouth full of cake, Newt started in. "We was down to see her this morning."

Resting his armpit on the crutch and leaning to his plate, Earl snatched a pink and a blue mint and popped them into his mouth, mashing them until they were purple. "The doc said she's gettin' better, but she still has trouble remembering where she is and what happened."

Newt added, "They're runnin' tests on her heart. Said she ought to have more umph than she does."

The rescue unit had hauled Ramona, Newt, and Earl to North Platte as soon as they'd arrived on Tree Horn Ridge.

Ramona had been weak, dehydrated, and hypothermic, but overnight in the hospital had taken care of that. I'd been able to get her admitted to the mental health facility with Kim Matthews's help.

They'd admitted Newt, but by the time Earl had his leg set, the two brothers had enough of incarceration of any kind and had begged to come back to Grand County with me.

I'd planned to go to bat to have Yvonne Cartwright removed, but she'd resigned, and Verde Mesa seemed to be in an uproar.

Newt swallowed and opened his mouth to speak but forked in more cake at the same time. He sounded muffled. "Doc says it's good we come down."

Earl's tongue was purple. "When she's better, she maybe can come back and live with us. Doc's gonna see if she can."

"How does Ramona feel about that?" I asked.

Newt shoved the remainder of his cake into his mouth and turned around to plop another piece on his plate.

Earl reached for the mints, then seemed to rethink his plan and grabbed a handful of nuts instead.

Newt nodded at me. "She's wantin' to come. We're the only family she's got."

"And the doc knows we take good care of her," Earl added.

"Even docs know that love is the most important thing."

Earl looked thoughtful. "It might take a bit of time before we get her here, though. She's upset when she gets to remembering. That bad Ramona got her twisted in her thinking, saying they were locked up because they killed their husbands. And their husbands were bad men."

Newt interrupted. "Which we don't think Bob Blakey was a bad man. And Mona, I mean, Ramona don't, either."

"I think maybe she's got a touch of All Timers, but Doc don't call it that."

Newt frowned at Earl for that and kept talking to me. "Ramona says she remembers coming around and getting scared of that other one. And that's what happened in Big Springs at the truck stop. She stole the keys from the bad one and got out to the car but then got confused."

"We're lucky she came to our house," Earl finished.

That made sense. From what I'd pieced together from Brenda King's murder, she'd pulled into the truck stop to fuel up. Of course, she'd have planned to keep going east toward North Platte. But that truck stop was the last place to get gas before heading up to Hodgekiss. Rami and Ramona had stopped there, too.

The night of the bad rainstorm, Ramona had gone into the truck stop to use the bathroom and somehow ended up with the car keys in her hand. She'd walked out, become disoriented, and driven off to Newt and Earl's, abandoning Rami.

Rami had been hanging out at the truck stop since Ramona had peeled away. My guess was that Rami had been eating out of the Dumpster or panhandling. Whether she'd had a plan to get to Hodgekiss or not, fate had sent Rami a golden opportunity. It was Brenda King's misfortune that Rami spotted her.

I glanced toward the kitchen, where Dad always took his position as beverage manager. If he wasn't on the rails, Dad could be counted on to dole out the Coors Light, coffee, and Pepsi at every Legion Hall gathering. Today, he was flanked by Deenie Hayward, Wanda Jenkins, and Trudy Drake. Even though he appeared charmed and tipped back a beer of his own, I wasn't sure I caught pleasure in his eyes.

I searched the crowd to find Louise. She glared at me and thrust her chin toward Dad, as if she blamed me some more.

Love. We all needed it. "I'll talk to the doctor and see if that can be arranged."

Twyla scooted from the kitchen and waved her hands in a shooing motion. "You damned coyotes have had enough. Save some for the rest."

With conspiratorial grins, the brothers hunched their shoulders. Newt made a lunge and plopped another piece of cake on each plate. He picked them both up. Earl had already started for the back door that led into an alley, and Newt beat him to it, and with both hands holding the plates, he leaned back to open it. It wasn't a smooth or fast escape, but it worked.

Carly stood toward the back of the room. I wound through people eating cake and watching Zoe open gifts while sharing gossip and opinions about the value of each offering. With a tug on Carly's arm, I motioned for her to follow me. We slipped through the front door into impending dusk and the sound of kids in full-throttle romp.

"I need your help carrying some stuff," I said, already on my way to Elvis parked behind the courthouse.

I lowered the tailgate and scooted a cardboard box to the end. A quilted baby blanket covered the top. "Take this one, and I'll get the rest. Unpack it on the gift table for Zoe to open."

She frowned at me. "Did you get Zoe a gift on your own? That'll make the rest of us look cheap."

I fought a smug smile. "Just some hand-me-downs. Nothing important."

She lifted it, surprised at the weight. "What's in here, a lifetime supply of bronzed baby shoes?"

I leaned into the bed of the pickup for another box, much bigger but only holding one item. "Just go, before she gets done and people leave."

We lumbered up the hill, and Carly finally spoke. "So, what about the foreman job?"

I'd been seesawing on the idea and hadn't come to a decision, so it surprised me to answer quickly and with confidence. "Think I want to stay sheriff."

She appraised me with sympathy. "I'm going to get temporary help until after the election, in case you change your mind."

"Or in case I lose and need a job?"

She frowned as we climbed the steep hill in the middle of the road. "Dahlia isn't going to stop."

I hugged my box. "Oh, I think Dahlia will stand down."

Carly studied me but didn't say anything.

We shuffled to the front door, and Shorty Calley looked through the glass and opened it for us. "Looks heavy."

People made room for Carly as she worked her way to the table in front. Zoe had nearly finished with the mountains of presents, so there was room to set the big box down. While the older ladies in the folding chairs in front oohed and awed over a frilly dress that would no doubt scratch little Olivia, Carly pulled the baby quilt off the top of the box.

Her eyes opened in surprise before shimmering at me in amusement. "Would you look at this."

38

Like Vanna White revealing the puzzle, Carly pulled out the item on top and set the bronze sculpture with the flame-like curves on the table. A murmur sounded from a few people standing close by.

While the conversations died in a wave starting with those closest to us and making its silent progress toward the back of the room, she lifted a flowered pillowcase that clanked and rattled. Reaching inside, she closed her fist on a bunch of teaspoons and pulled them out to place them on the table.

I wove through people and set my big box on the floor. The flaps made a slapping sound as I flipped them open and pulled out a sword in its scabbard.

Cindy Doak hollered on her way from the kitchen. "There it is!"

I stepped back and searched the crowd for Dahlia. She stood close to the kitchen, a cake plate suspended in a shaking hand. Her mouth open in something like horror, and she stared at me.

I didn't feel that sense of justification I probably should have. A part of me felt sorry for her mortification, though, and unless she forced me to do otherwise, her secret would stay with me.

Merle met Cindy at the table, and they couldn't hide their happiness while he lifted the sword and Cindy picked up spoons one at a time.

The conversations rose, and people surged toward me, asking questions and giving me atta girls. I kept my eye on Dahlia while she clutched a Coors Light can and gulped it, making a gallant effort to appear unfazed.

Carly grabbed my hand and tugged me toward the back door where Newt and Earl had disappeared. Not stopping to explain or comment to anyone as we scurried for our escape.

The door barely clicked shut before she turned on me and shouted, "Arrest her."

"I can't arrest her without proof."

Carly pointed to the Legion. "You have proof. All the stolen goods. You had to get them somewhere."

"I needed to get some kind of probable cause before I could search legally. Now the chain of custody is all messed up, and I'll never be able to prosecute her."

Carly tilted her head. "Get real. You'll never arrest Dahlia."

Diane strolled around the corner of the building. Some kind of fashion magician, she didn't totter in her spiky pumps on the dirt road. Maybe she'd seen me take off after Carly and had come out the front to head us off. "Actually, not arresting Dahlia is smart. After Mom getting away from you and Jeremy not facing charges, it would be political suicide for you to lower the boom on Dahlia."

I pointed at Diane. "Mom got away from *you*."

She shrugged and dropped an arm around Carly's shoulder. "At any rate, well done. We couldn't have done better ourselves. How did you figure out where she kept the goods?"

Dahlia would never be my friend, but I couldn't be intentionally cruel, so I didn't see the need to tell them I'd figured it out from one thing Dahlia had said. "They're history."

That made me remember a time not long after Ted and I had married. Ted was teasing me about having children, and we were arguing about toys. He said his mother had a doll collection, and if we had a daughter, he assumed she'd want to give it to a grandbaby. He'd turned to Dahlia and asked her where it was. She'd answered, "Oh, they're history."

Fast-forward two or three years. Ted, Sid, and I were moving bulls to the Brenner pasture. Dahlia stayed at the ranch, her horseback days long over by then. But we'd run into some calves that needed doctoring, and I rode back to the ranch for penicillin and the vaccine gun.

Dahlia hadn't been in the house when I'd gone to the fridge for the penicillin, and I'd wondered where she'd gone but didn't pay a lot of attention. Until I walked back to where I'd tied my horse outside the barn.

I heard a noise that stopped me. When I stood still to listen, it sounded like a woman singing a lullaby. Intrigued, I followed the sound to an old shed that had been a chicken house many years ago. We used it to store old machinery and other bits and pieces we didn't need but didn't want to toss.

I eased open the door to a dark space. In the shadow, it felt chilly and creepy with the sound of singing, now clearly Dahlia's voice, growing louder. It came from the back wall, and I tiptoed in. I'd never noticed a gate in the far corner, probably because I hadn't been at the ranch long enough to explore all the nooks and crannies. As I inched closer, I could see a camp lantern through cracks in the wall.

Inside, Dahlia sat with her legs crossed, an old baby doll nestled in her arms. She rocked back and forth singing "Rock-a-Bye Baby." More dolls were arranged on a blanket covering a dirt floor. A plastic storage bin was in the corner with its lid off. The doll collection looked more like the present than history.

I'd felt embarrassed and guilty for intruding on a private moment. I figured everyone was entitled to harmless secrets and never told a soul about Dahlia's playtime.

Technically, me going to Frog Creek when Sid and Dahlia weren't home and rummaging in that old chicken house could be a B & E—but without the breaking, because there were no locks. But it wasn't any worse than what Dahlia had done to the Doaks. And I felt confident she'd never call me on it.

When I didn't cough up the story, Diane and Carly hugged tighter. They wore satisfied smirks like two cats fat on cream. Carly said, "We're Foxes. One for all, all for one."

Before they could see the tears that surprised me, I turned around and headed back to the door. I wasn't used to that brazen unity, and it undid me after the encounter with Michael and Louise's accusations about destroying the family.

Since Sherwood Temple wasn't a local, he hadn't put in an appearance at the shower. Too bad he'd missed the drama. I'd take the sculpture out to him later.

I considered a piece of cake and decided against it. Opted out of a beverage as well, since I didn't want to get too close to Dad and somehow end up in his drama. So I stood close to the back wall.

Garrett Haney pulled away from the group of neighbors who ranched up north. He kept his eyes on me as he maneuvered through the crowd.

Roxy might have been way off mark when she'd tittered about Garrett and me being a pair. But I had to admit, he seemed much different than I'd expected. Not the powerful and arrogant Scottsdale lawyer who'd forgotten his raising, but a vulnerable man trying to be a good father. And with that smooth, chestnut hair and expressive brown eyes, he wasn't short on looks, either.

When he finally got to me, he said, "I let Tony play outside with those fiendish little nephews of yours. I'm having a hard time not running out there every two seconds to supervise."

I laughed. "Believe me, if there's too much blood, someone will let us know."

His smile looked uncertain. "Guess I'm going to have to get used to this rough-and-tumble."

Sarah bounced cranky Brie on her hip and scowled at me from where she'd been recording Olivia's presents so the parents could send the hundred or so thank-you notes.

It sounded like he was trying to tell me something, but I didn't get it. "Why?"

He sent a sheepish, almost apologetic look in Sarah's direction. "I'm moving back. Well, Tony and I are. Sheila and I are divorcing, and I'm getting custody."

I didn't wish divorce on anyone. "I'm sorry about that."

May sauntered up in the crisp Levi's and flowered polyester button-up she wore for special occasions, her hand patting the cigarette pack in her breast pocket. "Too bad you didn't come up with that loot before Monday."

"Too bad it was stolen in the first place." I located Dahlia in a corner by the back door, her color a little healthier and a suspicious gleam in her eyes. That made me nervous, since I'd thought she'd be cowed by knowing what I knew.

"I think we all know who done it," May said, following my gaze.

Garrett lifted his eyebrows in question.

"Guess we also know nothing can be proven, so there's not much point in accusing," I said, watching Dahlia.

Dahlia lifted her chin and sighted me down her nose. She knew I couldn't nail her for this, but that shouldn't cause her to look so smug.

May kept that blue heeler focus on Dahlia. "I told you to be careful of that ol' snake. But even I didn't think she'd get this low."

"Setting it up to make me look bad is one of her villainess powers. She'll try again even if it didn't work out for her this time."

May cocked her head and gave me a quizzical smirk. "You ain't heard."

Garrett, clearly lost in the conversation, shifted from me to May.

My stomach did a sour loop. "Heard what?"

May cackled. "The way that Ethel Bender spites you, it'll pain her to not be the one to tell you. And you know what, I like the idea of that, even if I don't like the news I'm delivering."

The acid started to eat into my gut. "What news is this?"

May drew in her head like a snake readying to strike. She narrowed her gaze on Dahlia with a look designed to kill. Then she focused on me. "Welp, I hate to inform you, but there's a *re*-call filed on you."

Garrett stared at May.

Oh, is that all? "Sherwood Temple is an entitled blowhard. He can throw his two-bit temper tantrum and cost the county a ton of money, but no one's going to listen to him."

May Keller puckered up her face in confusion. "Don't know what the Sam Hill you're spoutin' about. You sound like that loony chippy of Newt and Earl's."

"Sherwood Temple. The general manager of the Creekside Golf Club. He'll probably withdraw the recall as soon as he gets the sculpture back."

May's weathered face showed irritation. "Still don't know what you're babbling about, but Who's-What's-It got nothing to do with the recall."

If Sherwood Temple wasn't behind it, did Dahlia decide to go bold and do it herself? That would only be good for my chances at reelection, since

Dahlia causing that kind of a mess in the county wouldn't sit well with voters. "Doesn't matter. There are enough Foxes around that a recall won't pass."

Now May shook her head as if giving up. "Not if they're a house divided."

Okay, now I was the one confused.

She seemed to make sense of it now. "Oh. Well, this makes it double hard to break it to you. There ain't no outsider in on this mess. The one that filed against you is Louise."

BULL'S EYE
Kate Fox #8

Was his death a tragic accident—or a murder in cold blood?

Caught between juggling her dysfunctional family and a looming recall election, Sheriff Kate Fox feels like she's on a bucking bronc with one hand stuck in the air. When a top bull breeder is mauled to death at a rodeo, Kate quickly realizes that this so-called accident hides a much darker truth.

Dropped from the case to protect her upcoming election bid, Kate is forced to cowboy off on her own when she fears the victim's wife is being targeted unfairly. After her snooping reveals a list of shady suspects, each with their own reason to want the victim dead, Kate finds herself caught up in a deadly web of lies and fraud at the heart of the competitive world of rodeo.

But when her investigation takes a terrifying turn, Kate starts to question everything. How deep does the corruption go? And who will be left standing when the dust finally settles?

Get your copy today at
severnriverbooks.com

ACKNOWLEDGMENTS

Not to be too much of a whiner, but writing books is hard. And the world of publishing can be brutal. The only way I could possibly navigate this life is with a crew of the best people backing me up. From pondering to plotting, scraping up the smatterings of an ego, to celebrating milestones, no one could boast a more supportive, smart, or inspirational cabal. So, I acknowledge with my deepest gratitude, Janet Fogg, Wendy Terrien, Jessica Lourey, Lori Rader-Day, Erica Ruth Neubauer, Susan Calkins, Terri Bischoff, and Mark Stevens. A big thank you to my hiking and drinking buddy (not usually done at the same time), Kate Matthews, who is always on hand to bring me back to the real world when my made-up one threatens to drown me.

I don't want to make anyone jealous but I do have the best agent, Jill Marsal, who answers emails with freakish speed. I don't know how I got so lucky to be published by Severn River Publishing, but their faith in me, not to mention their care and feeding of the books, has been phenomenal. A special thanks to Mo Metlen for taking care of all that stuff I don't wanna do, and Amber Hudock for lots of things but especially for the title.

Shawn Hebbert is indispensable to the Kate Fox series. Not every writer is fortunate enough to have the exact expert on speed dial, but I'm grateful I do. A big thank you to Sharon Connealy, who is great for filling in Sandhills details and for always making me laugh, even when she doesn't intend to.

Thank you to the Goddess of Developmental editing, Jessica Morrell. And if readers saw the manuscript before Editor Wizard Kate Schomaker cleaned it up, they'd add their effusive thanks to mine (Go Big Red).

To my daughters, Erin and Joslyn, who continually cheer me on, keep me laughing, and inspire me every single day. I'm so lucky you still like to hang out with me. But if you ever take me to Applebee's for my birthday, you're out of the will.

Mostly and always, thanks to Dave. You make everything possible.

ABOUT THE AUTHOR

Shannon Baker is the award-winning author of *The Desert Behind Me* and the Kate Fox series, along with the Nora Abbott mysteries and the Michaela Sanchez Southwest Crime Thrillers. She is the proud recipient of the Rocky Mountain Fiction Writers 2014 and 2017-18 Writer of the Year Award.

Baker spent 20 years in the Nebraska Sandhills, where cattle outnumber people by more than 50:1. She now lives on the edge of the desert in Tucson with her crazy Weimaraner and her favorite human. A lover of the great outdoors, she can be found backpacking, traipsing to the bottom of the Grand Canyon, skiing mountains and plains, kayaking lakes, river running, hiking, cycling, and scuba diving whenever she gets a chance. Arizona sunsets notwithstanding, Baker is, and always will be a Nebraska Husker. Go Big Red.

Sign up for Shannon Baker's reader list at
severnriverbooks.com

Printed in the United States
by Baker & Taylor Publisher Services